FOLLOW YOU ANYWHERE

WESTON PARKER

BRIXBAXTER PUBLISHING

Follow You Anywhere

Copyright © 2019 by Weston Parker

First Edition.

Editor: Eric Martinez
Cover Designer: Ryn Katryn Digital Art

FIND WESTON PARKER

www.westonparkerbooks.com

CHAPTER 1

NOLAN

The divorce had been final for several months, and now the custody battle was finally behind me as well. The tightness that had lived in my chest for the last two years had eased, but it wasn't gone. *Not by a long shot.*

Scarlett wasn't done fighting or making my life hell. I just didn't know when the next hit was going to come. All I knew was that my ex-wife wasn't about to give up or lay down her weapons just yet.

Sighing into the warm steam that filled the shower, I tried to focus on the positives. I was in a period of relative calm between storms and I planned on making the best of it. I'd lived on autopilot since Scarlett and I had separated, feeling like I was fighting for my life every damn day.

It felt like the blinkers were slowly coming off now, like I was coming back to life and could finally breathe again. Standing under the pulsating stream of hot water, I filled my lungs with air and allowed the tension caused by all her bullshit to leave my body when I released it again.

My mind wandered, finally able to think of something other than work or the fuck up that had come from my marriage. Not surprisingly considering that I was naked and alone, it eventually landed on sex.

The next thing I knew, my cock was so hard I could hammer in nails with it. Almost like it was desperate to remind me of its existence. *God, how long has it been since I last jerked off?*

I didn't even remember. No wonder my dick was suddenly doing its best impersonation of the stone the damn shower was made of.

Reaching down to wrap my fist around my shaft, a half-hiss, half-groan escaped into the steam that filled the glass cubicle. I stroked once, twice before I released myself and put my hand on the wall for balance.

My fingers curled into my palm and a loud moan escaped when my free hand slid back down. It had been so long that it only took a few images of luscious curves and a slick pussy flashing through my brain before I felt pressure beginning to build at the base of my spine.

I wanted to drag it out, but I couldn't. I pumped faster, tightening my grip as my head fell forward. I imagined sinking my fingers into the glistening folds I pictured, running my tongue over the hardened nipple of an ample breast I conjured up.

Moans belonging to the nameless, curvy woman in my imagination filled my mind and my breathing became rapid. My hips bucked as I fucked my hand faster, and my eyes screwed shut. I couldn't fight it anymore. My orgasm was coming for me and it felt so fucking good.

The woman was now crawling to me on her hands and knees, her sexy lips pouting and her belly soft. She beckoned to me, her beautiful pussy hot and wet and aching.

Aching for me.

When she sank down on my shaft, her tight walls clenching and so fucking slick, I couldn't hold back anymore.

My balls tightened and shudders wracked through me as I came so damn hard I saw stars. An epic climax that just sucked me dry.

It took me several long minutes to recover, but damn if I knew why I hadn't done that in so long. Some me-time was probably something that had to go on my to-do list.

When I finally finished up in the shower, I had to admit I felt good. Better than I had in a long time. My limbs felt loose and languid and the tension I'd been carrying in my muscles for years had melted away.

I emerged from the shower smiling and ready for whatever the day held for me, or so I thought.

Unfortunately for me, I was wrong. *So very, very wrong.* The bombs started dropping almost as soon as I walked into the office, and the biggest one of all was yet to come.

"I'm getting too old for this," Wayne announced when he walked into my office just after I arrived. My righthand man had been with me since I first started renovating the hotel chain I now owned.

It had made me billions and he hadn't done too badly for himself either. Well enough to act as a pretty decent incentive to put off retirement for another couple of years, or so I'd thought.

I looked up from the plans for our latest renovation and rolled my chair back a few feet, bringing my arms down on the padded leather armrests. "A wise man once told me that age is a matter of the mind, Wayne. A wise man who looked a lot like you actually. If memory serves, it might even have been you. Less than a year ago. In this very office."

He threw back his graying head of hair and laughed with his signature guffaw. It came straight from his beefy belly and would be a sound everyone in the office missed when he left.

"Maybe he wasn't so wise." He crossed to the chair opposite my desk and heaved himself into it. I almost started when I noticed how much slower he was moving than he had been the last time I'd really paid attention.

It had been a while since I'd last taken a proper look at the man who had quite literally raised me in this business. Wayne's hair was almost totally gray now, with only a few strands of pepper between the salt.

The crinkles beside his brown eyes were deeper and more defined, as were the laugh lines around his mouth. Even his mud-colored suit looked older, more worn. No matter how many times I'd tried to send

3

him to my tailor, he still insisted that his own suits were better than any new one crafted for him would be.

Hell, that might even be the same suit he'd been wearing when I met him nine years ago. He straightened his yellow tie and tore his eyes away from the view of the Capitol building in the distance behind me.

"Here's the thing, Nolan." He shook out one of his legs and placed his ankle over his knee, his foot immediately beginning to bounce. "I'm getting to an age where I want to enjoy the years I have left with my wife."

"You're saying you're going to retire?" I'd seen it coming regardless of the fact that I hadn't been watching him too closely recently. I hadn't been blind. My focus simply hadn't been solely on the people on my team.

Sitting in the head office at a hotel chain was much more hectic than people imagined. There wasn't time for daily or even weekly catch-up sessions.

Wayne smoothed his tie again and his foot finally stilled. "It's time, Nolan. I'll probably be back here begging you to rehire me within a year, but I need to slow down."

"I get it." I didn't really. Slowing down didn't seem appealing to me at all, but then again, at sixty-two, Wayne was thirty years my senior. Maybe my outlook would have changed by the time I got there. "There's nothing I can do to change your mind, is there?"

I hadn't worked side by side with him for almost a decade without learning a thing or two about the man. He shook his head swiftly, his lips turning up into an apologetic smile.

"It's been an honor to see you turn the hunk of junk this place used to be around, but I owe it to myself and to my wife to make the best of my sunshine years."

"What about if we offer a job to your wife? You can live out your sunshine years here together." There was no way in hell he'd take the offer, but I had to try.

As I expected, the lines around his mouth deepened when he laughed. "Thanks, but no thanks. The missus and I have been talking about taking an RV around the country for years. We can finally afford to do it."

Fuck, I should've paid him less. But no, Wayne had earned every dime he'd ever made. I couldn't take that away from him, no matter how much I didn't want to see him leave.

"I understand. We're going to be lost around here without you though, my man." Truer words had never been spoken. If it hadn't been for Wayne, who knew how it would have worked out?

When I graduated with my shiny new degree in business, I'd started looking for my own success story. I had determination, a dream, and a plan to make it my reality.

I'd met Wayne a year after graduation when I walked into his office and made a similarly earth-moving announcement to the one he'd made when he'd walked into my office minutes ago.

My name is Nolan Yates and I've just bought this hotel. Wayne had looked around his shoddy office and blinked at me for a solid minute before he'd replied.

It's nice to meet you, son. He'd risen from his chair and held out his hand for me to shake. *Wayne Scott, and I'm sorry you wasted your money.*

I hadn't corrected him that it had been the bank's money and not my own. I didn't have two dollars to throw at the renovation I wanted to do, but I had that handy degree and a mouth that could sell ice to an Eskimo or sand to the desert.

Fast forward to the present day, and I owned the entire chain that hotel had belonged to. We'd restored it to its former, higher-end glory and were now revered as a landmark in every city we had a branch in.

I'd have loved to take the credit for our success, but being disingenuous just wasn't me. Wayne had been with me every step of the way. He'd advised me, critiqued me, stood up to me, and called me out when I needed to be.

He still did all those things for me, which was why I'd kept him on as my righthand man and compensated him accordingly. He shook his head at me now, a knowing smirk curving his lips.

"You think I'm going to leave you high and dry?" He exhaled on an exasperated sigh. "Maybe I haven't taught you as well as I thought I had. I'd never do that."

"What are you suggesting?"

"I'm going to hire someone to keep you organized." It was stated as fact. He wasn't asking for my approval or permission, simply giving me a heads-up on what he was going to do.

"Go ahead." Organization was not one of my strengths, and Wayne knew it. "I trust you to find a good candidate for the job."

"Of course you do." Wayne laughed again, pressing down on the armrests of his chair to push himself up out of it. "You wouldn't know organizational prowess if it bit you in the ass."

As much as I wanted to argue with him, I couldn't. "I'd get the hint if it was a big bite."

"Maybe." Wrapping his fingers around the back of the chair, he leaned on it. "To be on the safe side, I'll find you someone so good that there won't need to be a bite. Big or small."

"I appreciate it." No one would be able to replace Wayne, but an executive assistant might keep things from falling apart. "Tell Mrs. Scott hi from me. Also, tell her I said happy retirement. We'll have a party eventually, of course."

He nodded. "She's been worried about how you were going to react to the news. Thought I might put it off another year or two just to stop me from breaking your heart."

"I don't have a heart." I smirked. "Not anymore."

Wayne's expression turned sympathetic. I hated the look on anyone but him. He'd been there with me every step of the way.

When my marriage started falling apart, he'd been there. When Scarlett started staying out all night, he'd been there. The day I'd found out she'd been cheating on me, he'd been there. Through the couples counseling, the rehab, her admission to psychiatric institutions and having to explain to our daughter where her mother was, he'd been there.

Wayne understood better than anyone else what Scarlett had put Karina and me through. His sympathy was genuine. It came from a place of understanding instead of pity. It had taken me a long time to be able to distinguish between the two. *Thank you, Dr. Haversham.*

"Speaking of which," he said. "How did the final court date for custody go? I should've led with that, but Mrs. Scott's been on my ass to tell you the news. I needed to get it out before I changed my mind."

I didn't understand how Wayne had made it for forty years with his wife, but I knew that she was the center of his world. Whatever she wanted, she got. I'd never said it to Wayne, but I considered theirs to be an anomaly for relationships.

"It's okay. She'd have kept your dick in a vise until you spoke to me." True story. Wayne's wife was a goodhearted ball-buster. "It went as well as we could have hoped. I was granted full custody. Scarlett has no rights to Karina."

He whistled under his breath but held up his hand for a high five. Not a fist bump, an actual high five. I gave it to him because it had been a long, hard road to get to this point, and if Scarlett had her way, it wasn't over yet.

"Your lawyers are miracle workers. Karina's only five. I mean, obviously, I get that Scarlett doesn't deserve custody, but Karina's a little girl and she is her mom."

"It wasn't easy," I said quietly. My chest still burned when I thought about everything we'd been through in the last two years. I still couldn't quite believe it had worked out this way. "The judge agreed that Scarlett couldn't provide a stable home for Karina. Thankfully, we could prove a lot of our motivations for asking for supervised visitation, and he agreed with that, too."

"Supervised visitation?" He punched the air. "What a win. Supervised by who?"

"Scarlett's mom." We'd lost the argument that visitation should be supervised by me or my proxy, but I supposed we couldn't have won them all.

Besides, I really did want Karina to know her mother and her grandmother. I never wanted to be the person responsible for preventing them from forming a relationship with her. I only wanted it to happen in a safe environment.

"I'm really glad to hear it went your way." Wayne offered me a hug. A real one, not a bro, back-slapping farce masquerading as a hug. "Scarlett wasn't, well..."

I couldn't help but laugh as I stepped away from him after returning his hug. "Yeah, I know. It didn't hurt our case that she kept threatening to, among other things, come after me for half of the company."

"Can she do that?" He might have resigned, but I saw the flash of worry darkening his eyes.

I gave my head a firm shake. "No. Everything she's entitled to was divided and distributed when we got divorced, but it sounds like her lawyers are making her promises to keep cashing my checks."

"Sounds about right," he said. "I'm really glad it went your way."

He started walking backward, heading out of my office. "Just because I resigned doesn't mean I'm not here for you and Karina, okay?"

"I know." A genuine smile curled the corners of my lips. "Thanks, Wayne. Tell Mrs. Scott we'll have dinner sometime soon, okay?"

"You got it." With a final wave, he turned and left my office.

When the door slammed shut, I slumped into my chair and tried to contemplate the company's future without Wayne.

We'd be fine. The company was made up of more than one person. Fuck, not even I was irreplaceable, but we'd sure be worse off for seeing him leaving.

But that wasn't even the worst part of my day.

The worst part of it happened at lunchtime when I got a frantic call from Karina's school. "Mr. Yates? This is teacher Betty calling from Bright Beginnings. I'm sorry to bother you at work, but I'm afraid we have a bit of an emergency situation here."

My heart, blood, and extremities turned to ice, and I shoved to my feet, feeling like the world was about to be ripped right out from underneath me. "Is Karina okay?"

"She fine's, sir, but there's a note on the file that we're not to release her to her mother. Mrs. Yates is here though, and she's insisting on taking Karina with her. She's yelling and making a scene out front. Security has tried to talk to her, but she refuses to budge."

I was already running out of my office as fast as my feet could carry me, dread churning in my stomach.

Scarlett had gotten enough money in the divorce to be able to disappear with Karina if the school let her take our daughter home with her. Her threats to do exactly that had been one of the deciding factors in the custody case.

My heart was in my throat, my knuckles white from my tight grip on the phone as I practically flew down the stairs to the parking garage. "I'm on my way. Just, whatever you do, don't let Karina go with her."

"We'll do our best, sir," the teacher promised. "But, sir? You should hurry. We've hidden Karina in the bathroom, but we can't keep her in there forever."

CHAPTER 2

LACIE

Peachtree, Georgia. Population: 35,186 according to the latest census. It wasn't the most exciting of places to wake up, but it was home to me.

Besides, there was no place else I could wake up to the smell of my mother's famous breakfast. Well, famous in *our* family anyway. *Bacon, sausage, hash browns, grits, biscuits and gravy.*

If we were able to craft our own heaven, mine would smell like waking up at my mother's house. Fortunately for me, I woke up to the scent of my personal heaven at least two mornings a week.

Unfortunately, it showed in my waistline. Also, being twenty-four and in possession of not only my degree but also a Master's in Business Administration made me feel a little lame to be waking up in my mother's house at all.

Obviously, life hadn't exactly gone my way, but I was keeping my head up and my wits about me. *Change can come any day now.*

I reminded myself of Mom's mantra as I rolled out of bed and followed the smell of heaven down the stairs and into the kitchen. She was standing behind the stove, fully dressed with her hair pulled into an elegant updo at the nape of her neck. The sad thing was that my mom had probably spent only a few minutes getting her hair like that, whereas a similar do would take me at least an hour.

I plopped onto a stool at our farm-style kitchen island before grabbing a piece of freshly cut apple and popping it into my mouth. Mom turned with her treasured spatula in hand, eyes sparkling with laughter as she saw me sitting there in my pajamas.

"I love that you're in your twenties and you still feel comfortable enough coming down to breakfast in your pajamas."

"Shouldn't I?" I frowned and poured a glass of juice from the pitcher in front of me. "I kind of thought parents signed up for that before we're born. Isn't there a form that gets passed around where you sign all your rights to decorum within the sanctuary of your home away? I'm imagining something along the lines of 'thou shalt not require children to have any propriety within your home until they're eighty-five.'"

She rolled the light green eyes I'd inherited from her, and the corners of her mouth pressed in. "I think what you meant to say was 'thank you, Mother, for the lovely breakfast you've prepared for me.' Also, if I recall correctly, the form said 'children are excused from propriety until age six, around which time they should know better if you've taught them properly.'"

"You just said you loved my pajamas."

"I said I love that you're still comfortable enough around here to wear them to breakfast," she corrected gently. "Am I going to get that thank you for breakfast?"

She slid the oven open and made me a plate, just like she'd done all through my childhood. Guilt burned a hole through my esophagus. "Thank you, Mom. It smells heavenly and delicious and I don't know what I did in a previous life to deserve it."

She laughed at my rambling, just as she had when I was little. Sure, her hair was gray around the temple and the lines in her skin was more pronounced, but she was still Mom. Seeing her in the kitchen like this always made me feel like I was ten years old—at most. Maybe that was why I never gave a second thought to the pajamas.

"You're welcome, sunshine." Her eyes crinkled on a smile. Then she slid my breakfast over to me.

I lifted up the cutlery she'd already set out and waited for her before I dug in. Twenty-four or not, Mom was big on manners.

Once she'd made her own plate and sat down with me, she nodded at me. "Have at it, Lace. I know how much you hate to wait."

Grinning my appreciation, I tucked into her delicious food. I'd never understood how my mother kept her stick figure with her cooking, but I sure hadn't inherited that.

My own body type was more big and beautiful, and I was perfectly happy with it. I'd long since accepted that the size-zero life wasn't for me. I wasn't obese or unhealthy. I just wasn't built small. Add Mom's cooking and Dad's genetics to that, and my curves were more plentiful than a mountain pass.

I loved a good mountain pass, though. There was nothing quite as scenic as a nice, long, slow tour down one. The view, the feeling of "oh, that's where I'm going to be soon," and the moment when your breath caught because what was in front of you was magnificent.

I'd been told that it was the same for men who appreciated curves, but I hadn't yet experienced it for myself. My mountain was ridiculously, seriously, depressingly unexplored.

Yeah, that's right, girls and boys. We have a virgin in the house.

I blew out a huffed breath, which only resulted in one of my black locks getting stuck to my lip. I tried blowing it away before giving up and shoving it behind my ear.

"Thanks, Mom." I smiled around my annoyance at my own unruly hair. "And thanks again for letting me stay while I figure things out."

Last month when I'd graduated with my Master's, I'd been all starry eyed and optimistic. I'd taken every class my professors had advised, applied for jobs with every company they'd claimed to have influence in, and so many other random things.

Everything they'd told me to do, I'd done. Extracurriculars? Check. I'd been captain of the debate team for two years, joined the dance club and the chess club. Academics? Check, check, and another check.

My GPA survived all my extracurriculars intact, and I'd graduated near the top of my class.

My social life had been a little lacking. There hadn't been any time to join a sorority and go all *ra-ra for sisterhood.*

Joining a sorority might have been more effective when it came to job hunting, though. At least I'd have had contacts then, if my understanding behind the purpose of joining was at all correct.

Instead, I was back at Mom's house with a mountain of job applications sent out and no luck yet. As if she was reading my thoughts, Mom's head tilted and she peered at me above her specs, which she'd somehow kept clean of grease while cooking all that oily food.

"What are your plans now, Lace?" she asked in that tender voice of hers. "You have your Master's degree. Surely, you have something planned."

The worst thing of all to me was that there was no rush or judgment in her tone. She was being her usual supportive self, and that made it all the harder to admit that my plans had brought me nowhere.

"I'm looking into selling drugs or going into prostitution." I shrugged a pajama-clad shoulder.

Mom gave me a look that should've been patented. It said *you're not funny,* but *maybe you're a little bit funny,* but also *where the hell did I go wrong?*

That look was a serious talent.

I was trying to shake it off when she cleared her throat. "A guy I know in Washington D.C. called me the other day."

I grinned, spearing a piece of perfectly crisp bacon with my fork. "Is my mother really dating a man in the big city?"

"I'm not dating him," she scoffed. "It's not such a big city, either."

"It's the political capital," I argued, though I had no idea why. "If you're not dating him, why are you bringing up a call from him?"

It was easy enough to joke about it, since my mother would never entertain the thought of another man after my dad died. The two of them had been the ultimate couple. I'd tried to encourage her to get back up on the proverbial horse for years, but she'd shot me down every time.

"I'm bringing it up because he didn't want to talk about me," she said. "He wanted to talk about you."

"Me?" I nearly choked on my bacon. "Why?"

Her shrug was far too elegant to be happening in our little kitchen. "I've told him about you over the years, and he thinks you could be perfect for a position he's trying to fill."

If it was anyone other than my mother I was talking to, I'd have made a joke about the position he wanted to fill. Since it *was* my mother though, I held back my comment. "Okay, but why?"

"We were friends in high school, but we've kept in touch. He's actually married to Wendy."

"Wendy, as in your best friend from high school, Wendy?" I'd heard stories, but I'd never met her.

Mom smiled. "Wendy Ambrose, now Wendy Scott."

"Okay." I tried to wrap my head around it. "So her husband has a job available?"

"Not him, but his employer. They're looking for an executive assistant for the moment, but there are opportunities for growth, and the starting salary isn't bad."

The way she grinned, I knew that the starting salary was a lot better than *not bad*. "What's the company?"

"NY Hotels."

My eyes widened. "They're situated in New York?"

"No." Her eyes mirrored my own. "It's the initials of the owner, I think. It's definitely not New York. Wayne is definitely based in Washington."

"Oh." I'd go anywhere for a job at this point and do anything. Being at Mom's house was awesome, but I couldn't stay there forever.

It was supposed to have been temporary for me, but my email inbox was empty. As was Mom's mailbox—the address I'd given for postal replies.

Yeah, my options are very limited. "I'll check it out. Thanks, Mom."

She looked at me expectantly, making me realize that she wanted me to check it out right then and there. I pulled my phone out of the small silk pocket of my pajama pants and pulled up the company she'd mentioned.

My jaw nearly hit the floor when I saw how luxurious the hotels were. The suites cost more per night than I'd made a month at my college job as a bookstore clerk.

What surprised me more was the "about" page. It featured a person referred to as a "kid" who had taken a failing hotel chain and turned it into pure gold.

There were links to this "kid," but they honestly didn't matter to me. I wasn't looking to marry a twenty-three-year-old kid or something, but working at the company looked damn promising.

The employee reviews were raving, and it looked like they even had proper breakrooms. *I could totally get behind a company that has reading nooks with their napping pods.*

Mom saw my glee when I read that part of the description. "You want me to call Wayne back for you?"

"No," I said quickly. "I'll call him myself."

It wasn't pride or being stubborn that made me insist, but rather the assertiveness that Mom had instilled in me from the moment I could form cohesive thoughts.

"Sure, baby. I'll give you his number whenever you're ready."

"Will this job also be based in Washington?" Would I even take a job that far away from Peachtree? I'd even gone to college based on it being weekend-driving-distance away from Mom.

"I believe so, yes." Her lips pursed.

"What do you think about me applying for a job so far away?" I'd never go without her support. Plus, if I got to wake up to her breakfast forever, that wasn't a bad thing for me either.

"You have your own life to live, Lace." She smiled. "You have to find your own way and step out of your comfort zone. You've got a lot of life to live to make up for what you should have at twenty-four, baby. If not this, then what?"

15

CHAPTER 3

NOLAN

The soft rustling of bedding woke me up, followed by the tiniest of dips in the mattress. A sleepy smile formed on my lips before I'd even opened my eyes. *Thank God I'd gotten to her on time.*

It had been one hell of a showdown, but my baby girl was safe and home with me. There wasn't a single doubt in my mind that Scarlett still wasn't laying down her arms, but I'd be ready for every attack she ever launched if that was what it took to keep my daughter safe.

"Good morning, sweetheart," I murmured, so damn relieved that she was here with me that I felt dizzy, even while lying down with my eyes still closed.

Karina's small palm landed on my cheek, stroking it gently. "Shh, Daddy. Go back to sleep."

I readjusted my head on the pillow so there would be space for hers and hooked my arm around her to pull her body close to mine. "Five more minutes, okay?"

Her quiet giggle rang out into the early morning stillness of my bedroom. I felt her nod when she settled down next to me, her body relaxing as it curved with mine.

The new shampoo her and I had picked out the last time we went shopping smelled like vanilla and lavender. Her hair tickled my nostrils, but I breathed in deeply. This was definitely my new favorite scent. Then again, anything that reminded me of Karina instantly became my favorite.

She turned under my arm draped around her. My eyes were still closed, but I could practically feel the intensity of her gaze on me.

"Daddy?" she whispered.

"Mmm?" Like most kids, Karina didn't sleep in. Not even on Saturdays. Now that she was awake, she was going to stay that way. She might let me lie in bed for a little while longer, but there was no way I was getting back to sleep.

I cracked open an eye to find her hazel ones fixed on me. Various hues of blues and greens swirled into golden brown in her irises.

Karina was a female, mini version of me, so I knew the serious look in the eyes she'd inherited from me meant business. I lifted an eyebrow and brought up a hand to stroke it through her chocolate-brown hair.

Mercifully, Karina was completely oblivious about what had gone down at her school the day before. The teacher's aide had taken her to the bathroom and made up a game to keep her occupied and as far out of danger as she could get her.

Which was why I didn't really understand why she was looking at me the way she was. "What's up, baby? You're looking way too serious for this time of the morning."

"I woke up in my bed again," she said, as if that explained everything.

"Okay. I woke up in my bed, too. Our beds are where we're supposed to wake up."

Her little brow wrinkled. "No, it's not. I fell asleep on the couch with you."

"I know, but you're going to have to help me out here, Kare-bear. I'm not following why waking up in your bed is a problem." I covered my yawn with my hand and rolled onto my back.

Karina propped herself up on her elbow and leaned over to peer into my eyes, her face only inches away from mine. "You always take me to my room when I fall asleep."

God, it's way too early for this. I barely suppressed a groan. Karina was my entire world, but sometimes, her five-year-old brain worked in ways I couldn't comprehend, especially not seventy-three seconds after sunrise—or at least, that was what it felt like.

"I do take you to your bedroom when you fall asleep, but it's there in the name. It's *your* room and it's got *your* bed in it. Don't you like your room?"

"The room is fine." She sighed. "I don't like waking up there because you're not there."

Shit. Okay. I mentally slapped myself on the cheek a few times to wake my groggy brain up. I'd been warned that she might experience separation anxiety at times after the divorce, and it seemed like this was one of those times. All I had to do was remember the play therapist's tips.

Okay, I've got this.

Elbows hitting the mattress, I lifted my shoulders until I was in a half-sitting position, and I looked into Karina's eyes.

"I'm always going to be right here, sweetheart. There's nothing to worry about when you wake up in your bed. I'm right down the hall. You can always come to me, just like you did this morning."

She tilted her head and pondered my answer, tapping her thin index finger on her lips. "But why can't I sleep in here with you?"

"My room isn't half as much fun as yours. You have toys, your princess tent, your princess bed, and your pink curtains. Mine doesn't have any of that." I sat up fully and spread my arms to my sides, gesturing at the space around us. "See? There's not even one teddy bear in here."

She looked around as if seeing the master bedroom of our Georgetown home for the first time. The tension in her narrow shoulders finally relaxed and her nose crinkled. "You need some toys, Daddy. Everything is gray. Why don't you have any pink?"

She was a hundred-percent correct. Everything was gray. Curtains, bedspread, pillows, sheets, even the towels in my en-suite bathroom.

When I'd bought this place after Scarlett and I officially separated,

I hadn't really been focused on decorating the room. Now two years down the line, a part of me was still waiting for Scarlett to walk in after one of her crazy shopping sprees and spruce the place up.

"I don't have any pink because I'm old and boring." I winked at Karina before I rolled to my side and grabbed her, hauling her close to me to tickle her tummy. Her laughter was music to my ears.

"You're not that old, Daddy," she managed to gasp out between giggles.

Not that old, indeed. It just feels that way most of the time. Thirty-two wasn't exactly middle-aged, but it sure felt like most of my life was behind me. *The relationship part of it definitely is.*

"I'm too old to have pink in my bedroom." I let her go when she wiggled free. Then she jumped off the bed and ran to the door.

She paused when she reached it, turning back to face me. "I think I like my room more. If you don't want pink, you should at least get some toys. Really, Daddy. Your room is boring."

"Yeah, I know." I heaved myself out of bed. It was probably time to get breakfast started.

When Karina saw my feet hit the hardwood flooring, another peal of laughter burst from her, and she ran down the hall, calling out over her shoulder. "I'm going to play with my toys now because I've got them. You don't."

I chuckled as I watched her go. Then I looked around my room too. Karina had been right. It was dull as shit in here.

The room itself was fine, but I hadn't done much to it to make it feel like it belonged to a real-life person. In fact, it looked very similar to the way it had when it had been on show.

I'd fallen in love with the place the first time I'd walked in, immediately feeling like Karina and I could make a home in the one-of-a-kind, renovated, waterfront penthouse. It had three bedrooms plus a den and spectacular panoramic views of the river from just about every room. We had a large terrace, a private heated pool, and even our own garden on the roof.

The building was safe and in a neighborhood that was home to a world-class school. The area was quaint and quiet, and it had cobblestone streets and eighteenth-century architecture. I honestly couldn't imagine a better place for Karina and me to start over.

My bedroom, however, could probably use a touch of personality. Soft sunlight shone in through sheer curtains covering the windows that made up half of one wall, giving everything that early-morning glow.

I never thought I'd have to start over in my thirties and much less that I'd have to do it as a single father with a toddler in tow. But those had been my breaks. I had to live with them, and getting something done about my bedroom felt like as good a place to start as any, now that all the legalities were finally behind me.

I start focusing on the future. A future in which I'd still be living in this bedroom, alone, when Karina went off to college. *Hopefully close by*.

With a heavy sigh, I walked to my bathroom and turned on the faucet in the shower. The modern, stone monstrosity had two heads, one of which I'd never used, and some fancy settings I'd never even played around with.

Fuck, these last couple of days are just full of realizations about how much of a robot I've been for the last year. Between work and the battle royale for custody, I'd just been trying to get through it all. Nothing mattered except keeping the company on track while dealing with the shitshow that was my personal life.

The most important of all was getting custody of Karina. I ate, slept, and breathed that custody case, regardless of where in the country I'd found myself for work on any given day. Even getting to take a quick shower now without having to obsess over it was like a mini vacation.

After I was done, I dressed and headed out of my room.

"Hey, Kare-bear!" I called from the kitchen, opening the fridge to see what our options were. "Do you want some breakfast?"

I heard Karina's footsteps before the little ball of energy herself barreled into the kitchen. "Yes, please. I want to help you cook it. Cooking is fun."

"That, it is." I grinned at her and pulled out a carton of eggs, a jug of milk, a bottle of juice, and some butter. "But if you help cook, you have to help clean up. You remember our deal, right?"

"Right." She nodded and pulled a stool from the breakfast bar closer to the counter, using it to get to her usual perch on the marble next to the stove. "Are you going to work today?"

"Nope. It's Saturday, so I'm all yours."

She clapped her hands excitedly. "Yay for not working today. You always work on Saturdays."

"Not always," I argued. Then I frowned as yet another realization sank in. "Okay, maybe these last few months have been rough. I'm sorry I've been gone so much, baby. I'm hoping it's going to get better soon, though."

Leaning over to press a kiss to her forehead, I allowed my eyes to close and made a silent vow that I would do everything I could to stop traveling so much for work. Being here for Karina was my number-one priority.

Work had always been a close second for me, especially since things started going to shit with my marriage. This past year, it had been even more of an escape for me than before. I threw myself into it not only because that was what it took to run a bona-fide hotel empire, but also because burying myself in work was a coping mechanism for me.

The mere thought of losing custody of Karina had torn me apart, so I hadn't allowed myself to think about it. When I wasn't working, though, it was all I could think about, so I'd go back to work.

"I like it when you're around, Daddy," she said, drawing me out of my depressing thoughts. "But it's okay when you're not, too. I get to hang out with Uncle Alec. He's cool."

"Yeah, he is," Alec's voice piped up from the door as if he'd been waiting for his cue to walk in. My best friend wore his trademark grin and tossed his keys down on the counter as he joined us. "What's for breakfast, party people?"

I rolled my eyes, but I couldn't hold back a chuckle. "Who still says 'party people'?"

"I do." He shrugged his broad shoulders and smirked at me, green eyes twinkling in that mischievous way he had. "Since I'm the coolest guy you know, that means you have to follow the trend I'm setting and bring it back."

"I'm a party people," Karina said, eyes filled with adoration as she looked up at Alec.

He reached out and ruffled her hair, his smirk transforming into a tender smile when he held up his fist for her to bump. "Yeah, you are."

"A party *person*, baby," I corrected gently. "You're one person, so you can't be *people*. Just person."

Karina and Alec exchanged a look, something they did often, and folded their arms in unison. Her lips even pulled into a smirk that matched his. She shrugged, the motion again resembling his almost perfectly.

Alec was a brother to me in every way but blood. We even looked kind of alike. He looked after Karina whenever I had to travel, and considering how often that had been lately, he was basically co-parenting her. We joked about it often.

She'd even picked up all those little mannerisms of his, though I hoped to God that when she got older, she didn't pick up any other mannerisms from him. The guy was a player with a capital P—when Karina wasn't with him, of course.

But then again, he was in his early thirties, single, not bad looking, and didn't come with ten tons of emotional baggage. I couldn't exactly blame him for living it up. At least I occasionally lived vicariously through his misadventures.

"How's work going, bro?" he asked before grabbing the bread and carrying it over to the toaster. Alec came over so often, it felt like he lived here sometimes. He even had his own key. He was totally at home at our place, which again was the cause of many jokes.

Between that and the co-parenting stuff, maybe I should have just married Alec. Lord knew I'd have saved myself a lot of heartache.

He tossed me a look that let me know he knew what I was thinking and winked. "Put the ring back in your pocket, sweetheart. I ain't ready for no proposal. Seriously though, how's it going at work?"

"I'd never propose to you, bro. You're way too high maintenance." I laughed and shook my head. "On the work front, not great actually."

He frowned. "Why? I thought you guys were, like, rock stars over there."

"We're not. Wayne is, but he's retiring."

"You can't call Wayne that. He's old, but you can't call him retarded."

"*Retiring*, you idiot." I slid my eyes to Karina. She didn't call me out on the bad word that had slipped through, but she wasn't listening to us. She jumped off the counter and sped out of the kitchen, clearly bored of our conversation.

Picking up the spatula, I started breaking eggs into the pan. "He's looking for a replacement for himself, but I don't know how anyone is going to do everything he does."

Alec perked up as he tossed the first pieces of toast on a plate. He looked at me over his shoulder. "Make sure his replacement is hot. A girl with a body like a back road."

I glared at him, but he just shrugged.

"What?" he asked. "You can't deny that you need some curves in your life."

I flipped Alec off. I couldn't quite help but have a flashback to my brief fantasy the day before, though.

Maybe he was right. Getting laid didn't have to mean starting a relationship. It sure didn't mean that for him. It was another thing I'd have to consider adding to my list, but not now. *Not yet.*

Alec distracted me from the depressing realization that I wasn't ready for even just sex yet by telling me hilarious anecdotes about his job. He worked as a D.C. tour guide and it seemed like tourists never stopped getting up to stupid shit.

We finished making breakfast and cleaned up after eating. When Alec went off to work, Karina and I decided to go to the movies.

Whatever revelations I might have come to as I tried to take back control of my life, the fact was that Karina was the most important thing in it. And right now, she needed me to be present in the moment and to spend some quality time with her.

Everything else could wait.

CHAPTER 4

LACIE

Toto, I've a feeling were not in Kansas anymore, I thought as I stepped off the plane in Washington D.C. Of course by Kansas, I meant Peachtree. And by Toto, I meant, well, me.

There were hundreds or maybe even thousands of strangers around me, but I didn't know a single person within hundreds of miles of here to talk to. I didn't even know the man I'd flown here to meet, my mother's friend Wayne.

Putting blind faith in someone when I didn't even know what they looked like didn't come naturally to me at all. My type-A personality much preferred for everything to be well organized and in my control, but on the other hand, that very same personality made me impatient, proactive, and incapable of sitting and waiting.

In the end, I'd accepted his offer to purchase a plane ticket for me, and I hopped on the next flight out. He wanted to meet me, and I didn't see why that couldn't happen immediately.

The airport in Washington was huge—by Peachtree standards anyway. It was a hive of bustle and activity that made me feel like a shot of adrenaline had been injected straight into my heart.

I hadn't checked any luggage, so I skipped the throngs of people heading to the carousel and wheeled my small bag out to the arrivals terminal. There was man standing near the front, wearing an impeccable suit, who had my name on a small placard.

My heart jumped into my throat. *Is that Wayne?*

He saw me staring at him and nodded as he came forward and held out his hand for my suitcase. "Ms. Cole, I presume? I'm David and I'll be your driver for the duration of your visit."

"My driver?" People had those in real life? I thought those kinds of people only existed in books or movies. "You don't have to do that. I can just grab a cab."

"Nonsense." He flashed me a polite smile and gently took my case from me. "Mr. Scott sent me himself. He said to give you the VIP treatment."

I felt my eyes grow to at least double their usual size. "He did? Why?"

"I'm just the driver, ma'am. I don't ask any questions. Feel free to take a cab if you want, but I'll just follow you to the hotel anyway."

He took off walking toward the exit, and since he now had all the possessions I had brought with me, I rushed to catch up. David's eyes sparked with something like amusement when I fell into step beside him.

"Decided against that cab?" he asked.

I nodded, my brain racing to absorb everything going on around me as well as keeping up the conversation I was in. "Did Wayne really ask you to drive me around for both days I'll be here?"

"He did, yes." He tipped his head at a sleek, luxurious black car parked right out front. "That's us. May I?"

He pulled ahead of me and opened a rear door. My protests about how I could open my own doors died on my lips when I caught a glimpse of the interior. The seats looked like genuine leather, and the temperature seeping out from inside felt like a hug coming out to greet me.

The weather here was crisp and cool, that bite of the impending winter already in the air. The car was nice and warm inside, though. When I slid into it, David shut the door behind me. I ran my hands along the soft seats and wondered if I should have washed my shoes before I got in. It sure felt that way.

I'd never had a serious boyfriend, but the one guy I'd been getting to know back in high school had always made me take off my shoes before I was allowed to get into his car. It hadn't been even a quarter as nice as this.

I had the strangest urge to sit on my hands so I wouldn't be tempted to touch anything. There was a screen separating me from David, and the one thing I allowed myself to touch was the button that seemed to operate it.

"I'm here for an interview," I told David. It just felt too weird to be driven around and not to talk to the person doing it. "Got any tips for me?"

He glanced up at me in the rearview mirror. "Interview tips?"

I nodded. "My interview is later today and I'm really nervous."

There was a lot riding on me getting this job, not the least of which was finally being able to afford to stand on my own two feet. I was anxious to start making my own living, and the competitive streak inside me had been screaming at me constantly since I graduated that we were already behind.

Twenty-four. Virgin. Unemployed. Living with Mom. What my subconscious perceived as my failures played over and over again in my mind, refusing to let me forget any of it for even a minute.

If I got this job, it would mean moving here and being as far away from my mother as I'd ever been. I was still nervous about that, but it wouldn't make me turn Wayne down if he offered it to me. I'd been psyching myself up all week, and I was ready to go.

David eased us out of the airport and onto a busy motorway. *Note to self: if I move here, I'm using public transport.* I couldn't imagine driving in a place with so many cars on the road.

Once he deemed us safe, he glanced up at me again and cleared his throat. "You shouldn't be nervous, ma'am. Mr. Scott and Mr. Yates are both good men. It's a great company to work for. Joining the team was the best move I've ever made."

It was comforting that he genuinely seemed to feel that way about his job. In my mind, I imagined working for such an empire to be like one of those reality TV shows Mom liked to watch, where people got fired for breathing too loudly in the wrong place.

It didn't scare me, and it wouldn't make me back down, but I did relax a little knowing that it might not end up being like that. "How about Washington? I've never been anywhere like this before. I can't imagine what it must be like to live here."

"I've lived here all my life. Never wanted to live anywhere else." His chest puffed out. "It's the best city in the world."

"I'm pretty sure everyone says that about their city." Well, everyone who didn't come from Peachtree. "What makes this one so great?"

His eyebrows lifted. "Even the leader of the free world lives here. Think about it. The President could live anywhere and yet they all choose to live here."

"Because that big white house they all get happens to be here," I pointed out.

David shook his head emphatically, a ghost of a smile touching his lips. "I refuse to accept any one of them would have chosen anywhere different for that house to have been built. We have the Smithsonian, Arlington, the Capitol, and the Library of Congress. You can even experience real Japanese cherry blossoms at the Tidal Basin in Spring. There's nowhere else like it."

"You make some valid points," I conceded.

"I raised my three daughters here." He looked at me in the rearview mirror again and winked. "I couldn't figure out how to make a boy, but if I had, I'd have raised him here too."

I laughed at his joke and held my hands up in surrender. "Okay, okay. You win. So if I do get this job, you think moving here will be worth it?"

"Absolutely."

The car started to slow. I looked up at the hotel we were pulling up outside of, and my mouth went dry.

From the outside, it looked like the old-world Washington elegance I'd seen pictures of. Gorgeous exposed brick made up the outside facade, but there were traces of modernity in the arches and the abundance of windows.

"Mr. Scott has arranged for you to stay in the Club Suite," David said. "You're going to love it." He pulled up behind another car waiting under the porte cochere for the occupant to climb out. "He also wanted me to let you know that he'll meet you here this afternoon."

"My interview is going to be here?" When did my voice get so squeaky? I caught a glimpse of myself in the window as I stared up at the luxurious interior of the lobby. I could only just make it out from where we were waiting, but I didn't think they allowed dirty shoes in there either.

My eyes were wild, my pupils blown. David chuckled when he looked at me across his shoulder. "Don't be nervous. You're going to do great. Just be yourself."

I didn't bother to point out that he didn't know me and therefore couldn't know that I would be great if I was myself. David was being polite, and I would be too. "Thank you, and thanks again for the ride."

He nodded. "Mr. Scott thought you might like to do some sight-seeing before your flight out tomorrow afternoon. I'll collect you in the morning and show you around?"

"That sounds great." I smiled, desperately trying to ignore the way my heart was thundering in my chest. "I'll see you then."

"Good luck," he said as a suited man walked down the stairs and opened the door for me. Another walked to the back of the car to retrieve my suitcase and waved at David.

Clearly, the staff here had been told I was coming and were more than ready for me.

The VIP treatment continued all the way to my suite. I didn't even have to go through the check-in process. Even if I didn't get the job, this was an experience I knew I'd remember for the rest of my life.

My mouth gaped open when I walked into the suite. I blinked a few times, trying to find my voice to ask the man who'd showed me up if he was sure this was meant for me.

Surely, there had to have been some mistake. This room was

gorgeous. There was no way they'd put a lowly job applicant up in someplace like this for the night.

"Are you sure this is—" I stopped mid-question when I turned around to see the man had quietly taken his leave.

I was alone. In a suite the size of Mom's house. I pinched myself, but the opulent suite didn't disappear. *Holy crap. This is real.*

With a squeal, I took off running toward the gigantic bed and threw myself onto it. Fancy pillows went flying to the floor as I rolled around, running my hands over the starched fabric.

Once I'd had my moment, I got up to explore the suite. The bathroom was stunning, with polished white tile and a claw-footed bathtub as big as a hot tub. I figured at least four people could fit in the shower. What anyone needed such a big shower for was beyond me, but it sure was going to be fun to use it later.

Plush gray carpet sank down beneath my feet as I walked back into the room. I had a balcony with a view of what felt like the whole city. The living room featured a large dining table, a gas-lit corner fireplace, and couches with a flat-screen TV mounted on the wall.

Time sped up as I carefully tried to examine and take in every inch of my room, and before I knew it, it was time to get ready to meet with the illustrious Wayne Scott.

At the exact minute my interview was supposed to start, there was a knock at my door. One of the staffers asked me to follow him and led me down a few floors to a walkway that formed a bridge between this building and the next.

About a minute later, the environment changed from relaxed hotel with soft jazz flowing through the speakers to sleek, modern corporate headquarters. My head spun at the immensity of the change and how it had come seemingly out of nowhere.

The staffer leading me to the interview offered me an understanding smile but didn't say much. He deposited me in front of a door, knocked, and then wished me luck before he disappeared back the way we had come.

Before I had time to process any of it, the door swung open, and a meaty man with silver hair and a large grin held his hand out to me.

"Lacie Cole, as I live and breathe. I'm Wayne Scott. Come on in. I'm so glad you could make it."

"Likewise." I shook his large hand and followed him into an enormous office. Just like my suite, it had a fantastic view, but Mr. Scott didn't seem to notice it at all. Instead, he was looking at me with such fondness in his expression that I felt suddenly like I was looking at my grandfather.

"Have a seat," he said, making a sweeping motion at the sitting area he had set up in his office. "What can I get you to drink? Coffee, water, juice?"

"Coffee, please." I definitely needed something stronger than water to get me through this. I was more nervous than I'd ever been yet strangely comfortable with the kindly man with the flushed cheeks who held my future in his hands.

He dialed in an order for two coffees, then came to take the seat across from me. "How was your flight?"

"It was fine. Thank you so much for the ticket."

He waved his hand with a dismissive flick of his wrist. "Don't mention it. It's company policy to pay for travel and accommodation for applicants and employees. If you want the best of the best, you have to enable them to get to you."

"That's quite a policy to have," I said, wondering how much money they must make to be able to afford something like that.

Wayne grinned, and another flash of genuine fondness brightened his eyes. "Nolan insists that it shouldn't cost people money to get the shots they deserve in life. He also knows that the people he needs aren't always going to be based around here."

I assumed he was talking about Nolan Yates, owner and CEO of NY Hotels. The kid I'd seen mentioned on their website. "That's mighty generous of him."

"Yep. He's a good person and a better boss." Wayne's expression when spoke about this Nolan person was a lot like what David's had been when he'd been talking about his daughters. "Anyway, how is your mother? Wendy and I miss her so much. I don't know if you will remember, but we actually knew you as a child."

Thanks for the warning, Mom. "Please don't take offense, but I'm afraid I don't remember."

"It's not a problem." Wayne was still grinning. The lines on his face clued me in that it was something he did often. "I don't blame you. You were only a few years old when we moved. I don't remember exactly, but I didn't think you'd know who we were."

I felt terrible about not remembering. I also had a feeling that this was a person I'd have been able to learn a lot from if he'd stuck around Peachtree. "It's nice to meet you now, anyway. I wish I did remember you."

He waved his hand again, then paused the conversation when a woman with blue hair brought in our coffees. Her teeth were stained with lipstick when she smiled at me, but she also made me feel welcome here. At ease, even. It was an odd feeling to have during a job interview.

"It's nice to meet you again too, Lacie. I've been meaning to reach out to you for quite some time, but something has always come up before I got around to doing it. When I heard you were graduating with your Master's in Business Administration though, I knew the time had come to make a plan to meet you. If you're anything like your mother, you'll be perfect for what I have in mind."

He explained the role to me and what would be expected of me. To most people, it might have sounded tedious and boring, but to me, it sounded wonderful, like a dream come true. "Would I be working for you?"

He shook his head sadly. "No, you'll be working directly under Nolan. He's not here today, but you'll be his executive assistant. I'm retiring as soon as we find someone to take over my place at his right hand."

"Wow." I was stunned. When I'd agreed to take the interview, I hadn't known or expected that the job would be for the person at the very top of the hierarchy. Anxious anticipation and excitement zapped through me. So what if the CEO was a kid?

He obviously had a good head on his shoulders to be able to do what he did with this company. My research had shown that the chain had been on the brink of bankruptcy when he'd taken over.

Wayne smiled. "Yeah, wow is correct. Do you mind if I ask you some questions?"

"Go ahead," I said before I picked up my coffee and blew on the surface, causing little swirls of steam to rise up and float away.

I answered Wayne's questions as best I could, and twenty minutes later when he stood up, holding his hand out to me again, I expected him to say they would call to let me know.

"Congratulations, Lacie. Take the next couple of weeks to arrange whatever needs to be done in order for you to move here. You got the job."

My heart skidded to a stop, and blood drained from my face before everything inside me kicked into overdrive. I got the job. I couldn't believe it.

Watch out, Washington. Lacie Cole is going to be here soon.

CHAPTER 5

NOLAN

"Come look at my pictures, Daddy." Karina looked up at me as we walked into her kindergarten class, tugging on my hand to lead me in the direction of a purple plastic kids' table. "We painted with our fingers yesterday."

I stole a glimpse at my watch as she dragged me over to her seat, noting that I only had a few minutes to spare. I followed her anyway, dropping to my haunches at her table to look at some of the things they'd been doing in class. I didn't mind being a little late for her.

"These are great, sweetie. Is that us?"

She nodded proudly, pointing at the painted stick figures. "The blue one is you, the green one is Uncle Alec, and the yellow one is me."

Removing the picture from the top of the pile, she moved on to show me the next one. It didn't escape my notice that Scarlett wasn't present in any of them. "There's Granny and Grandpa with us and the animals at the zoo."

"Did you really do these yourself?" I asked. "I don't think you did. They must have been done by an artist."

Karina giggled and gave my shoulder a little shove, her hazel eyes wide as she shook her head. "No, Daddy. It wasn't an artist. It was me."

"Then you're a real artist." I grinned before pushing to my feet, then bent over to give her a kiss on the forehead. "I have to go, but I'll be here to pick you up after school."

She pouted a little but cheered up when one of her friends arrived. "Okay, Daddy. Bye bye."

"Goodbye, angel face. Have a good day." I reached out to ruffle her hair, but she had already turned and was running to her friend.

Oh, how times have changed. It felt like yesterday that I'd dropped her off for the first time and she'd refused to let go of my leg. Now she couldn't hang around to say goodbye properly. It was bittersweet, but I was smiling as I made my way to the car.

When I got to work, I went into my office and stopped dead in my tracks when I opened the door to find someone I didn't know inside. My arm froze in mid-air as I went to hang up my jacket on the stand just inside the door.

The woman in front of me looked like she had walked right out of one of the fantasies I'd allowed myself to indulge in a little more often since I'd first started coming out of robot mode two weeks ago.

Jet-black hair hung down her back in a braid that almost reached her round ass. Some of it had escaped, and the loose tendrils framed a heart-shaped face with pale, smooth skin and rosy cheeks.

Light-green eyes surrounded by long eyelashes blinked in surprise at my intrusion, a pink tongue darting out to wet her plump lips. My cock stirred at the sight of it, immediately making the connection between the similarities that the woman in front of me had to the ones I'd been thinking about when I was alone.

To quote Alec, she had a body like a back road. There were bumps and curves in all the right places. Although most of those curves were hidden behind modest clothing, I could see enough for my mind to be able to fill in the blanks.

My eyes raked from hers, across tits that looked to be a little more than a handful, and I noticed she was holding a stack of my folders. My mind was ripped from its lustful thoughts when those folders reminded me that I was in my office and she was a stranger—a stranger who seemed to be reorganizing my stuff.

"Who are you?" I asked before finally shrugging my jacket the rest of the way off and hanging it up. "And why are you in here?"

"I'm Lacie," she replied in what had to be the sweetest voice I'd ever heard. Almost the exact same voice that purred in my fantasies for me to fuck her harder and faster. My dick recognized it too, starting to swell behind my zipper.

Jesus Christ. Get it together, Yates. "Okay, Lacie. What are you doing in here?"

A delicate hand with a simple, silver ring around her middle finger found her hip, and a manicured eyebrow arched. "I'm tidying up. I don't think I've ever seen an office in such a state of disarray. It's a nightmare."

"Right." What in the ever-loving fuck was going on? To say I was confused was an understatement. "This is my office, though. What are you doing in it?"

"I just told you what I was doing. I'm organizing." She blew out an exasperated breath before she froze, the whites around her green irises becoming visible. "You're Nolan Yates?"

I nodded. "And you're Lacie, the organizer. I still don't understand why you're in my office."

"Lacie Cole," she said, coming toward me with her hand extended. "I'm so sorry. I didn't realize you were, well, you. You were supposed to be a kid."

I frowned. She was saying all this like it was supposed to clear up my confusion.

It didn't.

"Obviously, I'm not a kid." Seriously? Was I being pranked or something?

I leaned back to check the corridor outside, but there was no one waiting to yell *we got you*. Backing up to the door, I forced a tight smile. "Excuse me for a minute, please."

Wayne would know what was going on. Nothing happened in this company that he didn't know about. I needed to find Wayne.

He was in his office when I got there, and he looked up when I entered. I closed the door behind me and put my hands on my hips. "Who the fuck is Lacie Cole, and why is she in my office?"

I didn't mention that I thought she was the sexiest woman I'd seen in a long, long time or that I'd never met anyone quite like her. In a single one-minute conversation, she'd criticized me, basically called me a disorganized slob, become frustrated with me, and told me that, for some unknown reason, she'd thought I was a kid.

Wayne beamed at me. "Remember that conversation we had when I told you I was going to hire someone to keep you organized when I was gone? Lacie Cole is the woman I hired for the job."

My eyebrows shot up. "She's my executive assistant?" How the fuck was I supposed to concentrate on work when the very embodiment of my dirty fantasies was right beside me? "No, that can't be right."

"It is." He flashed me a grin that showed off all his teeth. "Isn't she great?"

"I don't know. I just met her." *And eye-fucked her.* "Why didn't I know she was starting today?"

Sighing heavily, he gave me a pointed look. "I made a note of the interview on your calendar two weeks ago, and I put her on it as starting today just after I hired her. She needed some time to make preparations to move here. I even sent you her file before the interview."

Fuck. I hadn't been paying much attention to my calendar lately. "Okay, well, I'd better get back. Thank you for finding someone."

Lord knew how I was going to work with her by my side twenty-four-fucking-seven, but I was going to have to figure it out. If the girl had moved to take this job, I couldn't exactly reassign her just because I was attracted to her.

Plus, Wayne had hired her to take over for him. If he trusted her with the job, then so did I. I knew I wouldn't find anyone better than the person he had chosen, and that person was Lacie Cole.

My dick was just going to have to learn to live with it. It was a damn inconvenient time for her to be starting, giving that it had just rejoined the party, but there was nothing to be done about it. I wouldn't fire her or reassign her. That would be way too petty and childish.

Wayne called after me as I left his office to go back to my own. "Let me know how she works out, Nolan. I really think she's the one, though."

Taking a deep breath before I opened the door again, I sat my imagination down and gave it a firm talking to. There would be no thinking about Lacie in any appropriate ways and no more drawing of parallels between her physical attributes and those of the nameless women I conjured up when alone.

I found her still working on straightening up when I finally walked back in. She looked up, her cheeks flushing a deeper rose as she held out her hand again. "I didn't mean to offend you, Mr. Yates."

"Nolan, please. You didn't offend me. Don't worry." This time, I didn't leave her hanging. I took her small hand in mine and tried to ignore how soft it was. "Maybe we should go grab something to eat so we can get to know each other before we get to work, okay?"

"Okay," she agreed, giving my hand a quick but firm squeeze before withdrawing hers from it. "I've heard that the signature food I have to try here is called a Half Smoke. We should go get that."

I blinked at the bossiness in her tone. She was bossy, but she was also polite. It left me confused as hell as to what her personality really was, but I supposed there was only one way to find out.

"Sure. I know where we can find some of that." I motioned toward the open door and grabbed my jacket, putting it back on. "Let's go."

CHAPTER 6

LACIE

"Hi," I greeted the hostess at the diner Nolan had chosen for us. "We'd like a table for two, please."

He stood beside me, his mouth closing without a sound having come out of it. I could see that he was taken aback by my assertiveness. Men were so used to being the ones doing things like getting tables when they were around that they were often intimidated by women who did it for them.

I snuck a peek at my gorgeous boss, trying to determine if he was just surprised or whether he truly was intimidated. If it was the latter, I was so screwed.

The man might look like sex on a stick, much more like a model than the CEO of a billion-dollar company, but that didn't mean he didn't have bite. And not the good kind of bite, either. The kind that got you fired on your first day for being more forward than women were "supposed to be."

To my relief, I only saw surprise in his expression. There was none of that male aggression that tended to shine through when their masculinity was threatened.

I wasn't a feminist by any means, but Dad had passed when I was barely a teenager. His premature and untimely death had left Mom and me to fend for ourselves. My mother had quickly learned what it would mean for us to keep standing on our own two feet. She didn't take crap from anyone and didn't allow people to walk all over her.

A lot of people had tried to take advantage of her over the years, but she'd gotten through it all with her head held high.

Assertiveness is your ability to act in harmony with your self-esteem without hurting others, Mom had always told me.

I smiled as I remembered the inspirational quotes she used to stick up on our fridge. I still didn't know if they'd meant more for me or for herself, but they'd stuck with me anyway.

The hostess nodded and led us to a booth near the back, setting menus down on our table and telling us that a waitress would be with us shortly. Nolan slid into the booth with curiosity burning in his eyes.

"So, Lacie, I'm sorry about earlier. I didn't realize you were starting today." Perfectly straight white teeth showed when he grinned. "I didn't mean for us to get off on the wrong foot."

"We didn't," I assured him. Sitting across from him like this, it was a little more difficult to formulate words than usual.

The man truly was stunning. Since I'd been expecting a guy much younger than even my twenty-four years, I'd pictured a boy who'd had a run of good luck. *So not the case.*

This was no boy sitting at the booth with me. Nolan was all man, and a pretty damn decent specimen of one, too.

Eyes like a swirling vortex of blue, green, and gold were intelligent and alert, so intense that my entire body had heated up beneath them earlier. Short dark-brown hair curled ever so slightly around his ears and at the nape of his neck.

The charcoal suit he wore couldn't hide what was sure to be an incredibly sculpted body. I could tell from the way the material stretched and clung, from the planes and bulges being exactly where I wanted them to be.

At somewhere around six foot four, he was taller than anyone I'd ever had regular contact with and at least a foot taller than me. He towered over me, but instead of making me feel threatened, it made me feel safe somehow. As cool and confident as he came across, he also exuded this air of warmth and comfort.

It was a heady combination of qualities to have. I couldn't deny that it made him even more attractive to me. And that was without his broad shoulders and lean, tall frame. A swimmer's build. *Hands down, my favorite build on a man.*

While I couldn't deny that my panties had gotten unnaturally damp when I'd first seen him, especially since I'd seen the heat that had flashed momentarily in his eyes, I also knew I didn't have to worry about anything happening between us.

He was so far out of my league, he was playing a different sport altogether. The heat I'd seen had disappeared so fast that I knew he knew it, too. Also, he was my boss. I was pretty sure all workplace relationships were frowned upon, and that didn't seem like a good way to start my career.

"Tell me about yourself," he said, startling me out of my inner ramblings.

I placed my hands in my lap and sat up straighter, hoping that I appeared confident, capable, and professional. "I graduated with a degree in Business Administration and obtained my Master's last semester. I've been working since I was thirteen, mostly in administrative or sales positions."

Bookstore clerk was an administrative position for purposes of this discussion, as was babysitting. I'd helped the kids with homework and logistics, so it wasn't a lie. I just wasn't going into a lot of detail.

"A Master's degree?" Nolan whistled under his breath, more impressed by my education than my work history. "That's impressive. Why did you apply for a job as an assistant?"

"Executive assistant," I corrected him firmly, cocking my head. "What's wrong with that position?"

He frowned, confusion evident on his brow. "What? Nothing. I didn't mean that there was anything wrong with it. I meant that people with your educational background usually apply for jobs in management or on the higher levels of analysis, at least in my experience."

"Oh." It was a good point and one that I knew to be true.

Sucking in a deep breath, I forced myself to tone it down. I had a tendency to be a touch defensive at times, and this guy had me all rattled and tied up in knots.

It wasn't right that he was obviously really talented at what he did, richer than my hometown, and looked the way he did. *Pick one, damn it. Let the rest of the population in on some of what you've got.*

The waitress saved me by arriving to take our order. Nolan smiled at her, and I swore I saw her knees buckle. *Welcome to the club, girl.*

"I'll have the biscuits and gravy, please."

My hand shot out to stop her from taking his menu away. "You shouldn't order that. It will raise your cholesterol."

"So will the Half Smoke you came here to order," he said, then looked back up at the waitress. "Biscuits and gravy for me, please. The lady will have the Half Smoke with mustard slaw and crispy onions."

She didn't look at me to confirm, having eyes only for Nolan while she jotted down the order and asked about drinks. I couldn't say I blamed her.

"Wayne hired you to be my assistant you know, not my mother," he said once the waitress was gone. A muscle in his jaw ticked and his shoulders were rigid.

It didn't take a genius to figure out that he was getting irritated. I gave him the sweetest smile I could muster. "It's kind of the same thing."

"No, it's not." He ran his hands through his hair, closing his eyes as if sending up a prayer for patience. "Mothers are allowed to nag and have an opinion about your personal life, your lifestyle choices, all those wonderful things they like to harp on about. Assistants are supposed to assist, not make things more difficult."

"I was assisting with your diet," I argued because there was something wrong with me and I just couldn't back down now. *Damn you, stupid knots!*

Logically, I knew that he was right and I was wrong to have interfered with his choice for breakfast, but it felt like taking a knee now would set some kind of precedent for the future of our relation-

41

ship. Those damned knots were just making everything come out wrong.

"I'm an all-rounder," I said. "I'm happy to assist in all aspects of your life."

Nolan raised a dark brow, a smirk forming on his lips while I replayed my own words and realized what they sounded like out loud.

My cheeks became balls of fire, but I refused to take it back.

"Really? All aspects of my life?" His voice was so much huskier. I was sure of it. *Oh my greatest, garbled gosh. Why in the name of a certain frustrated virgin who shall not be named do I have to find him so sexy?*

I swallowed back my humiliation, my urge to apologize for how that sounded, and most importantly, my lust, but I stood my ground. "Absolutely. Anything you need, I'm here for you."

The amusement that danced in his eyes was like a bucket of ice poured over my overactive libido. Knowing he was out of my league and seeing him basically laughing at even the insinuation of him needing anything like *that* from me were two very, very different things.

"Would you care to give me some examples of things I might need that you'd be happy to take care of for me?"

"Oh, you know." I waved my hand around. "Just, whatever you need. Laundry, gastronomical recommendations, the number for a dietitian."

"You think I need a dietitian's number?" His smirk manifested fully, and it was as alluring as it was annoying.

"If you're eating biscuits and gravy for breakfast every day, then yes." *Why, hello pot. Have you met kettle?*

"I don't eat them every day. I'm having them today because we're here, and while this place has some of the best Half Smoke in the city, they also have the best biscuits and gravy."

"Well, I'll be sure to get you the number for a good doctor then, too. When your cholesterol catches up to you, we'll need someone who can get all the facts from an objective source."

"You're going to be the objective source?" he asked with more than a tinge of disbelief in his voice. "You don't seem entirely objective to me so far."

"Of course, I'm objective." The nerve of this guy.

He folded his arms on the table and ducked to look into my eyes. "It doesn't quite seem that way to me."

Just as my mouth started opening to form a protest, the waitress brought out our food, along with two cups of coffee. I thanked the gods of caffeine for the much-needed fortification and tucked into my breakfast.

The Half Smoke wasn't half bad. It was a confused sausage-type thing made with half beef and half pork. It also definitely wouldn't be good for my cholesterol, so I kind of got where he'd been coming from with that.

Nolan and I kept up the banter while we ate. When he pushed his plate away and drained the last of his coffee, he pulled out his wallet and tossed a few bills down on the table.

"Thank you for agreeing to come grab a bite with me, but I don't need an assistant."

Oh no. No. Nonononononono. I was not about to let his company drag me halfway across the country only to send me packing again. "Really? Did you know you have a conference call in twenty minutes?"

His face fell and he cursed under his breath. Maybe he hadn't answered my question, but it was clear that he hadn't known about the call. "Fine. Come on. We need to get back to the office."

Looking at me over his shoulder, he strode about two paces ahead and sighed. "Look, I'm not happy about this, but I guess I do need you. Try to keep up, okay?"

"Okay." Despite his grumbling and everything else that made him less than ideal as a boss, I followed him out of the restaurant with a smile on my face. *I still have the job and he admitted to needing me. That's a win, right?*

CHAPTER 7

NOLAN

"Why on God's green earth did you hire that woman?" I asked Wayne as he sat down at the coffee shop we used for our meetings sometimes.

Both of us liked to get out of the office, and this place made a great home brew that we were partial to. Although given what I'd recently learned of Wayne's taste, maybe I had to reassess whether the coffee really was good.

A line appeared between his brows, but he smoothed it away quickly. "Her mother has always been a good friend of the family. She was Wendy's best friend in high school, and they never lost touch."

"Okay, but why hire her? She's going to be a massive pain in the ass."

He tucked his chin closer to his chest, crossing his arms. "No, she's going to be what you need to keep the company moving in the right direction. Why do think she's going to be a pain in the ass?"

My eyes narrowed. "She's infuriating. She's a bossy, interfering know-it-all who's only polite when it suits her. She criticized my office within her first five minutes in it. Then she tried to tell me what to eat. I think she accidentally propositioned me but then didn't have the balls to bring it up or address it. It's pretty clear that she has no professional experience. She's just all over the place."

Wayne chuckled as I listed my issues with her, sitting back in his chair when I was done. His arms were still folded, and he was wearing an amused expression.

"Tell me, Nolan, when did you develop a problem with strong, assertive women?" he asked.

"I don't have a problem with strong, assertive women. I have a problem with her."

"Considering what I saw from her and what I know about her mother, she is a strong, assertive woman. I didn't take you for the kind of man to be afraid of that."

"I'm not afraid of it." In fact, I preferred people who stood up to me and for themselves. I liked people who spoke their minds and said what they meant. "What she is isn't assertive, Wayne. She's insane."

"Actually." He cleared his throat. "She reminds me a lot of you when you first took over the company. I had many of those same problems with you when I met you. You even tried to tell me what to eat, remember?"

"You wanted pizza, and I insisted that Chinese was healthier."

He nodded and formed a gun with his fingers, miming pulling the trigger. "Exactly."

When he gave it a minute to sink in, my eyes widened. "You're not serious. She's isn't anything like me, and I know for a fact that I never propositioned you. Not accidentally or otherwise."

"You didn't, huh?" He let his head fall back as he laughed. "You told me you'd suck my dick if we got that Italian marble for the bathrooms at a discounted rate."

"I didn't mean it," I protested, nearly choking on my first sip of coffee.

Wayne gave me a look. "From what you just said, neither did she."

Fuck. He had me dead to rights on that one, except... "Yeah, but I also said she didn't have the balls to face it. If memory serves, I offered to give you that blowjob when you got us the rate."

45

He rolled his eyes. "Well, I think that one little discrepancy is warranted under the circumstances. Don't you?"

"Yeah, okay, but I still don't think she's anything like me."

"You need to give her a chance, Nolan. She could do great things at this company if you let her. I didn't hire her on a whim or only as a favor to her mother. She wasn't the only candidate I interviewed, but she was the only one I seriously considered."

Searching Wayne's eyes, I nodded slowly. I didn't listen to a lot of people, but he was one that I had a lot of respect for. His judgment had played a key role in getting the company to where it was today, and his advice had saved my ass more than once.

If he said I had to give her a chance, I'd do it. There was also the fact that Mrs. Scott might actually remove my balls with a blunt butter knife if there was a delay in Wayne's retirement after he'd found his replacement.

I couldn't make him wait any longer, and I kind of liked my balls where they were. "Okay, I'll give her a chance."

"Good." His easygoing grin appeared. "After coffee, I'm going home to spend the day with my wife. We want to do some renovations to the house, and she wants me with her when she goes to pick stuff."

I couldn't quite believe he was really retiring, but he was. There was no reason why he had to be at the office every day now that Lacie was. I was going to miss the hell out of my friend and mentor, but I had to respect his wishes.

"Sure. Tell Mrs. Scott hi from me."

"Will do," he replied and picked up his coffee. "Let's get this show on the road, shall we? There are tiles out there somewhere with my name on them, and I'd really like to get them picked out today."

Understanding that he needed to get going, I launched into the agenda I had in my head for our meeting. We finished much faster than usual, presumably because Wayne really was in a hurry, and we were done before I could ask when he planned on leaving the office for good.

When I got back to the office, I was in a bad mood. Seeing filing cabinets lining the wall of the outer office to my own, which was the space that was becoming Lacie's office, made me feel even worse.

"What is this?"

"They're called filing cabinets," she said. Although the words were snarky, her tone was sincere. This woman confused the shit out of me.

I ground my teeth and sucked in a deep breath through my nose. "I know what they are, Lacie. What are they doing here?"

She finally raised her head out of the drawer where she'd been in the process of hanging those ancient files with the metal rods in them. "I need to keep your records somewhere that I can find them. Since you didn't seem to have any logical system going in your office, I took the liberty to create one myself."

I physically had to bite my tongue to keep it from saying something. I'd promised Wayne I'd give her a chance, and firing her on the spot for fucking up my system that I'd had going for years didn't qualify as giving her a chance. I breathed out through my nose and reminded myself what Mrs. Scott would do to me if I fucked with Wayne's replacement.

Lacie opened her mouth to keep explaining her reasons for wrecking my office, but I wasn't listening anymore. I walked into the space that felt positively empty now, thanks to her "organizational skills," and fell into my chair.

Obviously, she wasn't very good at reading people since she didn't leave me alone after that.

After giving me only a couple of minutes of silence to collect my thoughts, calm down the thunderstorm raging through my body, and try to stop myself from going off on my assistant for the first time in my life, the door cracked open.

Lacie's head popped in, a tablet computer clutched in her hand. "Have you got a minute? We need to go through your schedule for the rest of the week."

She walked in without waiting for an answer and took a seat on the edge of the chair across from me. Her back was so straight, I was convinced there really was a stick up her butt.

"Sure. Come on in. Have a seat."

"Thank you." She smiled politely. Lifting up the tablet, she tapped on the screen to bring it to life and rambled off a list of things I already knew about. "You also have a meeting with some of the general managers on Friday morning. They're flying in from four of the locations to discuss site inspections, upgrades, and a couple of other things. I've emailed you the updated agenda."

Okay, so a list of things I'd already known about and that meeting —which I'd set up months ago and had promptly forgotten about. I really needed to start using my calendar again. I also had a new appreciation for what Wayne had been dealing with when it came to keeping me on track for the past couple of years, despite my personal issues.

"Thank you. I'll take a look at it."

"No problem. Just let me know if you'd like to add anything." The reminder that I'd just gotten of why Wayne was right and I did need her made the irritation about the cabinets and my system fizzle out.

It honestly hadn't been much of a system. *More of a general idea, a wish, and a prayer.*

The cabinets weren't that bad, either. Sure, they belonged to a different era, but if they'd been good enough to serve in every company around the world for years, they were good enough for me.

Feeling some of the haze clearing from my mind, I noticed for the first time what Lacie was wearing today when she stood up and smoothed out the... dress?

She stepped away from the chair, and I realized it wasn't a dress. The legs were joined together. It was honestly so damn shapeless and baggy that I didn't even know if that type of garment had a name.

In fact, with as loose as it fit, I wasn't even sure that it was a garment meant for being worn on the human body. It wasn't only that, but the thing was a terrible shade of burnt orange too.

Holy hell. My one hand dragged through my hair while the other scratched the stubble on my chin. "Thank you, Lacie. There is one more thing, actually."

She lifted her eyebrows, along with the tablet, tapping it back to life as if expecting to have to take notes. "Sure, what's up?"

48

"I don't know how to put this delicately," I started, rolling my lips into my mouth.

The green in her eyes became brighter when she was amused apparently. "I'm not a flower, Nolan. You don't need to put things delicately around me."

I nodded.

She was right.

She could dish it out, so I might as well see if she could take it. "Fine. If you're going to be around the office and coming to the meetings and stuff, you need to dress more appropriately. Go get some suits, maybe some dresses that were made to fit humans and not whatever that thing was made for. Take Maureen if you want. If you don't want to take her, go down to the fifth floor. Track down Maggie Harper. She used to be in charge of hiring personal shoppers before she started here."

Fire appeared in Lacie's green eyes before they narrowed to slits, her glare piercing and dark. Before she could climb on her soapbox about her appearance after literally just telling me that she didn't need me to be delicate, I pulled a company credit card out of my wallet and handed it over to her.

"Your appearance matters, Lacie. You need to look professional and not like a student going through an alternative, grunge phase. Take the card and swipe it until it catches fire for all I care, but take the day and go get some clothes."

I lifted my chin when I was done, ready for whatever challenge she was about to throw down. She glared at me for another long minute, her mouth opening and closing several times before she plucked the card out from between two of my fingers and stormed out of the office.

Okay, so maybe it wouldn't have killed me to have phrased that a little more delicately. What could I say?

She should have given me a fucking minute.

CHAPTER 8

LACIE

Shopping for clothes was only fun for thin people. I was sure of it. Since I wasn't one of those people, it really wasn't fun for me. In fact, I hated it with a passion that was only rivaled by my hatred of taking a sip of coffee, only to discover that it had gone cold.

Most of the clothes I owned, I'd bought purely out of necessity and, for the last few years, only online. At least buying clothes online was slightly less traumatizing than having to face harsh lights in changing rooms, seeing something I liked only to find that it didn't come in sizes anywhere near mine, or dealing with the judgmental stares of salespeople who only wanted to direct me to the outdoor section of their store. *You know, the place where they keep the tents.*

I huffed out a frustrated breath as I flicked through another rack of clothes that looked like it had been made for stick figures. *Go shopping, he said. It will be fun, he said.*

Well, okay, Nolan hadn't actually sent me shopping for the fun of it. He'd sent me because apparently, I dressed like I was going through a campus grunge phase. It stung like I'd walked face first into a hornets' nest to know that the hottest man I'd ever seen thought my appearance wasn't up to par.

I wondered if he was going to try sending me for plastic surgery or liposuction next. *Don't be dramatic, Lacie. Just buy a damn dress.*

Another rack later, I realized that this shopping spree wasn't going to work out for me. I didn't want to be out shopping. I wanted to be in the office doing the job I'd come here to do.

Screw Nolan Yates and his opinion about my clothing. The only opinion of his that mattered to me was what he thought about the job that I was doing, and I actually had to do it before he could form that opinion.

Thrusting my chin into the air, I marched my jiggly butt right out of the store and back to the office. All the way there, I tried to breathe through my anger over him sending me out to buy clothes in the first place.

Who did he think he was, ordering me to go shopping like that? Well, I had tried to tell him what he could and couldn't eat, but this was different—or at least I felt like it was.

And okay, to be fair, he had given me a company card to do my shopping with, which was pretty considerate of him since he wasn't responsible for buying me clothes to come to work in, but still.

I was furious at him for suggesting that I needed new clothes. What was wrong with what I was wearing? Absolutely nothing.

It wasn't inappropriate, immodest, or totally worn out. I didn't look like a beggar or a stripper or anything else that I shouldn't have looked like in his fancy corporate offices.

So, okay, my outfit today might have been the wrong size when it arrived, and it might not have been what I thought it was when I ordered it, but it wasn't that bad. Glancing down as I stomped to the office, I realized that the color also wasn't great.

Honestly though, I really didn't care too much what I wore. As long as it covered me properly and was comfortable, I was happy with it.

It wasn't that I didn't look after myself. I kept my hair and nails neat and wore simple makeup. I just didn't have an obsession with fashion the way some other people did.

When I walked back into Nolan's office without any shopping

bags, he arched a dark eyebrow as he lifted his head. "I could have sworn I told you to take the rest of the day off to go shopping."

"You did." I turned to shut the door firmly behind me, not wanting anyone else to accidentally witness this. "But I didn't come to D.C. to worry about my clothes. I came here to work and I would very much like to get back to it. I don't need a shopping spree, your card, or your fashion advice."

Reaching into the front pocket of my pants, I pulled out the heavy black credit card and placed it down with a decisive click on his desk. Nolan looked from me, to the card, and back again.

"That thing has pockets?"

I nodded, folding my arms across my chest. "It does because it's a perfectly practical, perfectly appropriate garment for work."

His lips curved into a gentle smile. Not a smirk, an honest to god smile, and it was beautiful. "You just called it a garment. You don't even know what it's really called, do you?"

I opened my mouth to argue, but then I realized that I couldn't. My shoulders slumped. "No idea. It wasn't what I thought it was when I ordered it."

"I know the feeling," he said, that stunning smile still on his lips. "I ordered a shirt once, and when it came, it was a pillowcase."

I was so surprised by his admission that I laughed. "Really?"

"Really." He chuckled and closed the file in front of him, motioning with long fingers at the chair across from his. "Have a seat, Lacie."

It occurred to me that for the first time since I met him, we were have having an amicable conversation. It felt nice not being at odds with him or trying to sell myself to him. *Not in* that *way. Jeez.*

I sank into the leather chair and actually felt welcome there this time. Well, more welcome than when he hadn't invited me to sit down.

Nolan sat back and looked into my eyes, making me momentarily lose myself in his once again. With the blue, green, and gold fighting for dominance, I couldn't quite decide which there was more of. Just that the overall effect really was gorgeous.

"Why didn't you buy any clothes, Lacie?" he asked. There was no hostility or judgment there, only curiosity. "I don't think I've ever met a woman that I could give my company credit card to and not have it come back a smoldering hunk of plastic."

A small smile tugged at the corners of my lips. "Well, now you have."

"Yeah, it seems so. You didn't buy anything?" He cocked his head, a lock of his dark hair barely falling across his forehead. "Like, not a single thing?"

I shook my head, my teeth sinking into my lower lip. When I didn't say anything else, he prompted me again. "Why not?"

"I don't need new clothes. I have enough clothes. All I want is to do my job."

"While that's admirable, I'm afraid I'm going to have to insist that you get some new clothes to do your job in." He wasn't being rude about it anymore, but his voice was firm.

"Why?" I was genuinely curious. It seemed like this was important to him, and I didn't understand it at all.

"Appearance is important to the people who come into the office and who we deal with." He motioned toward his own suit, dragging my attention to his abdomen.

For a second, I found myself wondering what he looked like underneath the expensive fabric covering him, but I caught myself before I started drooling or something equally embarrassing.

"Our hotels are at the higher end of the pricing scale," Nolan was saying when I tuned into the conversation again. "Luxury and class are literally our business. We sell extravagance, opulence even. To be able to do that, we need to look the part."

"I'm your assistant. It's not like I deal with clients."

"You're my *executive* assistant," he said, making the same correction that I'd made when we went to breakfast. The way his lips curled up told me he remembered it, too. "You may not deal with clients on a daily basis, but there will be times when you will need to deal with them. It's not just about the clients, though. It's about the image we portray of the company to the world. Trust me. If we owned a couple of low-budget motels, I'd be the first one to show up at work wearing jeans and a T-shirt."

"Do you even own jeans and a T-shirt?" Try as I might, I couldn't imagine him wearing anything but his immaculate suits—or nothing at all—but I didn't need to be thinking about the times my imagination had strayed there right now.

Nolan's eyes crinkled as he laughed, the sound rich and melodic. "Of course, I do. I just don't get to wear them as often as I'd like. Now, how about if I go shopping with you tomorrow? We need to get you some clothes that show you're a professional in a professional business. I'll show you what I mean."

Maybe it was because I was entranced by his laugh, or his eyes, or just about everything about him when he was like this, but despite my intense hatred of shopping, I nodded.

"Perfect," he said, placing his hands back on the folder he'd closed when I came in. "In that case, you may get back to work."

"Thank you." I flashed him a relieved smile and then practically sprinted out of his office. The effect of him when he was being nice, when he wasn't snapping or glaring at me, was almost too much.

If he was going to be like this more often, I was going to have to start keeping dry panties in my office. God, I really needed to do something about depriving my nether region. It was becoming a serious distraction, especially with a boss who looked like mine did.

Forcing myself to stop wondering what it would feel like to have him inside me, giving me that soft smile as he moved above me or cuddled with me after, I buried myself in work. It was a pretty effective technique to distract me from Nolan and sex and sex with Nolan. *Which I really shouldn't even be thinking about.*

When I got home that night, I'd managed to complete everything that had been on my to-do list for the day, and I hadn't had another brief moment of hormone-induced insanity. It had helped that Nolan had been in meetings all afternoon and I hadn't really seen him again.

After making myself a cup of tea, I stretched out on the couch in front of the bay window in my apartment and admired the lights of the city twinkling below as I pulled out my phone. It was time for my promised weekly call to my mother.

We got all caught up before she asked what was bothering me. I'd tried to keep my voice light and airy, but it didn't sound like I'd been as successful as I thought.

I sighed, wishing that the phone had a cord I could play with like the one she was on did. "I'm worried about my job."

"Why?" Surprise clung to her tone. "I spoke to Wayne earlier this week, and he told me things were looking great over there."

"It's not Wayne I'm worried about." Boy, it would have been much easier if I had been working for him. "I don't think my boss likes how assertive I am."

"Has he fired you?" she asked.

I didn't want to tell her that he'd tried. Besides, that wasn't what she'd asked anyway. "No, he hasn't."

"You must be doing something right then," she said. "Don't doubt yourself, baby. You're an asset to any company, and they're lucky to have you. Just stay true to yourself. You can't go wrong by being you."

CHAPTER 9

NOLAN

"Daddy, I can't find my penguin bracelet," Karina yelled from her bedroom. "It's gone."

"It's not gone, sweetheart," I called back to her, sliding the final pieces of fruit for our breakfast from the chopping board into a waiting bowl. "I'll come help you look for it now."

"What did she lose this time?" Alec asked as he walked into the kitchen and headed straight for the fridge. "If it's the red ribbon, I think I saw it under the couch the other day."

"If you saw it there, why didn't you pick it up?" I asked. "I swear, you're worse than her sometimes."

Alec laughed as he pulled a carton of milk out of the fridge and took a swig from it, proving my point. He wiped his mouth with the back of his hand after he swallowed. "Because then I wouldn't know where it was the next time she was looking for it."

"It's not the ribbon anyway." I rubbed my chin as I tried to picture the bracelet she was looking for. "It's the penguin bracelet. Why does something always have to be missing when we're getting ready for school?"

He shrugged. "The nature of the beast, I guess. You go help her hunt it down. I'll mix up the fruit salad and get the yogurt and muesli out."

"Thanks." I jogged out of the kitchen and went to track down the bracelet with Karina. We had less than forty minutes before she had to be at school, and she still had to have breakfast.

Thankfully, the bracelet wasn't as far gone as a lot of other things we'd had to find before she would go to school. It ended up being in her drawer instead of hanging from the little stand I'd gotten her.

Proudly sporting the bracelet made up of silver penguins linked together with small rings that we'd gotten at the aquarium, Karina followed me to the kitchen.

"Eat up," Alec said to Karina, sliding a bowl he'd already dished up for her to her usual seat. "I added an extra dollop of strawberry yogurt for you."

Her lips spread into a radiant smile. "Thank you, Uncle Alec."

"No problem," he said to her before turning to smirk at me. "I think I'm today's favorite."

I rolled my eyes. "You're the favorite every day because you don't need to dish out discipline or get her out of bed in the mornings."

"True." He chuckled, getting some breakfast for himself and joining us at the counter. "How's work? You seem to be in more of a hurry than usual."

"Yeah, I have to squeeze a shopping trip into my workday. It's not ideal."

A line appeared between Alec's raised eyebrows. "Why? What do you need to shop for?"

"My new assistant, Lacie. The woman dresses like she's never heard of corporate attire." Or attire that fit her properly at all. "I tried sending her out for clothes yesterday, but she came back empty handed."

His eyes slid to Karina, letting me know that he was letting me off easy with the interrogation because of her. "What's she like, this new assistant of yours?"

"She's organized," I said. I couldn't tell him any more than that with Karina here. Anything I said about another woman, even if there was nothing going on between us, could confuse her right now.

Alec nodded like he'd just realized the same thing. "Okay, well, I can take Karina to school if you want."

Relief filled my chest. "I'd really appreciate it. I have no idea how long this shopping trip is going to take, but I have a ton of stuff to get done today."

"Why not take your assistant another day then?"

"If you saw what she wore yesterday, you wouldn't be asking me that question." I honestly didn't understand why anyone with a body like hers would want to hide it underneath that shapeless sack. "It needs to be today."

"Okay." Alec grinned and nudged Karina with his elbow. "Hear that, kiddo? You're riding with me today."

She let out a cheer. "I love riding with you. We get to sing along to the Spice Girls."

My eyebrows jumped up as I shook my head at him. "The Spice Girls? Seriously, bro?"

"They were the cornerstone for our generation." Alec shrugged, totally unashamed of being busted for not only listening to the Spice Girls but also for singing along to their songs. "Those are our anthems, man. Don't even try to deny it."

With a roll of my eyes, I decided to shelve this argument for another day.

When I got to work, Lacie was already there. She sat at her desk, the corners of her lips turning down when she saw me. "I was really hoping you'd be sick today."

"What?" My head jerked back. I'd thought we'd made some progress in our working relationship with our conversation yesterday.

Her green eyes flared wide open. "I didn't mean that I wanted you to be sick. I just… We don't have to go shopping. It's not really my thing."

Oh. That again. "We're going shopping. Come on. There's no getting out of it now."

We got to the high-class department store down the block a few minutes later, but I'd practically had to drag Lacie with me. She was much more uncomfortable with this than I thought she would be.

"Would you relax already?" I asked as we stood in the elevator, being taken up to the top floor where the ladies' section started. "This isn't supposed to be a punishment."

Lacie's arms were crossed so tightly that her breasts were just about sitting under her chin. I tried not to notice them, but it was impossible, even in the baggy button-up shirt she was wearing.

She shot me a look in the mirrored doors we stood in front of. "That's easy for you to say. I bet you just have a ton of fun shopping."

"Hate it actually," I said cheerfully, trying to lighten the mood. "But since we're not here to pick out boring suits for me, this should be fun."

"Oh, yes, of course," she grumbled. "Because we're here to pick up boring suits for me."

"They don't have to be boring." I grinned, trying to hide that my mind had jumped to suggesting that we pick up a few things that were decidedly less boring than suits. *Like lingerie.* "We can get some interesting stuff too."

Lacie's gaze barely flickered to mine in the mirror, so it turned out that I shouldn't have worried that she might catch a glimpse of any less-than-professional thoughts from me. She didn't say anything when the doors slid open and we stepped into what had been Scarlett's version of wonderland.

Perfume from one of the floors wafted up, giving the air an intoxicatingly sweet but spicy smell. I'd hated coming here with my ex-wife, especially since she made me wait for hours while she tried on everything they had, but somehow, it didn't feel so bad being here with Lacie. Probably because I knew she didn't want to be here any longer than was absolutely necessary.

"Right, let's start over there." I pointed to where I knew the work wear was. "We'll get the boring essentials out of the way first. Then we look at the rest."

She nodded, a resigned look in her eyes. I led her to a saleswoman nearby before leaving them to their own devices while I went to browse. If Lacie was already uncomfortable with the idea of shopping, I couldn't image she'd want me standing anywhere near them when they started choosing sizes and that kind of thing.

Personally, I didn't give a fuck what size she wore. She was sexy as fuck as far as I was concerned, but I wanted to give her some personal space just in case she was worried about it.

The store was quiet at this time of a Wednesday morning, with only a few other shoppers around. I spotted a few things that I thought Lacie would look great in but purposely waited until she was in the dressing room before I pointed them out to the sales assistant.

When that was done, I went to sit outside the dressing room I'd been told she was in. "You okay in there?"

"Yes." Her voice was smaller than I was used to. "Do I have to come out?"

"If you wouldn't mind." I was dying to see what she looked like in clothes that fit her properly, but I wouldn't force her to show me if she didn't want to. I'd get to see everything she chose eventually anyway.

The door handle lowered, and it cracked open just before she peeked out. "Is it just you out there?"

"Pretty much." I looked up and down before nodding. "Nope, not even just pretty much. The other woman who was in here is gone."

Lacie tugged her lower lip between her teeth before pushing the door all the way open and stepping out. "Well, what do you think?"

My mouth dried up, and all the blood in my body flowed south. Yeah, I definitely couldn't be honest with her about exactly what I thought. "You look good."

She looked beautiful actually. But it probably wasn't an appropriate thing to say.

The black pencil skirt hugged her hips and thighs, showing her shape off in a way I'd never seen before. On her feet were red heels that had her toes peeking out at the front, elevating her and making her legs look two miles long.

A fitted black blouse clung to her waist and showed just enough cleavage to hint at what lay beneath without being too in your face. *Unfortunately.*

"You really think so?" Her lip was a little swollen from having been bitten so much this morning. I put my ankle over my knee since I couldn't really adjust my growing problem with her standing right there. "You can tell me if it's too tight."

"It's not too tight." I frowned at the uncertainty that flashed in her eyes when she heard my response. *What the hell?*

Lacie was the last woman I'd have pegged as insecure about anything, much less a figure as stunning as hers. Mankind had done something terribly, terribly wrong if she thought she had anything to be insecure about in that department.

Rising from my seat, I went to stand in front of her. Not giving a shit if it was inappropriate, I put my hands on her shoulders and bent slightly at the knees so I'd be able to look into her eyes. "It's not too tight, Lacie. I promise. You're gorgeous, and that outfit is going to knock any man who comes within a hundred feet of you off his feet. If you're uncomfortable in it, then don't get it. But if your only worry is whether it's too tight, then you should know that it's not."

"It's not uncomfortable," she replied quietly but more confidently than she'd sounded before. "You're a man within a hundred feet of me though, and you're still on your feet. I appreciate you trying to make me feel better anyway."

"I'm only still on my feet because I'm the ultimate professional." Seriously, it was taking all my self-control not to fuck her up against the wall in the changing room. "I wasn't trying to make you feel better. Why would I do that?"

She shrugged, some humor finally sparkling in her eyes again. "That's a good point. You wouldn't. You're not nice enough."

"Hey. Ouch." I brought my hand to my chest to clutch my heart. "I'm plenty nice enough. I just didn't have to be right then because what I said was true."

Lacie's green eyes rolled, a smile playing at the corners of her lips. "Whatever you say, boss. Wanna see the next pick?"

"Yes." I would sit up and beg like a dog to see her in more outfits that showcased her body like that one did if that was what she wanted. It was going to be hell not to draw on them in my imagination later, but I'd deal with that problem when the time came.

Lacie tried on a few more things, coming out to show off each one to me. I said every complimentary thing I could think of that didn't cross any lines and was feeling pretty proud of myself when she relaxed into it eventually.

I even managed to make her laugh a few times. When she came out wearing her own clothes, there was a huge pile of new stuff over her arm. I took it from her, carrying it to the register.

"You know, you're not really what I expected upper management of a company like NY Hotels to be like," she said as we walked, looking up at me with the most unguarded expression I'd seen from her.

I shrugged my shoulders but couldn't hold back my grin completely. "Did you just compliment me?"

"No." She gave me a playful bump on the shoulders and laughed. "Okay, maybe it was a compliment, but it was true too."

"What did you imagine upper management to be like?"

That damn lip went back into her mouth, which I really had to stop noticing. "Stuffy, old, mean maybe."

"Why would you think that?" I frowned. Had she really come to work for me with that idea in mind? The woman was braver than I'd thought if she had.

"I've never really been around anyone in upper management before, and especially not in a company like yours. I've watched some reality TV shows though, and they didn't paint a pretty picture."

"Yeah, they don't," I agreed. I prided myself on being a decent human being to each one of my employees. Maybe I hadn't really been to Lacie thus far, but I liked to think I was making up for it now.

It really felt like we'd made some kind of breakthrough in the last twenty-four hours. Enough of a breakthrough for her to ask me a question I could see she'd been thinking about for a while.

"How does the management structure work at the company? I know you must think I'm an idiot for not knowing, but all of this happened so suddenly, and then Wayne wasn't around often, and you were, well, *you*."

"You're not an idiot." I set the clothes down on the counter and handed over my card. "I'm glad you're feeling comfortable enough to ask me, though."

The sales assistant rang us up and started loading up paper bags with Lacie's purchases while I turned to face the woman in question. "I'm the apex of our management structure, but I set it up so our corporate governance keeps even me in check. We're not top heavy, and we have enough checks and balances in place that no one could take advantage of the company."

"That's interesting." I could see the gears in Lacie's big brain turning. "What kind of checks and balances?"

"How about I take you to dinner tomorrow night and we can discuss it all?" I wasn't even flirting. Lacie needed to be ready, and I was the one who had to get her there. "I'd be happy to tell you. I just don't feel like the middle of a department store is really a conducive environment for this discussion. I'm in meetings all day for the rest of the day and the whole of tomorrow, so tomorrow night is the soonest I can do."

Karina would be having a supervised visit with Scarlett, so I had some time to take Lacie to dinner to answer all her questions. It should have occurred to me before that she'd need to have all this information, but with everything going on, it honestly hadn't.

Lacie nodded as we were handed the bags containing our purchases. "Sure, that sounds good. I've actually got quite a lot of questions for you."

"I'll do my best to answer them all." I shook my head when she tried carrying all the bags herself, taking some of them off her hands. "You ready to get back to work?"

She eyed the bags I'd taken, then sighed and let it go. "Yeah, sure. Let's do it."

CHAPTER 10

LACIE

"Bye, Lacie," Nolan said as he walked out of his office and into mine, shrugging into his midnight-black jacket as he shut the door. "I'm not coming back after my last meeting. It's at a venue close to my house, so I'll see you in the morning."

"Okay." I lifted my hand in what I hoped was a casual wave. "See you in the morning."

My heart thundered in my chest and blood rushed to my cheeks when he smiled at me before leaving. *God, I hope he doesn't notice.*

He didn't. After returning my wave with a relaxed gesture of his own hand, he spun around and headed out. Meanwhile, I tried to do my best not to watch him walk away. But damn, it was hard to keep my eyes off his beautiful backside.

When he'd been a bit of an asshole to me, it had been easier to ignore the attraction I felt to him. I was seeing him in a totally new light now though, and that was making it more difficult than ever. Because he was actually a really nice, really decent man. *The kind of man a girl could totally fall for.*

I'd nearly fainted when he'd touched me in that store earlier, and he'd only touched my shoulders. I couldn't imagine what I'd do if he ever *touched me*, touched me. My best guess was that it would be something really embarrassing, like ugly cry or beg him to marry me on the spot.

I knew I shouldn't be attracted to him, but I couldn't help it. No matter how hard I tried to fight it, it was there. Especially since he was showing me a side of himself I'd never have expected to exist.

Nolan was an enigma. A gorgeous, smart, sweet, cocky, confident, arrogant, douchey enigma. And for some inexplicable reason, I loved it.

There was so much more to him than I'd ever have thought. A depth that I was desperate to explore, not that it would ever happen. Which was also why I wasn't worried about whatever really embarrassing thing would happen if he ever touched me properly, because it wouldn't happen.

Sure, he'd said some really nice things to me when I was trying on those clothes, but it hadn't meant anything. I could see he was being sincere, but the compliments he'd given me were purely to boost my self-esteem. Just because he thought I might knock a few guys off their feet dressed like that didn't mean he was one of those guys.

Despite what he said about only still standing because he was a professional, I couldn't picture him being knocked off his feet by anything or anyone. He was just one of those people who seemed totally in control at all times, steady and unshakable.

I appreciated what he'd done for me, though. He really had made me feel good, sexy even. For other men, anyway. So much so that I'd ended up enjoying a shopping spree for the first time in forever.

I was comfortable in my own skin and happy with my figure, but buying clothes for myself just wasn't fun. In the size-zero culture we lived in, everyone's self-confidence took a knock at times. Mine definitely did, and those times were always only when I had to go shopping.

Unless I had Nolan by my side apparently. He'd managed to track down my temporarily misplaced self-esteem and happily returned it to me.

I was so lost in thought about the man I totally wasn't crushing on that I didn't notice the blonde woman walking into my office at first.

She cleared her throat to get my attention, an amused smile playing on her lips. "Excuse me?"

I blinked out of my Nolan-induced trance and felt my heart sink to my shoes. The woman was a knockout and she was at my boss's office. Shit, was she his girlfriend? I couldn't believe I didn't even know if he was taken or not, and here I was, daydreaming about him.

I'd checked his hand for a ring when we'd first met, but just because he wasn't wearing one didn't mean he wasn't married or didn't belong to another woman. Shame colored my cheeks as I offered her a smile. *Mother definitely didn't raise me to fantasize about other women's men.*

It definitely wouldn't fit with the manners she'd taught me, and she took them very seriously. "I'm sorry. I spaced out for a second. Can I help you?"

She waved her hand dismissively when I apologized, a stunning smile spreading on lips painted the color of a juicy red apple. "I'm a bit of a space cadet myself. Don't even worry about it. It's nothing urgent anyway. I was just wondering if Nolan was around."

Guilt churned in my stomach. Not only was his girlfriend beautiful, but she was nice too. I was really going to have to stop this crazy attraction I felt to him somehow.

"He's already gone for the day," I said. "You just missed him."

She snapped her fingers, painted the same shade as her lips. She seemed like one of those perfectly put-together women, which made sense if she was with him, considering that he was exactly the same way.

"Dang it. I wanted to say hi. I'm Anna, by the way." She walked up to my desk and offered me her hand to shake. "I'm the general manager for the California branch of NY Hotels. I probably should have started with that, but like I said, space cadet."

I stood up and shook her offered hand, noticing for the first time that there was a diamond ring sitting on a very important finger. One that Nolan didn't wear. *She's not his girlfriend. She's married.*

It didn't mean he wasn't taken, but it still sent relief flowing through my veins. At least I hadn't been caught fantasizing about him by his girlfriend.

It also suddenly made me feel much warmer toward this smiley, kind, beautiful woman. "It's no problem. It's nice to meet you. I'm Nolan's new executive assistant, Lacie Cole."

"It's nice to meet you, too." She squeezed my hand before releasing it. "Good luck keeping up with that man by the way. He works like a machine."

"Surprisingly, it's been okay so far."

Her tinkling laughter met my ears. "I'm sure you just started at a good time. Trust me. There is a lot of travel and a lot of late nights in your future."

Wayne had mentioned something about travel and extended working hours in my interview, but that had been before I'd met Nolan. Traveling with him and spending late nights alone with him were certainly going to test the limits of my ability to hide my attraction to him.

"Speaking of travel," I said. "If you're the GM out in California, what are you doing here?"

"I'm here for the meeting on Friday. I know it's a couple of days early, but I wanted to take some time to see some of D.C. on this trip. Every time I come here, I go from the airport to the hotel, to whatever meeting I'm here to attend, and back to the airport. There are so many landmarks here that I've always wanted to see, and this time, I told my husband I was taking the time to do it."

"I'm new to the city, so I haven't seen many of the landmarks either. I think it's great you're taking the time to do it. I might take a page out of your book and take some time to do it myself this weekend."

Anna glanced down at her watch. "I don't mind waiting until you get off work if you want to come do some sightseeing with me? It's so much more fun if you're not doing it alone."

"You really don't mind?" Excitement bloomed in my chest. "It would be great to explore with someone."

"I've got some work to finish up myself. If I do it now, I won't have to do it tonight." Anna smiled. "You got somewhere I can set up my laptop?"

I nodded and showed her to a conference room down the hall. We worked for a couple more hours, then set off together to see the sights.

As we traveled on the big red bus that stopped at all the important landmarks we wanted to see, Anna and I got to know each other. I learned that she was thirty-five, had been married for nearly ten years, but didn't have any children. She had worked for the company for five years and only had good things to say about it.

"You're kidding." She laughed when I told her what Nolan had said about my wardrobe. "I hope you tore him a new one."

I shrugged, smiling as the bus started slowing to a stop. "I wanted to, but then he sat me down and explained. It made me understand where he was coming from."

"So he took you shopping?" she asked, her eyes wide on mine. "I'm having trouble imagining him in a women's clothing department. He's such a *man*."

"Yeah, he is." I swallowed the urge to tell her about the electricity I had felt between us in the store.

Anna and I were getting along well, but I'd only met her earlier today. Telling her about my silly crush on our boss probably wasn't the greatest of ideas. "Did you want to get off at this stop?"

"I always want to get off." She winked as she stood up, her good-natured humor shining in her eyes. "But I'll settle for seeing the sights since my husband isn't here."

I laughed and followed her off the bus, happy to have someone to explore the city with. We took a ton of pictures, and by the time we arrived at the final stop, I felt like I had made a true friend in her.

"Thanks for today," I said as I slung my purse over my shoulder and made sure we hadn't left anything behind on the bus. "I haven't had a friend I liked spending time with since high school. Today was fun."

"It really was," she agreed. "I'm happy to get to be the friend you like spending time with. I liked spending time with you too."

"It's too bad you live so far away."

She nodded but tossed me a grin as we made our way to the front of the bus. "Don't feel too bad about it. We'll see plenty of each other. You're bound to come to California with Nolan at least once every few months, and I'll come out here in between."

"Does he really spend that much time traveling?" A shiver of excitement shot through me. Sure, it was going to be difficult to hide my attraction to him if I had to go away with him so often, but on the other hand, I'd always wanted to see the country.

"He's very hands on at the branches," she said. "He likes to make sure that the lines of communication are open and that everything is going the way it should. So yes, lots of traveling."

When Anna and I climbed off the bus, she turned to face me on the sidewalk. "Would you like to hang out again tomorrow night? It's my last night in town for this trip."

"I'd love to, but I have a dinner with Nolan." I pursed my lips. I really did want to spend some more time with her. "Maybe I can call you after? We can get together if it's not too late."

"Sure." She smiled and opened her arms to give me a tight, warm hug. "I'm looking forward to getting your call already. I haven't had a good girls' night out in ages, and since I've got the time before I go back to my life, I'd really like to go grab a few cocktails and let my hair down. I hope Nolan doesn't keep you busy too late."

"Yeah, so do I." Well, depending on what he kept me busy with. *Stop it. It's not going to be like that between you two.* "I'm sure we'll be done early. We'll have time to go grab those cocktails. I'm sure of it."

CHAPTER 11

NOLAN

"You're going to get to see mommy tonight." I looked up into the rearview mirror to meet Karina's eyes. "Are you excited?"

"No." Her gaze fell to her lap, her fingers fumbling with the restraints on her car seat. "I don't like going over there."

After easing us into a parking space outside of her school, I twisted around to face her. "I'll pick you up before bedtime. It'll be fun. Grandma's going to be there, too."

The corners of her lips turned down; her expression despondent. "Do I have to? It's not fun there. I like being with you or Uncle Alec better."

"Mommy misses you, baby." I gripped the steering wheel so tightly, I wouldn't have been surprised if it snapped in half, but it kept the tension off my face so it would have been worth it. "Grandma misses you, too. They're making you a special dinner. You're going to have so much fun."

Although the words tasted like bile on my tongue, I forced them out with a smile. Having this talk with her was tough for me. I wanted Karina to be happy at all times, but she had to maintain a relationship with Scarlett as well.

The court had granted her a certain amount of visitation hours per month, but even if it hadn't been legally ordered, I'd still have done my best to ensure that Karina saw her mother as often as I reasonably could.

Despite everything she had done, Scarlett was Karina's mother, and I truly believed it was best for them to have at least some kind of bond, however much Karina didn't want to form one.

Since my former mother-in-law would be there to supervise, Karina's safety—my only concern while she visited—would be seen to.

I was still reeling from Scarlett's attempt to collect Karina from school, though. It made me feel like there were fire ants crawling all over my skin, poised to bite at any moment.

Before I'd arranged this visit with Scarlett's mom, I'd consulted my lawyer. Apparently, there was nothing I could do under the circumstances to prevent the visit from happening, outside of going to court. When I asked him to go to court, he advised against it.

Scarlett's visitation rights had been severely limited as it was, and he didn't think going to court after all she'd really done was show up at her daughter's school and ask that she come home with her was a smart idea.

Pointing out that she hadn't asked but demanded and caused a scene in the entrance hall hadn't changed his advice. He said I could come off as callous, spiteful, or even hellbent on ensuring that mother and daughter didn't see each other at all.

If that happened, he'd said that the judge might very well increase visitation or lift the supervision requirement altogether. I might have been prepared to take the gamble if the possible lack of supervision during whatever visits Scarlett might have with Karina after didn't make my hair stand on end.

Scarlett's mother was a layer of protection I desperately needed to have in place during Karina's visits with her mother. It helped that her mother was a law-abiding, God-fearing woman who would never disobey the court order that had been served on her. *Without that...*

I shook my head once to clear my mind of the ominous conversation I'd had with the lawyers. I wasn't going there. Karina had been placed in my custody, and she was going to stay there.

All I had to do was make sure I dropped her off right on time and arrived back to collect her early. I would wait to ring the doorbell until their allocated time for the visit had passed, but I'd make sure I was right outside just in case Karina needed me.

She let out a sigh into the silence of the car. "Do I have to go?"

"Yes, sweetie. You do." I hated making her go when she didn't want to and I didn't want her to either, but I refused to be responsible for alienating her from her mother. "I'll be at a restaurant nearby for dinner. If you need me, just ask Grandma to call and I'll be right there."

"No more than five minutes away?"

A smiled curled my lips as I nodded. "No more than five minutes away. I promise."

With a resigned nod, she shrugged her little shoulders. "Okay, but you also have to promise you'll come fetch me before it's time for bed."

"I will." I held out my pinkie finger to her and waited until she wound hers around it, looking into those hazel eyes. "I'll be there, baby. Promise."

We held eye contact for a second before Karina nodded again and let go of my finger. After she had, I climbed out of the car and opened the door to unbuckle her. We grabbed her backpack from the back and I walked her inside.

"If I go to dinner with Mom, can I sleep in your bed tonight?" she asked as I hugged her goodbye.

I grinned and pulled out of the hug so she could see my head shaking. "Nice try, but no. How about we compromise on me staying with you until you fall asleep?"

She rocked her head from side to side. I could see the smile she was trying to hide. "That's not a compromise. You do that anyway."

I winked. "What if I wasn't going to do it tonight?"

Karina laughed as if the suggestion was the funniest thing she'd ever heard. "You were going to. Story time is our special time together."

"It is." Story time was the only uninterrupted thirty minutes a day I could spend with her without either of us being distracted by anything else. "So, do we have a deal?"

"Okay." She held up her hand for a high five. "See you after school."

Bending over, I dropped a kiss on top of her soft hair after slapping her palm with my own. "See you after school."

Stress knotted my muscles as I drove to my office. The visits with Scarlett might be supervised, but I couldn't help feeling all tied up every time Karina had to go there.

Distracted by thoughts of just how fucked up my family situation had become, I barely noticed Lacie already sitting at her desk when I arrived. I caught her wave out of the corner of my eye as I darted through her office to get to mine. "Good morning, Nolan."

"Hey." I didn't stop moving. The only thing that would get my mind off the clusterfuck that was my personal life was work, and I had to get started if I was going to stop myself from going crazy in the buildup to the visit tonight.

Closing my eyes when I sat down at my desk, I let my head fall back against the chair and took a deep breath. My heart was doing insane things in my chest, my palms clammy.

Fuck. Nothing and no one got to me the way Scarlett did nowadays. The feelings of dread and terror she inspired were indescribable. I could face off with magnates and titans in boardrooms most people would never even step foot in without batting an eye, but the thought of my daughter spending the night with her mother rocketed me to the edge of a panic attack.

My eyes cracked open when I heard my door opening. Lacie offered me a hesitant smile. "Is everything okay? I don't mean to pry, but it looks like there's something on your mind."

"I don't want to talk about it." The words burst out of me, sounding harsher than I'd intended for them to.

Lacie took a step back but didn't leave. I watched as her shoulders rose and fell on a deep breath. Then they squared and she strode up to my desk. "Whatever it is, you need to get your mind off of it. My mother always told me that you have to starve your distractions to feed your focus."

"She sounds like a wise woman." What the fuck else was I supposed to say to that?

The strides Lacie and I had taken in our relationship were too fragile for me to tell her that she was presently keeping me from the only distraction I needed. Since I'd had a taste of how things could be between us without the hostility and headbutting, I really didn't want to go back to that.

There was more than enough of both of those things in my life. I didn't need it with those who worked close to me, too.

Lacie's smile grew warmer. "She's the wisest woman there is. Following her advice has brought me to where I am today. Want to follow it with me now?"

I lifted an eyebrow, suddenly wary over what she was going to suggest. A thousand possibilities flitted through my mind, some of them more enticing than others but none that could actually happen.

"What did you have in mind?"

She brought her index finger to her lips and tapped twice before she nodded. "I've been meaning to ask you if you would take me on a tour through the hotel here. I slept over there on the night of my interview, but I didn't really get a good look at it. I've learned that it's our flagship branch, and I think it would be useful for me to see it to get a better picture of what our business is all about."

I didn't need to think about it for longer than a second. "That's actually a really good idea."

Incidentally, walking through the hotel was something I did often when I was in need of a distraction. This had been the first branch I'd taken over, and not only did it remind me of my roots and how far I'd come, but there was always so much going on over there that it was impossible to dwell on whatever was bothering me. "Let's go."

Lacie started walking backward out of my office, keeping her eyes on mine. "Ready when you are."

"As cliched as it sounds, I was born ready." I grabbed the jacket I had hung over my coatrack when I walked into the office and put it back on as I closed the door behind me.

"It sounds cliched because it is a cliché." She walked over to her desk and jabbed her delicate finger down on a few buttons on the switchboard, activating the answering service. "Okay, let's go."

She fell into step beside me as we left the office. "Did you plan on acquiring this building as your head office when you first bought the hotel?"

"No." I chuckled, trying to imagine the look on my face if you'd told me then that I would own half the block in less than a decade's time. "All I planned on was not losing all the money the bank had loaned me to buy it."

"You were loaned the money for it?" She turned her head to look up at me as we walked. "How did you manage to convince the bank to give you that much money when you were, what, twenty-three?"

"Have you seen my smile when I turn on the charm?" I joked. "I just made sure I waited for a female banker."

Lacie's eyes rolled, but the corners of her lips tilted up as she put out her hands. "Okay, fine. I surrender. Don't tell me all your secrets. You never know when I might try to buy the hotel from you. I'm already a year behind where you were at the time age-wise, but I'm confident I'll be able to grow the chain so fast that I will more than make up for it."

"It's worth significantly more now than it was then." I laughed. "But I don't doubt that you could."

Amusement glinted in her eyes as she stepped through the door that led to the bridge adjoining the buildings. "It's good to know that you're confident in my ability to carry out a hostile takeover."

"Who says it would be hostile?" I teased, surprised by how well Lacie's distraction was working and how much I was enjoying talking to her. "I might just give it to you if you ask at the right time."

"I'll just have to learn when to ask then." She winked, but all traces of humor vanished as we stepped into the hotel. A professional mask slipped into place across her pretty features, and her spine straightened. "Tell me about the hotel. I know what the facilities are and all that, but I want the details I wasn't able to find online."

I nodded at Jeremy, a doorman who had been with us for almost as long as I had. My demeanor matched Lacie's now, but on the inside, the rush of gratitude that had surged through me when I realized that she had provided me with the perfect distraction was still there.

As a result, I ended up giving Lacie the most thorough tour of the hotel that I'd ever given anyone. She listened intently and only interrupted me to ask questions that surprised me with the depth of understanding they hinted at. She might only have started in this business, but she had caught up fast.

Impressed with the intellect she obviously possessed, I answered all her questions in detail, and by the time we got back to our office, I had all but forgotten about what tonight held. It was still lurking at the back of my mind, though.

"We're going to go to dinner a little early tonight," I said as I stood in the doorway to my office, my hand already on the handle to shut it behind me.

Curiosity burned in Lacie's eyes, but she didn't ask why we had to go early. "Sure, I'll be ready to go after work."

Evidently, she had learned that questioning me about my personal life wasn't going to get her anywhere with me. I vowed then and there that I would be eternally grateful to Wayne for having found me a smart and intuitive woman to take his place, and to Lacie for being the way she was.

CHAPTER 12

LACIE

From the moment Nolan walked into the office that morning, I'd known our dinner wasn't going to be a long one. In fact, I was so confident in the knowledge that I texted Anna when we got back from the tour of the hotel and told her that I would be able to meet her. We'd even chosen a place already.

All that was left for me to do was to let her know the time when Nolan and I were nearing the end of our dinner. What I couldn't have predicted, however, was that he'd gone so far as to call in an order for us before we left the office.

We arrived at the chic but relaxed bistro he'd booked a table at to find ice-cold glasses of water and appetizers being set down on the table. A mismatched array of china carrying all kinds of cold appetizers were set down on a royal-blue tablecloth with a single candle flickering in the middle of it.

To my surprise, Nolan himself pulled my chair out for me when we approached the table. The waiter had already had his hand on it but retreated when Nolan reached for it.

"Allow me," he said, the first smile I'd seen from him since we took the tour earlier tugging at his full lips. "Welcome to MooMoo, Lacie. It's the best kept secret in the city."

"I'll be sure to tell everyone all about it then." The joking had started naturally between us this morning. While it had come to an abrupt stop when we reached the hotel, it had been comfortable and fun to joke and tease with him.

With that smile still on his lips, he took the seat across from me and placed the cloth napkin neatly on his lap before leaning forward. "I hope you don't mind the rush this evening. I just have somewhere to be, and I can't be late."

I was burning to ask him where he was going and why he'd even arranged our dinner for tonight when he'd known all along that he wouldn't have much time. Something about the look in his eyes when I'd asked him this morning what was going on made me hold back.

Discomfort, pain, and even torture had glinted in those hazel depths before he'd blinked it all away. If my question had in any way been responsible for eliciting those feelings or making him feel them because of whatever demons were screaming in his head, I'd happily stay in the dark for the rest of my life.

Honestly, it didn't have anything to do with me anyway. My little crush was nothing in comparison to those things I'd seen in his eyes. Besides, my being attracted to him didn't mean he owed me any answers anyway. "That's okay. All of these look delicious, and I'm not fussy about food."

Relief swept across his brow as his handsome features relaxed a little. "Excellent. I've tried to order a bit of everything just in case you had allergies or are mortally offended by the thought of eating anything."

I laughed. "I'm not, but thank you for the consideration."

We made small talk as we worked our way through bite-sized pieces of heaven that contained everything from cream cheese and smoked salmon, to roasted eggplant and peppered chicken. My first impression had been correct. It was all delicious.

"What would you have done if I'd told you I was mortally offended by the thought of eating something?"

"Gotten a new executive assistant." He laughed and wiped his hands on his napkin before picking up his water glass and taking a sip. "Kidding. I ordered the vegetarian choices just in case. There were even a few vegan options."

"I noticed." I set down my silverware and straightened it before washing down my own last bite with some water. Our plates had barely been cleared away when our main course was served.

It was made up of tasting plates of the restaurant's specialties, filet mignon so soft it melted in my mouth and shellfish cooked with lemon and garlic.

A soft moan escaped me as I chewed, and my cheeks flamed when I realized Nolan had heard it. "These flavors are so crisp and clean."

"Yeah, they are," he agreed. The words were spoken in an even tone, but I'd have sworn that there had been a flash of heat in his eyes when he heard my moan. *Nah, you're imagining things.*

For the rest of the meal, I kept my sound effects to myself and tried my very best not to think about what I'd thought I'd seen from him.

When we'd finished our food, I took another sip of the wine that had been brought out with it and almost smacked my lips. Everything in this place was out of this freaking world.

I wasn't much of a wine drinker, but this one was great. My stomach was already feeling warm from the half glass I'd had, and my head was only about the rest of the glass away from becoming floaty. "If you're in a rush, we should get started."

Nolan didn't wait for me to ask twice, nor did he bother with platitudes about how he wasn't in so much of a rush. "We got a head start this morning in terms of company history, what we expect of our staff, and how the hotels run. The most important thing we have to talk about tonight is the meeting on Friday morning."

My head inclined. "The one with the general managers, yes."

"That's the one. They need to get a good first impression of you. Their first point of contact with the head office is you, so you're going to be working with them regularly."

"I've been reading up a little on their duties and responsibilities, so I think I'll be able to handle that."

"It will get easier as you get to know them. You just need to

79

remember that you don't work for them. It's quite the opposite actually. Be yourself when you meet them, and you'll be fine."

Nolan's nostrils flared as he shifted in his seat and pulled out his phone, thunder crossing his expression when he looked down at the screen. "I have to go. I'm sorry about this. I'll see you tomorrow morning."

He shoved back his chair and, with a tight smile aimed at me, turned around and walked to the front of the restaurant. I saw him handing over a few bills to the hostess and rush out the door without waiting for change.

Without him at the table, everything felt less warm and less... Well, just less. Following his lead by leaving my half-drunk wine behind, I texted Anna and went to grab a cab.

The cocktail lounge we'd chosen was near her hotel, and she was already there when I arrived. Pushing a bright pink concoction across the table to me when I got seated, she frowned. "That dinner was over in record time. I wasn't expecting you for at least another hour."

"He told me it was going to have to be fast and early. I'm not sure why. He didn't want to talk about it."

Anna's head tilted, and she cradled her chin between her thumb and index finger thoughtfully. "I know he just went through a tough divorce and that he has a daughter. Last I heard, he had been given custody of her. Maybe the rush had something to do with that."

I nearly choked on my first sip of the strong but pretty alcohol in my curved glass. "He has a daughter?"

She nodded, the thoughtfulness melting out of her expression as a smile spread across her lips. "Yeah. She's cute, too. I've only seen her in a couple of pictures, but she's adorable. She looks a lot like him."

"Wow." My mind conjured up a picture of a tiny, female version of Nolan, and I'd be damned if I didn't agree with Anna. "She must be gorgeous."

"Gorgeous, huh?" Her lips quirked. "Because she looks like Nolan?"

Heat flared out from my chest, up my neck, and settled in the apples of my cheeks. "No, I, um..."

Her manicured eyebrows swept up on her forehead. "Unless my

intuition is failing me spectacularly, I'd say someone has a crush on the big boss."

Damn you, alcohol. This was why I didn't drink often. The happy, floaty feeling almost always made my tongue way too loose. "Your intuition is failing you."

The lie didn't sound convincing, even to my own ears. Anna let out a girlish giggle that would have sounded ridiculous coming from me and waved her hand dismissively. "No, it's not. Don't worry. Your secret is safe with me. Plus, that's what girl friends are for, right? If we can't speak to each other openly and know that what we're saying will be kept in confidence, what's the point?"

Searching Anna's kind brown eyes, all I saw staring back at me was sincerity. Another woman might have laughed at the thought that I'd even entertain a crush on a creature as unobtainable and out of my league as Nolan, but not Anna.

It made me want to talk to her. Suddenly, my loose tongue didn't feel like such a curse anymore. It felt like a blessing that would allow me to finally spill my guts to someone and gain the opinion of a woman I was fast starting to consider a friend.

"Fine, I have such a crush on him. It's damn inconvenient."

"I'd say." She took a large sip of her cocktail before shrugging. "Can't say I blame you. That man is something else. If I'd ever look at another man except for my husband, I can't say it wouldn't have been him I was looking at."

She must have seen the unwarranted jealousy clenching my stomach reflected on my face because her eyes widened before she let out a soft laugh. "Don't look at me like that. My husband is the love of my life, and unlike you, I've never harbored any kind of crush on our boss. All I meant was that he's the kind of man that makes it difficult not to look or think about."

"Yeah, I guess he is." Which was exactly why I had to forget about my attraction to him. It was only going to cause trouble for me. "How do I get over it?"

Mischief crept into those kind eyes. "By getting under him."

The suggestion was made so offhandedly that all I could do was stare. Anna gave me a knowing smile. "Don't even pretend like you haven't thought about it. There's no rule against it at our company, as long as employees remain discreet and don't indulge in public displays of affection. Why not go for it?"

"He's my boss."

She rolled her eyes. "This isn't the middle ages. After his divorce, I'm not sure if he's ready for a relationship, but I am sure that he would appreciate a good roll in the hay as much as anyone else."

Another stab of that irrational jealousy speared my gut. Maybe it was the alcohol, but it was followed by a surge of anger. "Well, he's going to have to appreciate it with someone else. I don't do that."

"Don't do what?" She frowned, her brows jumping as she put two and two together. "No way. You're a virgin?"

"Yes." I drained the rest of my cocktail in one long sip. It went straight to my head, making me fuzzy instead of floaty. "I am. I don't roll in any hay, so he's just going to have to look for it elsewhere."

Anna looked at me the way I imagined she might look at a unicorn that suddenly walked into the bar out of nowhere. "You're way too beautiful to be a virgin. How on earth did that happen?"

I took a deep breath before I finally had the courage to hold her gaze again. Logically, I knew that being a virgin was nothing to be ashamed of. I was even proud of it most days, but today wasn't one of those days.

"While everyone else was off rolling in the proverbial hay and hooking up, I was in the library. I needed to make the grades to get the scholarships I was aiming for, and I threw myself into schoolwork to get them. Same thing when I got to college. I knew I wasn't going to get a good job unless I excelled, so I made sure I did that."

"That's admirable," Anna said. "And now, what's holding you back?"

"Lack of opportunities," I replied honestly. "Before you say that Nolan is an opportunity, let's be real for a minute. It's never going to happen, and it shouldn't anyway. Can we drop it now, please?"

"Of course." Her words said one thing, but the look she gave said another. It practically screamed that she disagreed and desperately wanted to keep talking about it. "Why don't you tell me more about Peachtree? That's where you're from, right?"

I nodded, relief mixing with all the alcohol in my veins. Anna and I talked about Peachtree for a while after that, but a part of my mind was still fixated on finding out that Nolan had a daughter.

Contrary to what I might have thought, the knowledge didn't dampen my attraction to him. If anything, something about him being a father made him even more attractive to me.

God, I really shouldn't have drunk that cocktail so fast.

CHAPTER 13

NOLAN

Heart racing at a pace that had to be unhealthy, I slammed on the brakes outside Scarlett's mother's house.

Karina came running to me from the porch where she was waiting and flung herself into my arms as soon as I opened the car door. Embracing my little girl as tightly as I could without crushing her, I took several breaths to calm myself down.

The text I'd gotten in the restaurant had made my phone vibrate against my leg, but it had felt like a live wire exploding in my pocket. My body had jumped into overdrive, my head barely managing to remind me to say goodbye to Lacie and pay our bill before I sped over here.

"Thank you for coming to get me, Daddy."

"Anytime, sweetie." I didn't know why Karina had asked her grandmother to send me a text requesting that I pick her up as soon as possible, but I could find out later. My priority right now was getting her home, where both of us knew she would be safe. "Let me talk to Mommy for a minute. Why don't you get into your seat?"

She nodded wordlessly. I opened the car door, she hopped in, and I shut it again once she was inside. I'd buckle her up after Scarlett went back into the house.

She had been standing at the door, waiting with Karina, but she was sauntering toward us now. The last thing Karina needed was to see her parents arguing—again—which was why I'd hustled her into the car so fast.

"Scarlett." I nodded in greeting at the bane of my existence. It was getting more and more difficult to remember a time I'd stood at the front of the aisle, waiting excitedly for the woman I'd believed I would be with for the rest of our lives.

"I didn't say goodbye yet," she said, her eyes not leaving mine. There was venom in her tone and poison flashing in her eyes. "You can't just take everything away from me, Nolan."

"I didn't take anything away from you. You tossed everything away yourself, Karina and I included."

I kept my voice low and measured. If I didn't force myself to remain calm during these encounters with her, all hell would break loose, and Karina would be there to witness it.

Scarlett raised an eyebrow and flipped her hair over her shoulder. "You still can't let it go that you had a little competition, huh?"

I refused to let her bait me, replying without losing my hard-won cool. "Yeah, Scarlett. Keep telling yourself that sleeping with every other man in the city after promising your fidelity to me is nothing but a little competition. I have to leave now. Good night."

Her arm shot out to stop me from opening Karina's door so I could fasten her buckles. "Not so fast, cowboy."

"You must have me confused with one of those other men. I'm not a cowboy." It would be easy enough to shove my way past her, but I didn't want to stoop to that level. Especially not with my daughter watching.

Scarlett's eyes narrowed to slits. "I'm not confused, Nolan. You're the only one who owes me billions of dollars. I'll never forget that or confuse you with anyone else."

I scoffed. "I don't owe you another cent. You already got a whole lot more than what you were entitled to."

As a no-fault state, Washington hadn't cared that Scarlett's infidelity had caused our divorce. She'd still walked away with half of fucking everything.

"I'm entitled to half of your company, and I haven't gotten it yet."

I shoved a hand through my hair and silently counted to ten. "No, you're not entitled to it. You've already gotten more than you should, so I suggest you just move on."

Done with rehashing the same old shit, I moved past her and ducked my head into the car to make sure Karina was all strapped in. Despite her earlier protestation about not having been able to say goodbye yet, Scarlett didn't attempt to do it now.

"You fucking owe me, dickhead." Her voice was shrill, carrying through the dark and quiet street her mother lived on.

As calmly as I could, I smiled at my little girl and shut the door again. "We're not going to do this here. If you have something to say, call your lawyers. They'll get in touch with mine. Good night."

Aggravation filled every part of me, but I had to keep it under control. Having it out with Scarlett wasn't anything new to me, but I had to do whatever I could to keep things from escalating around Karina.

Scarlett sure as hell never managed to keep calm in front of her. She'd even gone so far once as to say that the only reason she'd gotten pregnant was to get her hands on more money. Karina had heard her.

It had taken me months to reassure her that it wasn't true, that I loved her more than my life and that I'd always wanted her. The trauma she had been through because of that and so many other things that had happened was enough to last several lifetimes. I didn't plan on adding to it.

Ignoring Scarlett's rant as I sidestepped another attempt to stop me from leaving, I climbed into the car and locked the door behind me. Careful to ease us out of the parking since I knew Scarlett wasn't above throwing herself in front of my car if she thought that was what it would take, I held my breath until we were safely on the road.

Karina let out a sigh so deep that I knew she had done the same thing. It broke my fucking heart right in half. "Thank you for coming, Daddy. I couldn't stay there any longer."

"Anytime, sweet pea." I glanced up at her in the mirror when we stopped at a traffic light down the block from Scarlett's mom's. "What happened? Are you okay?"

She shook her head, and murderous rage turned my blood to mercurial levels. My hands shook as I tightened them on the steering wheel, but I swallowed it all back.

If they'd done anything to hurt her, there would be hell to pay. I'd raze the world to the ground to find them if they tried to hide, and then I'd burn every part of theirs all over again. But I wouldn't go flying off the handle if that shake of Karina's head didn't mean what it looked like it meant.

She played with the straps of her car seat again, a nervous habit she'd developed during the divorce. She knew not to loosen them, but they provided her with a sense of safety that she liked to touch. *Again, thank you, Dr. Haversham.* "I'm just happy to be back with you."

"Did something happen?" A green glow filled the car, forcing my eyes away from her and back to the road.

Pressing my foot down on the gas as slowly as I had to was torture since all I wanted to do was slam it down and race until my heart wasn't anymore, but I managed it. "It's okay, sweetie. You can tell me if something happened."

It took her a few seconds to reply. "Why can't I have a happy Mommy? The mommies who come to my school to pick up their kids are all happy. The teachers who are mommies are happy, but mine isn't."

Ah, fuck. Covering for Scarlett was something I had to do for now. A lot of the professionals I'd consulted during the divorce had warned me that Karina was too young to understand a lot of what was going on. It was especially true where Scarlett's mental health and state of mind were concerned. Neither were healthy and both were complicated.

"Everything is okay now, Kare-bear. We're going home, and when we get there, why don't you come sleep in my bed tonight?"

She perked up instantly, agreeing and then telling me that she was bringing her dolly too. As I steered the conversation away from her visit and her mother, I knew that Karina was going to be shaken up for the next day or so.

Whenever her visits with Scarlett ended this way, she tended to cling to me the way she had when she was a toddler going through separation anxiety. Sometimes, I could ask Alec to watch her during those times, and she would be okay with it.

I couldn't do that this time. She was still too pale when we got home, too quiet and withdrawn. Instinctively, I knew that she was going to need me tomorrow and not Alec, which meant I wasn't going to be able to make the meeting with the GMs.

A couple of them might have a coronary, but they'd just have to live with it. Karina had to come first, and I didn't give a fuck what anyone else thought of that. At least I had Lacie, who I knew was capable of handling the meeting on my behalf.

It was too late to call her now to let her know, so I'd have to remember to do it first thing in the morning. It was comforting to know I had someone who I could trust to have my back at the office. I'd been afraid that once Wayne retired, I wouldn't have that anymore.

Also, Lacie deserved a time to shine. People needed to know that she was smart and capable and to respect her. I hadn't planned for it to happen quite this way, but I supposed that even I couldn't control everything—least of all Scarlett's mood and rants.

It would be interesting to see what happened when I threw Lacie into the deep end without a life vest, but I had a feeling she was going to surprise me.

CHAPTER 14

LACIE

"Where are you?" I whispered into the phone with my heart galloping in my chest. The general managers had started to arrive for the meeting and were all having coffee in one corner of the boardroom, getting caught up with one another while I frantically tried to get ahold of my boss.

He hadn't answered my first few calls, and I'd just been about to send out a damn search party when he'd finally picked up. "I'm at home. I'm not going to be able to make it."

All the air left my lungs in a rush. "What?"

The question came out as a cross between a yelp and squeal that made Anna look up from her small plate filled with the continental breakfast spread I'd set up for them. I widened my eyes at her and shook my head.

She frowned but didn't come over. Instead, she grabbed the attention of another one of the general managers who'd been in the process of turning his head to look at me.

"I can't make it," Nolan said on the other end of the line, confirming my worst fears about what I'd thought I'd heard him say before. "You know what to do, Lacie. I need you to take care of the meeting for me."

"Prepping the agenda does not mean that I know what to do," I hissed. "Nor does printing the information for the packet and putting it all together."

"Printing all the information might not have, but you gathered all that information and typed it up." The calm reassurance in his voice made my hands slow their shaking to a tremble. I kept quiet and allowed him to continue. "You have a good idea of where the business is at and where we want to position ourselves. You've read everything there is to read about their branches, and you have all my notes on your tablet. We've talked all of it through, and a lot of what is in them were your ideas. So I reiterate: you know what to do. Do it."

A lump the size of a small country grew in my throat. I swallowed hard around it, but it didn't disappear. "Okay. I'll let you know how it goes."

"It's going to go well," he said. "Have fun with it. Let 'em know who's boss."

"You're boss, but okay. I see where you're going with this." I swallowed again, but my throat was still so tight that my voice was breathy. "Bye, Nolan."

"Bye." He ended the call.

I stood there staring at my phone for a beat after I pulled it away from my ear. I couldn't believe this was happening, but at the same time, a thrill of excitement traveled through me. This was real responsibility, a show of trust I hadn't been expecting so soon.

Regardless, it felt like I needed to run it by one more person before I took over the meeting. Walking across the room to the GMs, I smiled the most gracious smile I could muster. "We'll get started in a minute. Please help yourselves to some more coffee. I'll be right back."

Anna returned my smile, but there were questions in her eyes. "Of course. I might have another croissant. They're good, aren't they?"

Just like that, all the attention was back on her—for which I was eternally grateful—and I was free to hurry out of the conference room. Wayne was in his office when I arrived, looking up from behind the desk when I walked in.

"Lacie, this is a surprise."

"I know. Do you have a minute?" I stood in his doorway. I didn't know Wayne well enough to just go barging into his office.

He nodded and motioned me in. "Sure, what can I do for you?"

"Nolan has a big meeting with some of the GMs this morning. They've all arrived, but he hasn't. I just spoke to him, and he said I should take the meeting."

Interest flickered in Wayne's eyes, but so did something darker. "I hope everything is okay with him?"

"I don't know." The corners of my mouth turned down. "I'm assuming this isn't something he does often?"

Wayne let out a long sigh and removed his glasses to pinch the bridge of his nose. "There might be unforeseen circumstances keeping him away from the office more regularly than there used to be. Do you want me to handle the meeting?"

Questions burned the tip of my tongue, but I bit them back. I had no right to pry into what the circumstances might be that could keep Nolan away more often, no matter how much I wanted to know.

As it was, Anna had let all that stuff about his divorce and daughter slip last night. Anything else I wanted to know about his personal life, I'd have to wait to ask him when he was ready to start answering my questions.

I shook my head in response to Wayne. "No, he asked me to handle it."

"Really?" Surprise crossed his features before he schooled them again. Clearing his throat, he offered me a grin that reminded me of my grandfather so much that my heart squeezed a little. "Are you comfortable with that? If you want me to, I can step in. I'm not gone just yet."

"No, that's okay. It's nice of you to be willing to do that, but it's not necessary. I can do this." The way my voice cracked at the end of that sentence didn't make me sound as confident as I'd been aiming for.

Wayne's wrinkles deepened around a smile. "I know you can do this. That's why I hired you. Do you know everything that Nolan needed to talk to them about?"

I nodded. "I prepared everything for the meeting, and we talked about it while I was busy finalizing the agenda."

"Well, then." He sat back, loosely crossing his arms as his lips went up another inch. "You're going to be just fine. He would've called me to handle it if he didn't have faith in you. I only offered in case you didn't feel up to it."

I hadn't thought about it like that, but now that Wayne mentioned it, I knew it was true. A splash of confidence lifted my chin. "Thank you. Have you got any tips for me before I go in there?"

"Being confident is the most important thing with the GMs." His eyes twinkled as he studied my demeanor, letting me know he knew he would boost my confidence by pointing out the obvious. Gratitude warmed my veins, but before I could say anything, he spoke again. "Be confident, be assertive, and don't let them bully you."

"Okay." I wiped my hands on the front of my black slacks. "Thanks, Wayne. I really appreciate the pep talk."

"Anytime, kiddo." He slid his glasses back on and waved his hand in the direction of his door. "Go have at it. You can't keep them waiting too long."

A quick glance at my watch made urgency swell in my chest. "Good point. The meeting is scheduled to start in exactly a minute."

Wayne smiled again. "Better get back there fast."

I nodded before I spun around and hurried down the thick carpet in the hall, practically skidding to a halt in front of the conference room. I took a couple of seconds to catch my breath and reorder my thoughts before going inside.

"All right. Good morning, everyone. My name is Lacie Cole, and I'm Mr. Yates's new executive assistant." I walked right to the head of the massive mahogany table and motioned toward the chairs surrounding it. "If everybody will take a seat, we can get started."

"Where's Nolan?" one of the men questioned, a confused frown on his forehead as his eyes darted from me, to the door, and back again. "Isn't he joining us?"

"No, I'm afraid something has come up. He won't be able to make it today." Soft murmurs and grumbles met my ears, but everyone took

92

their seats. Once they'd settled, I made eye contact with each of them in turn as I talked. "Nolan apologizes for his absence. He really wanted to be here, but unfortunately, it's not possible."

"Where is he?" the same man from before asked.

Allowing a smile to form on my lips, I shook my head firmly. "I'm afraid I can't divulge that information. I can assure you that I am prepared for this meeting, and we will be able to finalize every item on the agenda in his absence. Why don't we start with introductions? I'm Lacie Cole, and you are?"

"Morton Keen from the Las Vegas branch," the man said. He clearly wasn't happy about Nolan not being here, but I wasn't either. *Guess we have something in common.*

"It's nice to meet you, Morton." I kept the polite smile on my lips as I greeted every GM in turn. There were only three present outside of Anna, who I obviously already knew. She winked at me when she made her introduction, causing some of the tension in my stomach to relax.

After the introductions, I directed their attention to the agenda and worked our way through it as efficiently as I could. Exhilaration flowed through me when I closed the meeting to a spontaneous round of applause.

"Well done, Lacie," Morton said. "I had my doubts, but I'm happy you stood in for Nolan. That went faster than it usually does with Wayne, and we covered everything comprehensively enough to understand. What do you say, guys?"

Anna and her colleagues nodded, all wearing smiles. One of the smiles dropped after the other man cleared his throat. Tristan Reyes was the manager of the Houston branch, and he looked as much like a bull as his personality resembled one.

"I don't disagree with Morton, but I do think that Nolan needs to come see us at our branches since he wasn't here."

My mouth opened, then closed before it opened again. "I can't promise that he's going to be able to do that anytime soon."

Tristan crossed his meaty arms and rested them on his belly, leaning back in his chair. "We were all summoned to meet with him to discuss our progress reports. If he really wants to know about the progress we've been making, he should come see our hotels."

"This doesn't happen often, but I agree with Tristan," Della Tolstoy of the Florida branch said. "You rocked this meeting, but that doesn't change the fact that our branches and our people are more than numbers on a page or ideas in Nolan's head. I was expecting him to announce another round of visits today anyway."

Sighing internally, along with maybe a curse or two thrown Nolan's way, I mentally reviewed his calendar for the next couple of months. It was jampacked as far as I could remember, but I also knew I couldn't let them leave here disappointed or discouraged. It would defeat the purpose of taking the meeting at all instead of simply postponing it.

"Okay," I agreed. "I'll make it happen. Keep an eye on your inboxes for information. I'll keep you up to date."

"Thank you," Della said.

Tristan and Morton joined her when she stood, shook my hand, and said their goodbyes. Only Anna was left in the conference room with me. She had her purse slung over her shoulder, and I knew that she had to get to the airport.

"Thank you for staying behind." I sagged into the chair I'd occupied for the meeting. "Whew. That was an unexpected crash course in how things are done at this company."

Anna's tinkling laugh met my ears, soothing my frayed nerves. "You did great, girl. You're going to be big in this company. I can tell."

"Thanks." I smiled, my eyes dropping to the watch on her wrist. "Do you need a ride to the airport?"

"No, I've got to return the rental there anyway." She opened her arms, signaling it was time for me to hug her goodbye.

I stood up and folded my arms around my new friend, wishing like never before that she didn't live so far away. "I'm excited to have you in California when you come for your site visits. In the meantime, call me whenever you need me. Okay? Promise?"

"I promise." I chuckled and hugged her a little tighter before letting her go. "Take care of yourself. I hope to be seeing you soon."

Apprehensive as I might be about traveling alone with Nolan, I'd kick him in the shin if he went to California without me. I really was going to miss having someone to talk to, even if my mouth still tasted a bit off as a result of all the cocktails we'd had while doing the talking.

CHAPTER 15

NOLAN

"We need to talk," Lacie said as soon as I walked into the office on Monday morning. I wanted to point out that I had a ton of work to catch up on since I'd been out on Friday, but her tone allowed no argument. Neither did the expression she wore.

Her jaw was set, her pitch-black eyebrows slightly raised. There was pure fire burning in those light-green eyes. With her hair pulled into a sleek bun at the back of her head, there was nothing to hide the fierce determination her body portrayed. *Or the curve of her neck, for that matter.*

Dismissing the thought before it led to me dwelling on the other curves visible in that fitted black blouse and pencil skirt we'd picked up for her last week, I nodded. "Okay, but make it quick. I've got work to do."

"Oh, you do, do you?" She propped her hand on her hip and took one step toward me. I caught a whiff of bitter orange, jasmine, and gardenia as she did. The scent I had come to associate with her dazzled and seduced, making me wonder if she tasted as good as she smelled.

Fuck. *Head in the fucking game, Yates.* "Yes, I do."

Her eyelids lowered as she narrowed her eyes. "Funny how a man with so much work to do managed to take a whole day off just last week."

I shrugged, trying to force my gaze away from her chest. She was clearly worked up, making it rise and fall faster and higher than usual. "I took a whole day off knowing I could make up for it today. I'm sorry I couldn't be at the meeting, Lacie."

Looking into my eyes for a beat, I saw a mess of emotion in hers that I couldn't make sense of. Her breathing started to even out. "Why weren't you there?"

Inhaling deeply, I decided to give it to her straight. I'd already decided over the weekend that I was going to tell her the truth. I just wanted to do it in person. "I have a daughter, and she needed me home with her."

All of her fight left her instantly, the fire in her eyes replaced with soft understanding. "Okay. I can't hold it against you if that was what it was."

"Thank you." I didn't know why that made a smile tug at the corner of my lips, but it did. "What did I miss?"

"Not too much. We covered all the items on the agenda. I recorded it on my phone for you, and Anna is going to draw up the minutes of the meeting."

"Sounds good. Forward it to me, and I'll listen to it when I can." I had the sudden urge to grab her hand and drag her into my office with me to listen to the meeting. I'd known she was going to do well, but now I wanted to hear her in action and see how her cheeks lit up with color when I told her how amazing she'd been.

Keep dreaming.

"One last thing," she said, winding her fingers together and twisting the ring she wore around her middle finger. "We have to go to each of the four branches since you missed the meeting."

"Yeah, we can't do that." A deep frown pulled my eyebrows together. "Let's see if we can add it onto the calendar sometime next year. I'm due out for another site inspection around all the branches around then anyway."

"That's not an option," she said firmly. "You need to sign off on the progress reports, and that needs to happen before the end of the year. I had a look at the calendar over the weekend, and the only way I can work this in is if we leave tomorrow."

"Are you fucking kidding me?" My eyes opened as wide as they could go. "I can't go tomorrow. There's too much to do here."

"We'll have to take our laptops and work remotely. I've already sent out apologies and alternative dates for all the meetings you had scheduled. If we leave tomorrow, we should be able to make it to the branches and back in two weeks."

Two weeks away from Karina right now felt like a mistake. On the other hand, she'd recovered faster this time than she had before, and she didn't have another visit scheduled with Scarlett for a couple of weeks.

Going away from her could only happen between her visits with her mother, which meant that this was as good a time as I was going to get. Those four branches were doing well, but all of them kept just missing the mark at being among the top one percent of hotels in their respective cities.

They had requested site visits months ago, but I hadn't been able to work them in around all the other trips I'd already had scheduled at the time, as well as having to be back for court dates. Thinking back, I remembered that I had promised them I'd come out after this meeting.

"Okay. Set it up." I dragged both hands through my hair, my mind sprinting at a million miles a minute. "I have some things of my own to set up if we're going to do this. If you let the GMs know we're coming, they'll set us up with drivers and accommodations. We're going to need iterni—"

Lacie's finger landed softly on my lips, silencing me as much with the feel of it as the fact that she'd put it there in the first place. "I know what to do, Nolan. You go organize your things. I'll see you tomorrow morning and email you the details during the course of the day. David will take us to the airport. If I have any questions, I'll ask you."

Electricity passed between us from the point of contact, acting like a direct line to my dick. It twitched to life as my eyes caught on hers.

Pupils blown wide, she stared into my eyes with as much attraction and bewilderment in hers as I was sure was in mine. Her finger slipped away reluctantly, like she wanted to keep touching me as much as I wanted her to do it.

The loss of her touch reminded me why her finger had been where it was. When I finally managed to find it, my voice was more gravelly than normal.

"If we really are leaving tomorrow, ask David or Wayne if you need help with the logistics. They'll be able to help you much faster than I will. I need to go make arrangements for my daughter."

The mention of Karina broke whatever spell had been cast on us, allowing some clarity to fill my mind. *Lacie. Executive assistant. Firmly in the no-fuck category because of it.*

"Sure." I wondered if she'd seen the thoughts flashing through my mind and was agreeing with those as well. "I'll get right on it. Please let me know if there's anything I can do to help with your arrangements?"

Firmly shaking my head, a genuine smile curved on my lips. "I know you mean well by offering, but I'll take care of the arrangements for my daughter."

One thing I'd promised myself was that I would never become one of those dads who thought he was so much of a big shot that his assistant had to organize everything for their kids. Karina was my responsibility. Having family and friends help me with her from time to time was one thing. Delegating her like she was a task to be carried out by my assistant was totally different to me.

Unease slithered into my gut at the thought of leaving her so soon after Scarlett showed up at Karina's school, after she made her so uncomfortable that her own mother had to text me to come pick her up.

The only thing that eased it was knowing that Karina was just about as safe with Alec as she was with me. He'd fight Scarlett tooth and nail if it came down to it, and he'd protect Karina with his life.

If this trip was too short notice for him, my parents would protect her the same way. They had retired to a house upstate about a year ago. It was a little over an hour's drive, which was why Karina stayed with Alec during the school year if possible. If not, I knew they'd step in anytime.

After leaving the office, I drove straight to Alec's work. His touring company had its head office near mine, and if Alec wasn't on a tour, he'd be there. I found him standing around the watercooler, flirting with a co-worker I knew he'd had a thing with some time ago.

When he saw me walking in, a frown formed on his face, and he made a beeline for me. "What's wrong? Did something happen with Scarlett?"

"No, it's nothing like that." I jerked my head in the direction of his small office. "Can we talk?"

"Sure, but you know they invented this thing called the telephone for that, right?" He smirked as he fell into step beside me. "Nowadays, there's even this nifty little version of the telephone and fits right in your pocket. Maybe you've heard of it? It's called a cellphone or a mobile phone."

A chuckle rumbled through my chest as I shook my head at him. "I just found out I have to go away for work for about two weeks. Figured I'd come down here in person to ask if Karina could stay with you while I was gone. The thing about your nifty little cellphone is that it doesn't yet transmit a holographic image of your best friend when he needs to have a discussion like this with you."

"I'm more than happy to help out with Kare-bear. You know that." He shut the door behind us when we reached his office, perching himself on the edge of his cluttered desk. "Why did you come down here to ask?"

"Because if it takes me getting down on my knees and begging you to keep her safe while I'm gone, I'll do it." I wasn't even kidding. I felt like shit for having to leave right now, but I did have to.

There was a common misconception that if you were at the top of the hierarchy in a company the size of mine, you could do whatever the hell you pleased when you pleased. Nothing could be further from the truth.

In order to keep a machine this size functioning at optimal capacity, the main mechanism needed to work smoothly. I was that mechanism. Without me giving it my all, no one else would do it either. I worked for my employees as hard as they worked for me.

Alec's smirk pulled one corner of his mouth higher. "That's not necessary, bro. I prefer the people who get on their knees in front of me to be women. Also, I'm not particularly into begging. I'm generous like that."

The smirk dropped when I didn't laugh. "Seriously, don't even worry about it. Kare-bear and I will have a blast. We always do. I'll drop her off for that visit with your parental unit this weekend and spend some time out there in nature myself before we head back on Sunday."

"You're sure?"

"Hundred percent." He reached out to slap my shoulder. "I couldn't love her more if she was my own, man. I've got this. Go."

Ten minutes of working out the logistics later, I was back in my car. I owed Alec a new car or something for Christmas, or maybe a farm upstate near my parents. He loved it there. No matter what I got him, I knew that it could never quite convey the full extent of the appreciation I felt toward him at times like these. He would also turn anything like that down, but I'd figure it out eventually.

I'd called ahead to Karina's school to let them know I'd be collecting her a little early today, and she was waiting for me in the office when I arrived. I signed all the necessary paperwork to take her home early, then shouldered her backpack after giving her a hug hello.

"Why aren't you at work, Daddy?" she asked from her car seat once we were on our way home. "You should be at work."

"I should, but I wanted to talk to you about something. Want to stop for some ice cream?"

A wide smile spread on her lips. "I always want to stop for ice cream."

Nabbing the last parking spot in front of our favorite parlor, Karina and I walked into the retro-style ice cream shop. We placed an order with the waitress, who skated away from us on her rollerblades to place it.

Karina was sitting on the edge of the vinyl-covered seat, eyes round as she stared at me. I reached for her hand and dragged my thumb across her knuckles. "Daddy has to go away for work again tomorrow. Are you okay staying with uncle Alec for a couple of weeks? He'll take you to see granny and grandpa this weekend."

"Will you come back when you're done?" she asked.

I nodded. "Of course."

"Then everything will be okay." She hopped off her seat and came to wrap her arms around my neck. "As long as you come back."

"I'll always come back to you, Kare-bear," I whispered as I returned her hug. "I promise."

CHAPTER 16

LACIE

"Wow," I breathed into the cavernous lobby of the Florida branch of the hotel. "This place is incredible."

It had all the luxury and style of the branch back in the D.C., but it was located right on a private beach and offered views of the sparkling ocean beyond the glass walls. That alone put it in a class of its own as far as I was concerned.

Nolan grinned beside me, setting both our bags down on their wheels. He'd insisted on bringing them in from the car himself. "I'm glad you like it, and I'm really glad to see all the improvements they've made."

Della spotted us from across the lobby, a welcoming smile breaking out on her face as she walked to us at a clipped pace. "Nolan, Lacie. I'm so happy you could make it. We've gotten your suites ready, and all my staff are prepared for the walkthrough."

Both of us shook her hand. Then she extracted it to motion to a porter while clucking her tongue at Nolan. "One day, you'll learn that everyone has a job to do. Carrying your bags is Eli's. He'll take them up for you. Would you like to freshen up, or should we get started?"

"We can get started," he said.

I nodded when Della turned her gaze toward me. Nolan had

warned me at the airport that we'd be getting to work as soon as we arrived at the branch, so I'd already reapplied the little makeup I was wearing and had brushed my teeth again for good measure.

"Okay then." She looked pleased that we could jump right in, about to turn around when she realized she'd lost Nolan's attention.

Eli was standing beside him, a grin on his face as he chatted with the big boss. "Thank you, sir. It's good to know that even us little people get noticed by those at the top."

"No one is a little person, Eli." Nolan flashed the man a winning grin as he shook his hand. "You're the first face the guests see when they arrive. The first impression they get of our service is from you. That's no little thing."

I watched as Eli's features and even his posture transformed. He stood up a little straighter, his shoulders a little wider and his eyes a little brighter. All because Nolan had taken a minute to speak to him and managed to talk him up so much in so little time.

If I was ever asked to define charisma, I'd only need one word to do it in. *Nolan.*

He was the kind of leader I'd learned about in college but had never gotten a chance to see or experience in real life. Della didn't seem to be as in awe of him as I was, but she still waited patiently for him to finish before leading us to the reception desk.

"As you can see," she said, "we've fully implemented the new booking system and our front desk gets the live notifications now."

Raising an elegant hand, she pointed at a woman wearing a headset talking rapidly into the attached microphone. "We've got round the clock live support from the website and any of the booking sites we're listed on."

"You've done all this fast," Nolan remarked, carefully taking in every detail. He didn't only look where she pointed either, immediately noticing every little thing that they'd changed. "I prefer these light bulbs to the old ones. They're warmer and brighter. You need to do something about those windows, though. In this light, the smudges on the outside are much clearer."

Della paled, but she made a note before we moved on. Nolan and

Della walked ahead of me, but it was because I was purposely staying a bit behind. I wanted to try soaking in this incredible view as much as I possibly could.

There was also an ulterior motive, though. I was becoming increasingly attracted to Nolan as he showed his authority in a subtle and respectful yet unfaltering way. My nipples had tightened to painful peaks, and since I was wearing a shirt chosen with the sweltering heat outside in mind, they were making something of a spectacle of themselves.

Della showed us every nook and cranny of the hotel, studiously making notes of everything Nolan pointed out. When we got back to the lobby, the poor woman looked exhausted.

"Let's pick this up again tomorrow," Nolan said. "We have all day here. Then we fly out the day after." He waited for Della to leave after saying goodbye, then turned toward me. "You must be dead on your feet, too. How about an early dinner before we turn in?"

"I'm way too excited and new to all this to be dead on my feet, but dinner sounds good." I couldn't wait to get up to our rooms to see my temporary home for two nights. The sooner I could get to check it out, the better.

Judging by the magnificence of the hotel in general and the opulence of the rooms we'd seen on the tour, I had no doubt it was going to be the most beautiful room I'd ever slept in. *I'll have to remember to take some pictures for my mom.*

"There's a seafood cafe just down the beach. Do you mind taking a walk?" He inclined his head toward the outer doors of the lobby.

"I've never been here before, so I'd like to walk." Usually, I only walked when it was absolutely necessary. That was why cars were invented, so we didn't have to walk everywhere.

However, when the walk in question would be on a white sandy beach just before sunset, it seemed more than worth it.

"In that case, follow me." He motioned for me to precede him, then fell into step beside me.

Hot, humid air whacked me in the face when we walked out of the air-conditioned lobby. It clung to my skin like a blanket, but I didn't mind. I inhaled a deep breath of fragrant ocean air and paused to take in the view.

Nolan came to a standstill next to me, bringing his hand up to shield his eyes as he looked out over the ocean where the sun was glowing like a ball where it met the water on the horizon. "It's quite a view, isn't it?"

"Yeah." My voice was barely above a whisper, but it felt like speaking any louder would intrude on the serenity of the moment.

Nolan seemed to agree, since he was using lower tones himself. "This is why they should be ranked among the top, if not at the top. It's hard to beat this view, even around here."

"It's seems impossible that it could be any better."

The azure waters of the Atlantic Ocean spread out in either direction as far as the eye could see. The resort was situated at the end of the road, and the beach was quiet here since it was private. In the distance, I could see people walking and children playing, but there were only a few guests on this part of the beach.

Waves gently lapped the shore, and the sand looked soft and inviting. Glancing up at Nolan, my lips curled into a playful smile. "I'm taking off my shoes for the walk. I hope you don't mind."

Instead of answering, he sat down on the step leading to the beach and started untying his own shoelaces. Once our shoes were off and dangling from our fingers, I followed Nolan as he started walking to the cafe he'd mentioned.

"I've never been anywhere like this before," I said, just about gaping at the scenery around me.

A lock of his dark brown hair fell across his forehead in the breeze. He pushed it back with his forearm. "I remember having the same thought when I came here for the first time."

"Did you know by then that you were going to own it?"

He laughed, his head falling back for a second. It made him look so young, so carefree. Almost like the ocean air had lifted the weight he always seemed to be carrying from his shoulders.

As if I'd needed anything to attract me to him even more.

"No, definitely not. Wayne and I flew down to meet with the

manager here when things started going well in D.C. The guy was a friend of Wayne's, and we were hoping to get some tips from him, but we were also hoping to enter into some kind of partnership."

"So it wasn't part of the chain?"

He shook his head. "The chain I took over at first had more than a few broken links and only a couple of properties. The company's shares had been sold and resold so many times that there were only two I had full ownership of at the beginning. I bought the rest of the properties we have now and made them part of the chain later."

The smell of a wood fire burning made me look away from him. We were coming up on a small cafe that had tables on a deck that stretched out over the sand. There was a man manning the grill, singing a song at the top of his lungs. I couldn't make out the words, but it didn't sound like he was singing in English.

"Here we are," Nolan said. "That's Bernard, the owner. He cooks all the food himself, and most of it is cooked on that grill right there."

"That's interesting." I definitely hadn't been anyplace like this before. "What's that language he's singing in? Also, can you see a hostess anywhere?"

"Bernard is Mauritian, so it's Mauritian Creole. As for the hostess, it doesn't work like that here. You just choose a table, and one of the waitresses will eventually notice you between rushing from the kitchen to the grill and back again."

"Okay then." We picked a table near the grill, but not so close that we could feel the heat coming off of it. Bernard looked over and called out a greeting to Nolan, who waved in response. "Wait, you actually know him? I thought you might just know who he was because he owned the place."

Nolan shrugged like it was no big deal. "In the early days when I bought this hotel and added it to the chain, I ate here almost every day for a month. Bernard used to come sit with me once the kitchen closed. He actually has shares in the restaurant in the hotel now. I gave them to him to thank him for all the advice he'd given me during that time. It was invaluable."

"You're full of surprises. You know that?"

A smirk rose on his full lips. "Only if you expect me to fit into some kind of mold. Otherwise, I'm just a regular old guy."

He definitely wasn't that, but I didn't say it. "What's good to eat here?"

"Honestly? Everything. I'd recommend having a platter so you can taste a bit of it all."

"Done." I smiled. "I can't believe I've never experienced anything like this before. It's just so different to what I was imagining."

"That seems true about a lot of things." His voice had changed. It was huskier now. When he looked into my eyes, there was something else in them too, though I couldn't put my finger on what.

Several long moments passed where we just looked into each other's eyes. The moment was broken when a waitress bumped into my chair. "Excuse me. Sorry. I didn't see you there. I'll be right back to take your order."

Nolan cleared his throat, and whatever had just been passing between us vanished. "If it's your first time, you should see something of Florida while we're here."

"That would be great," I agreed. It really would be, but my mind wasn't racing ahead to try and decide what I wanted to see while I was here.

All I could think about was the collection of moments we'd had so far today. It was almost like every once in a while, when we looked at each other, the world stood still and the air itself crackled with chemistry.

It was probably my imagination, but the more it happened, the more I wondered if that was true. Either way, this was only the first day of our trip. If the next two weeks were like this, our time away was going to be even more difficult for me than I had thought.

Hands to yourself, Lace. Hands to yourself.

How hard could it really be? I'd managed to do it all my life, hadn't I?

Yeah, but that was before you met Nolan.

Good luck, self. You're going to need it.

CHAPTER 17

NOLAN

"What is it with you and sunset walks?" Lacie asked, looking up at me as we leaned against the railing at the pier. "Yesterday, we walked to the restaurant, and now we've come here."

I lifted my shoulders and kept my gaze on the rise and fall of the swells before they crashed into the concrete barrier of the pier below us. Out of the corner of my eye, I could see Lacie's green eyes peering up at me.

"I just think it's a nice way to relax after working and being inside all day." It was true, but I didn't usually make a point of it. Having Lacie with me and having felt things I hadn't felt in a long time when we were walking back to the hotel the night before, I'd made a point of suggesting another walk. "Besides, it's not like we can walk during the day when we're supposed to be working. Unless you'd rather do all your exploring at sunrise, this is the only time we have available."

A quiet groan escaped her lips. "Sunrise is not a time human beings should be doing anything, let alone going for walks."

After having been dormant for so many years, my sex drive was back with a vengeance. Unfortunately, it seemed to be fine-tuned to Lacie. Every time she let out a sound similar to the one she just had, I wondered if that was what she would sound like if I ever got her underneath me.

Also unfortunately, Lacie was very vocal in her reactions and made these noises way too often for my deprived sex drive to keep up with. The attraction I had felt to her from the beginning had only grown with time.

At first, it had been only because she had the right kind of body type which happened to have fit in with the picture I'd conjured up on that morning I'd reawakened that part of me. Since then, I'd come to know her as a person, and that hadn't helped the attraction to lessen. Quite the opposite really.

I gritted my teeth and took a deep breath. What also hadn't helped was that sometimes when she looked at me, there was such raw desire in her eyes that I could barely resist going for it and giving both of us what we wanted.

But I couldn't do that. Not because she was my employee—well not only because of that—but also because I'd never make a move if I wasn't one hundred percent certain she wanted me too. It wasn't rejection I feared. I was a big boy. I could handle rejection.

What I couldn't handle would be her feeling some sense of obligation to be with me because she was afraid of losing her job if she didn't. I'd never fire her over something like that, but I knew it was a reality in the world we lived in that people did get fired over that kind of thing sometimes.

So, no. Until I could be sure I wasn't imagining things because of how much I wanted it to happen, I wouldn't do a single fucking thing about it.

Meanwhile, Lacie was blissfully unaware of my internal struggle. "I mean, I know a lot of people get up before sunrise to go to the gym or get breakfast or whatever, but there's something wrong with those people. Sunrise is for lying in bed, waking up calmly, and planning your day."

"It's very clear to me that you don't have any children." I chuckled, shutting down the monologue going on in my head and choosing to focus on enjoying the time we spent together instead. Because I really did enjoy her company. "Speak to me again once you do. There's nothing calm about sunrise once they're there and awake."

A soft smile curved her lips. "True. Although I look forward to that part of my life, too. It's a different phase, but it sounds so rewarding."

"It is. The kid part, anyway. The significant other part, not so much." I sighed. If only I'd had Karina with a surrogate so I wouldn't have had to deal with her mother and all the heartbreak she'd caused me.

Lacie didn't respond for a while, thoughtfully looking up at the gulls swooping and dashing overhead. "I heard about your divorce. I didn't pry or anything. Someone let slip about it."

"It's not a secret." One of the really bad parts about it was that it felt like everyone knew and everyone talked about it. Despite being my personal business, it seemed to have become a spectacle for public consumption. "What did you hear?"

"Just that it was really tough," she replied. "Do you want to talk about it?"

My head rocked first to one side and then to the other as I considered her question, feeling this unexpected, pressing urge in my chest to release some of the pressure that resided there. "Surprisingly, yes."

"Why is that a surprise?"

"Because the only person I've really talked to about it is my therapist," I said. "Okay, and Wayne, but I've only talked about the facts with him."

The feelings? Only Dr. Haversham knew about those. Alec knew about some of them, but more about the ones involving anger and rage.

Lacie's head jerked like she was taken aback, but she didn't ask why I'd want to talk to her about it. "Fire away. I'm a good listener."

"Divorce is difficult." I sighed, running a hand through my hair. "I've read enough about it to know that it's true for most people. It just plain sucks to have promised to spend your life with someone only to watch a relationship that used to be great crash and burn."

"I can't even imagine what that would be like."

I glanced down at her. "At least you admit that you don't. People love offering advice or saying that they know what it's like, even though they've never had one unhappy day in their relationships."

"I think they mean well mostly. They don't only do it with divorces. When my Dad passed away, there were so many people telling my mom and I what we should do, how we should feel, how we should move on."

"I'm sorry about your Dad."

Her eyes became watery, but she blinked back the tears and offered me a weak smile. "I won't say it's okay because it's not. But it was a long time ago. Thanks, anyway."

"Why do people always want to tell us what to do or how to feel?" I asked. "During the divorce, all my dirty laundry was aired for the world to see. My lawyers tried to be discreet about the whole thing, but court records are public. Anyone who might be interested or nosy can go dig that shit up. It's humiliating to have everyone know exactly what you've been dealing with when you've been dealing with what I have."

"I don't know," she said softly. "You don't have to tell me. I'm just trying to point out that your personal life is still private with some people."

My cheeks puffed up before I blew out a deep breath. "I'd rather you hear it from me than from someone else."

"I'll listen if you want to talk, but I promise I can wait. I won't go digging in the meantime."

The strange thing was that I trusted her when she said that. "Yeah, but someone will probably let it slip anyway. My ex-wife cheated on me repeatedly. She's borderline addicted to gambling and shopping. She blew through millions and always had some justification or another for it."

I had to stop to drag in another breath, releasing it slowly though my nose. "I was so blindly devoted to her that I didn't want to see it when my accountant first pointed it out. I told him it was her money too and that she could do what she wanted with it."

"That's really generous of you."

I chuckled, but it came out sounding bitter. "Yeah, so generous that I later found out I'd bought cars for two of her lovers and a place downstate where she could fuck the day away without having to worry about me barging in on her."

Lacie's cheeks drained of color, but the awful pity I'd expected to see didn't come. Relieved that she wasn't one of those people, I pried open yet another of the barriers I kept all the shit packed away behind.

"The humiliation and the heartbreak were what made me bury myself in work. The only person I'd come out of my trance for was Karina. Scarlett, my ex, realized that and filed for full custody of her. That woman didn't even know where Karina went to daycare at the time, but now she wanted custody of her?"

Just thinking back to the day I'd received that suit made my blood boil. My heart started beating out of control, and red spots clouded my vision.

A soft, cool hand landing on my forearm extinguished the flames lapping at my insides instantly, somehow restoring calm with nothing more than the brief contact.

Gaze dropping, I shouldn't have been surprised to see the hand belonged to Lacie. But I was. I'd been on the verge of getting carried away by the sea of pain that had become so familiar to me, and somehow, she'd brought me back.

"That's terrible, Nolan. I'm so sorry you had to go through that. You got custody though, right?"

"Yeah." I felt the vise around my heart relax its grip. "It's just still hard to even think about it."

"You know what always makes me feel better?" There was a glint in her eyes when she turned away from the railing.

"What?"

Out of nowhere, she took off running. Calling out over her shoulder, I saw she was wearing a smile. "Ice cream. Last one to get there has to buy."

She took off at full speed after that. No one could have been more surprised than I was at how she managed to make me laugh after I'd just cut my soul open and bled for her, but she did. I laughed until she was almost halfway down the pier, jet-black hair flying behind her.

If I tried, I'd still have been able to catch up and overtake her, but I decided I probably owed her ice cream after making her ears bleed the way I just had. Lacie and I changed the topic to something lighter once we had double scoops in cones, talking in between eating the creamy deliciousness from the ice cream truck on the pier.

I had a hard time keeping my eyes off her tongue when it darted out to lick her mint chocolate chip ice cream and an even harder time walking as a result of the way her tongue swirled and dipped into the cone.

Unlike the way it was with some, I could tell Lacie wasn't deliberately trying to be seductive. She was completely oblivious to the growing issue in my pants and that she was the reason for it.

Thankfully, the ice cream was done before we got back to the hotel, and I'd managed to get my thoughts to cleaner territory. Turning to face her in the elevator, my finger hovered above her floor number one above my own.

"Do you want to come have a nightcap with me?"

She tilted her head, sucking in a quiet breath. Indecision darkened her eyes before she nodded. "Sure, why not?"

Because I'm liable to rip your clothes off if I get you that close to a bed. But I could control myself. I wasn't a fucking toddler. "Exactly. Why not?"

Jabbing the number for my floor only, we rode up in silence. Paperwork for the site inspection was spread out across the desk in my suite, all marked colorfully by Lacie's post-its on the side.

"You've been good for the company. I don't know if I've told you that yet, but you really have. The people love you, you're organized, and you're getting things done so efficiently it makes my head spin sometimes. I'm really happy Wayne found you."

I heard her shut the door behind her, and when I turned again, she was standing so close to me that if I lowered my head, I could kiss her. Lacie's lips parted, that tongue of hers darting out to wet her lips.

"Sorry, I thought you were going to keep walking."

"No problem." Neither of us moved, our eyes leaving the other only to look down at each other's lips before sweeping back up.

The sexual tension that had been brewing between us suddenly felt so thick, I thought you'd be able to cut it with a blunt butter knife. Lacie's pupils dilated, a slight shiver traveling through her.

I could feel her breath fanning my neck and jaw, see the way her breathing quickened. If I'd been waiting for a sign that she wanted me too, I had it now. There could be no denying what was before my very eyes.

"I want to kiss you," I whispered, bringing my hand up to cup her cheek.

"I want you to kiss me," she whispered back and leaned into my touch, closing her hand over mine. "What are you waiting for?"

I let out a slow breath, keeping my eyes on hers. "Because I'm not going to want to stop at kissing. So before I do, you need to know that it's been more than two years since I've been with anyone."

"It's been more than two years for me too." Her tongue came out to wet her lips again. Then she sucked in a breath and closed her eyes. "So many more."

"How many more?" Our lips were so close together now that they brushed on every word we said.

"All of them." Vulnerability shone up at me from her eyes when she opened them. "I'm a virgin, Nolan."

"Shit." I went to take a step back, but she grabbed my shirt and kept me standing still. "When I said I wasn't going to want to stop at kissing, I didn't mean to put pressure on you. I'll be happy to kiss you for the rest of the night and do nothing else if that's what you want."

She was quiet for a beat before nodding once. "That's not what I want. I don't want to stop at kissing either. Let's not overthink it, okay?"

"Okay." Silencing the voice in my mind that was screaming at me to think about what I was about do, I decided to go with what she'd said to do instead.

So I didn't overthink it. I just finally pressed my lips to hers and wound my arms around her—perfectly fucking happy to take whatever she was ready to give me.

CHAPTER 18

LACIE

Nolan kissed me like the world was on fire and only we could make it rain. It was the kind of kiss I used to dream about as a teenager, the kind that made your foot pop and butterflies explode in your stomach.

One hand cupped my cheek while the other wound around the nape of my neck, his mouth moving with mine as if we'd practiced this for a camera a thousand times.

If we had been in a movie, fireworks would have been going off above our heads, if we weren't indoors, of course. The very last thing I wanted right now was for the roof to catch fire because of anything, let alone spontaneous fireworks.

I was about to lose my virginity, and nothing, except maybe for a spontaneous fire, could stop me. I couldn't exactly pinpoint the moment that I'd decided to give it up to Nolan if the opportunity ever presented itself, but I'd known it for days.

My decision had been made in abstract terms, considering that I hadn't thought it would become reality. Not because I didn't think he was attracted to me at all. I'd actually come to the conclusion that he could be during these last couple of days. I just thought that between the divorce, his daughter, work, and the fact that I worked for him, it would never happen.

And now, it was.

It was, in a word, dreamy.

Exactly like I'd dreamed it would happen, this insanely handsome, intelligent, genuinely nice man was kissing me, and his hand had moved from my neck to skate down my back.

It rested in the small of it, his thumb drawing tantalizing circles right above my butt.

I couldn't remember a time when I'd wanted someone to touch me more, for him to lift the ridiculously tight skirt he'd insisted on buying for me.

A low moan burst out of me, and I gasped when his hand strayed lower, brushing against the bare skin of my thigh when he slid it under the skirt. "Nolan, I..."

"What do you want, Lacie?" His lips brushed against mine, his voice rough and low.

"I don't know."

There was an insistent pulse between my legs, but my nipples ached for attention as much as my pussy. My panties were so soaked, I was pretty sure there was wetness running down my inner thighs. It was embarrassing how much I wanted him, especially now that I knew I was about to have him.

For the first time, I could let myself go there, let myself imagine what it was going to be like and know that I was about to find out. "I want you to touch me. I need you to, but I..."

I honestly didn't know where I wanted him to touch me first. It felt like my blood itself was on fire, setting ablaze every inch of me.

Nolan breathed out, sliding a finger under my chin to lift it so I would look into his eyes. "It's okay. I understand. Do you trust me?"

I nodded mutely, clenching my thigh muscles to find some relief. It didn't help as much as I wanted it to. He gave me a meaningful look, his eyes never leaving mine. "I want to give you everything you want. If you can't tell me what that is, I'll go with my gut, but I need you to remember something."

"What's that?" I whispered.

"I might be the one in control, but you have all the power. If you want me to stop at any time, tell me. If you don't, tell me that too."

"Okay."

"Okay." A devilish smirk curved his lips. "We need to get you naked."

I caught my breath but nodded. If I was about to be naked, that meant he was too. I couldn't wait to see if his body was as delectable as I'd imagined, but the thought of my own nakedness was daunting.

At least, it was until he'd undressed me and I saw the look of pure hunger in his eyes when they raked over me. It was enough to make my self-esteem soar and my doubts become a long-forgotten memory.

"So fucking beautiful," he groaned, reaching for the top button of his shirt.

On shaky legs, I closed the few feet of distance he'd put between us to get a good look at me and slowly rid him of his own clothes.

When I was done, I nearly fainted when I looked at him. That toned swimmer's body was everything I'd imagined and more, all the way to the washboard abs and the deep V between his hips. What was between them, however, made my mouth water and blood rush to my head. It rushed down south too, which made for the dizzying feeling that sent me reeling in the best way possible.

I'd seen a couple of cocks in real life before, not that I'd done too much with them. Even so, this one wasn't like the ones I'd seen before. It was thick and long and oh so hard, curving almost elegantly so that its tip rested at his belly button.

A drop of his own wetness made the head shine. I swallowed, suddenly desperate to get my mouth on him.

Nolan had other plans, though. He let out a primal growl and dragged me to the bed. "You need to stop looking at me like that, or I'm going to lose it."

More gently than I'd have thought after that noise, he laid me across his gigantic bed and crawled up over me, a lock of dark hair falling across his forehead. After kissing me breathless once more, he moved away from my lips to kiss my neck, trace his tongue over the shell of my ear, and make me feel like I was treasured by him.

Then he got to my chest and sucked a hardened nipple into his mouth, causing my thoughts to spiral and my back to arch as I cried out. He released me to look up, that wicked smirk doing things of its own to me.

"You like that, huh?"

I nodded but again couldn't find any of those pesky things called words.

"Excellent," he said, lowering his mouth back to me.

This time, when I felt the flat of his tongue against my sensitive peak, I also felt his hand making its way up my thigh. He sucked in a breath when he reached the apex of it, murmuring against my skin. "So fucking wet. God, Lacie. Going slow is going to kill me."

"So don't." Words! I'd found them, but then I lost them again when one broad finger slid into me and made lights explode behind my eyes.

"I don't want to," I barely heard him replying, "but we're going to do this right."

If by doing it right, he meant giving me one earth-shattering orgasm after the next, he definitely got it right. The first time I came was on his fingers, and the pleasure crashing into me was more intense than anything I'd ever felt.

Slowing down when it started subsiding, he flashed me a tight smile before kissing me senseless again. "Seeing you come is so sexy, I nearly came right along with you."

Despite the spectacular climax I'd literally just had, my inner muscles clenched around his fingers still inside me. His eyes flashed when he felt it, a soft moan parting his lips as he shut his eyes.

"That's my girl. Don't worry. I'm not done with you yet. Not by a long shot. I'm going to taste you now."

"What?" *Oh.* "Yes. Please."

Nolan planted one last kiss on my lips before moving down to where I'd never felt anyone's mouth before. It felt strangely intimate, but he quickly made me forget to feel self-conscious when his tongue licked me from top to bottom and back up again. His lips gave my clit a gentle suck, and my hips came off the bed. "Nolan! Yes, Nolan."

Bringing a hand up to my hips, he kept me anchored as he licked me again. And then again. It didn't take long before my second orgasm ripped through me like lightning through the summer sky, that brilliant first storm of the season that left you marveling at the beauty of nature.

And marvel I did, lying there panting and gasping as I tried to make my eyes come back into focus. I heard the sound of foil ripping and Nolan's breathing almost as ragged as mine before I could finally see accurately again.

What I saw made my breathing speed up again but for a different reason this time. Nolan was sitting on his knees between mine, his fist wrapped around his glorious shaft. "Do you still want to do this? No nodding this time. I need to hear you say it."

"Yes." I reached for his rock-hard cock with one hand and for his neck with the other, guiding him to me as I lay back down. "I want you. Please don't stop now."

There was a moment where we just looked into the other's eyes, our bodies positioned just right but completely still. I felt his blunt, broad head sliding through my slit as it twitched, clearly as desperate to be inside me as I was to want him there.

"Tell me if it hurts too much," he whispered, then brought his mouth to mine in a searing kiss as he gently, slowly fed himself into me.

Our voices blended in a cacophony of moans and shouts, tears only briefly stinging my eyes when I felt something give deep inside.

He noticed immediately, stopping though I could see in his eyes that it pained him to do it. "You okay?"

"Yes, keep going." I breathed through the pain, relieved when it quickly gave way to nothing more than discomfort. That, too, went away when he was finally buried in me to the hilt.

I felt him tremble beneath my hands when he stopped again, giving me time to adjust. "Still okay?"

"Yep." I shifted my hips and felt him slide a little deeper, both of us groaning when he did. My muscles tried to contract, but it only took me a second to force them to relax. "Okay. I think I'm ready. You can move now."

"Tell me if it hurts," he said, withdrawing slowly before thrusting back in more tenderly than I'd have thought he would. He let his head fall forward, another sound escaping him. "Fuck. Please tell me that didn't hurt."

"It didn't." I took his chin between my thumb and index finger to lift his head back up. "I promise to tell you if it does. Just stop holding back, please."

"You promise?"

"I promise." I lifted my hips again, and Nolan took my cue, withdrawing and plunging back in harder and faster this time.

"Oh, thank God," he bit out before doing it again.

On a few thrusts, I felt tiny bites of pain as my body stretched to accommodate his swelling and his increasingly wild movements. It wasn't bad enough to stop him, though.

In fact, it turned to pleasure before I could even think about stopping him. The inferno that started raging in my lower belly a few minutes later promised an orgasm that could rip me to shreds and put me back together better than before.

I'd read enough, prepared myself thoroughly enough for this moment, that I knew what to do. I knew I had to ride the wave and just let it go.

What I couldn't have been prepared for was the toe-curling, body-shaking euphoria that slammed into me when I did, causing my entire body to rocket to a state of bliss that nothing I'd ever felt before compared to.

I screamed his name and clung to his shoulders as I fell to pieces below him, barely aware of his own shout and the way his hips pistoned and his thighs trembled as he found his release as I did mine.

It felt like it took me forever to recover, for my breathing and vision to return to normal. Nolan had rolled off me at some point, disposed of the condom, and came back to bed to hold me in his strong arms.

Unfortunately, the warm glow of the aftermath vanished when I realized what had just happened. *I slept with my boss. I lost my virginity. To my freaking boss.*

"I'm going to let you get some rest," I said, panic taking the place of the pleasure that had swept through me only minutes before.

Squeezing his hand as I sat up and let go of him, I felt muscles aching in places I didn't know I *had* muscles. It was a delicious ache, though. An ache I'd been desperate to feel for such a long time that I couldn't wait to feel it again.

Nolan frowned, snaking an arm around me to hold me back when I tried to get off the bed. "I can get some rest with you here if you want to stay."

I did want to stay, but I didn't feel like I should. "That's okay. I have such a beautiful suite. It would be a waste not to use it for one of the only two nights I have it."

It was a weak excuse. One that the look in Nolan's eyes told me he didn't believe. Opening his mouth to say something, he closed it again and nodded instead. "Okay. If that's what you want, I'll see you in the morning."

Despite my protests that it wasn't necessary, he got up, dressed in pajamas, and walked me up to my room. After placing one more chaste kiss on my swollen lips, he said good night and walked away.

I collapsed onto my gigantic bed, my muscles tensing for a very different reason than they had been before as I lay there staring at the ceiling.

For some reason, I felt like I'd done something wrong.

Company policy didn't specifically prevent it from happening, but I'd just slept with my boss on a business trip. I wasn't this person. I didn't do stuff like this.

Correction: I'd just lost my virginity. To my boss. On a business trip.

Grabbing a fluffy pillow from the stack at the top of the bed, I pressed one down over my face and moaned into it.

What the hell was I doing?

CHAPTER 19

NOLAN

Reluctant to leave the sexy dream of the night before behind, I didn't open my eyes when I started waking up. I'd dreamed that Lacie and I had finally given in to the tension between us and—

"Fuck," I muttered into the silence of the room, wrenching my eyes open as I sat up. As I suspected, the evidence that it hadn't been a dream stared me in the face. I rubbed my eyes and checked again, but it was still there. "Holy shit. It really happened."

The comforter was still lying twisted on the floor at the foot of the bed, just as it had been in my dream. My clothes were in the haphazard pile they'd landed in when Lacie had shed them. The clincher was the foil wrapper lying in the trash can next to the night-stand. *Yeah, so that happened.*

And man, had it been incredible. Just thinking about it was going to make me hard again, and a quick glance at the time on the night-stand told me that I didn't have time for that.

It didn't stop my mind from wandering back to her anyway. How that woman had made it to twenty-four as a virgin, I didn't know. She was beautiful, fun, smart, sexy, funny, and too many other things to list without getting lost in it.

Although I'd never been one of those guys who chased virginities and collected them like trophies, I wasn't one of those who treated anyone like they were a leper either. Scarlett was the only virgin I'd ever been with before, back before she became borderline addicted to sex, along with all her other charming personality traits, and I'd been in seventh heaven back then.

But this had somehow been even better. Lacie had trusted me with something she'd never trusted anyone else with before, and I acknowledged it for the privilege it was. I just hoped she didn't regret it and, if she didn't regret it, that it would happen again.

Filled with a new, buzzing kind of energy for the day ahead, I practically flew through my shower and getting dressed, then headed down to breakfast. Disappointment slid through me when I got there to find Lacie wasn't down yet, but then I reminded myself that it was still early and she would be. It wasn't like she'd have flown back home in the middle of the night.

While I waited for her, I pulled my phone out of my pocket and decided to give Karina and Alec a call. I usually checked in with them every night or every morning. Since I hadn't checked in last night, it was time to do it now.

A tune played as I waited for the video call to connect. Then Alec's face popped up on the screen. "There's your ugly mug. How are you doing? How's the trip going?"

"Same old, same old. How's everything going there?"

Alec grinned. "It's great, man. Karina and I are having a blast, as always. We had a Disney movie marathon last night and stayed up until nine."

"Wow, that's hardcore." I smiled but pointed my index finger at him. "Don't go turning my perfect little angel into a bedtime-ignoring rebel now, you hear?"

"Can't make that promise, bro." He smirked before his eyes slid to the side. "Speaking of the little rebel in the making, there's someone here demanding to talk to Daddy."

My heart grew three sizes and leaped into my throat when Karina's face replaced Alec's on the screen. "Daddy, what's a rebel?"

"It's a very naughty child who doesn't listen."

Her hazel eyes widened. "I'm not a rebel. I listen."

"Yeah, you do." My arms itched to be able to give her a hug right now, to feel her little body cuddling into mine. "How are you, Kare-bear?"

"I watched two movies last night," she said proudly, her chest swelling. "I stayed awake until the end, too."

"Well done, baby." I lifted my finger and traced the line of her face, trying my best to keep mine stern. "But early to bed tonight, okay? Otherwise, you're going to be too tired tomorrow."

Then again, maybe Alec should have to deal with an overtired Karina once so he would finally understand the importance of bedtime. He usually stuck to hers because I insisted, but perhaps seeing why I insisted once would be good for him.

"I won't be tired, Daddy," she promised. "How's the work going? You're still coming home on the day with the sticker on the calendar, right?"

"Right, I'll be there. Promise." A soft sigh behind me drew my attention. I turned in my seat to see Lacie standing there, looking uncertain about whether to join me or wait for the conversation to end.

I waved her to her seat before going back to Karina. "I've got to go, Kare-bear. I love you and I'll see you soon, okay?"

"Okay, Daddy. Love you."

Alec's thumb came down from somewhere and ended the call while I set my phone down on the table.

Lacie offered me a shy smile. "You daughter is so darn cute. She has the sweetest little voice."

"Yeah, I think so too. I might be a little biased in her favor, though." I reached for one of her hands in her lap, watching her startle when I touched her. "Relax, it's okay. I just wanted to check that you were okay."

Heat bloomed in her neck and on her cheeks, but she nodded. "I'm fine."

"Are you sure? Because you don't look it. You don't have to hide anything from me, especially not after what we did."

Her eyes dropped to her lap, but her fingers finally opened and slid between mine. I liked the way her hand felt there, but I knew I couldn't really hold her hand for too long over breakfast in one of my hotels. I didn't give a fuck what people saw or thought, but I knew she would.

And I probably shouldn't indulge in public displays of affection when doing so was against the company's rules. I'd been the one to put those rules there, after all.

After about a minute, Lacie finally looked up at me again. "I'm okay. I'm a little sore, to be honest. I'm not sure how much walking I'm going to be able to do today before I start wincing."

"I'll call ahead to Houston and tell them we're taking the day to look around by ourselves. We can do the tour tomorrow." I squeezed her fingers once more, but seeing Della walking by with a few other senior staff members behind her, I withdrew my hand from Lacie's. "Is that all?"

She shifted in her chair, though I couldn't tell if it was because she was uncomfortable about talking about it or if it was just because she was sore. "No, I, uh—"

Della chose that moment to bring the other staff members over to say goodbye. After politely greeting them, I got them away from our table as fast as I could.

"You were saying?"

Her cheeks glowed, but she kept her eyes on mine. "Did we make a mistake?"

Dread slowly unfurled in my stomach. "I don't think that we did. Do you?"

Her teeth sank into her bottom lip and she shrugged. "I don't know. It feels like we've done something wrong."

"Did you want to do it?" *Please let her say yes. Please let her say yes.* I knew that she'd wanted to last night, but the harsh light of day was known for making people doubt things they'd been sure of only hours before.

"Of course, I did," she said to the flower in the vase in the center of our table.

127

I plucked it out and held it in front of my face. "Good. Now this time, say it to me."

She flushed, but a small smile was pulling at her lips. "Of course, I wanted to. You know that. But it still feels like I'm about to be called into the principal's office for doing something horribly wrong."

"We didn't do anything wrong and no one is going to call us in," I promised, making sure to keep my tone calm and my eyes on her green ones. They were filled with less uncertainty than they'd been when she sat down, but that was a far cry from feeling reassured. "We're both adults. We both consented. We both wanted it. I, for one, wanted it more than I can remember wanting anything in a long-ass time."

"You did?" Doubt clouded her eyes when she asked the question.

I hated seeing it there, so I lowered my voice and leaned in closer to her. "Yes, I did. You know that just as well as I do. Being inside you was fucking amazing, Lacie. If you'd stayed over, I'd have taken you again this morning to prove it if you'd have let me."

"So you don't regret it?" The clouds were parting, and I could see her usual confidence starting to take its place.

With a firm shake of my head, I put one hand to my heart. "I swear to you that I don't and I never could."

"Okay." She sat back in her chair, more relaxed than she had been since she'd walked in this morning. "Do you want to get some food? We should get to the airport soon."

"That's it? You don't want to talk about it anymore?" I felt a line forming between my eyebrows.

Lacie's shoulders lifted on a shrug. "No, I'm good. You're right. We're consenting adults and it happened after hours. Why? Did you want to keep talking about it?"

"No, but I..." I'd expected she would want to have more of a conversation about it than that, but she was surprising me once again. "I'm not the only one full of surprises, it seems. Well, if you do ever want to talk about it, just tell me. For now, let's grab breakfast. Our plane leaves in three hours."

Another thing I'd expected this morning was awkwardness. A

whole bunch of stomach-churning, gut-wrenching awkwardness. But there was none.

Lacie and I joked and talked our way through breakfast, went back up to our separate rooms to gather our things, and chatted all the way to the airport. It didn't feel like anything had changed between us, except that I felt closer to her. Strangely, getting to know her intimately had made her easier to talk to and not more difficult.

After getting on the plane, she leaned her head back and turned her eyes toward me. "Thanksgiving is next week. I figured it into our plans that we'd have to go home for the holiday weekend before resuming our trip."

A deep frown formed on my forehead. "We're not breaking up the trip to go home, only to set off again. It's a waste of time. The sooner we finish the trip, the sooner we'll be home for good. Well, by good I mean at least a few months."

Disappointment flashed in her bright eyes. "I've never had a Thanksgiving without my mother. Are you sure there's no way we can make a plan to see our families for the holiday?"

I turned my hand on the armrest between us and left my palm up. Lacie didn't hesitate to bring hers to mine. "I don't know. I don't think so."

She tightened her grip on my hand, nodded, and let me go. For the rest of the flight, she didn't speak much. I could see she was upset about missing out on Thanksgiving with her mother.

It wasn't like I was super happy about it, either. Alec and Karina had plans to go to my parents' house, but I knew Alec had been planning to visit his. It wasn't as big a deal to Alec as it was to Lacie, but the choice had effectively been taken away from him.

Seeing Lacie so upset about it, though, I knew I was going to have to make a plan about Thanksgiving.

I didn't know what that plan would be yet, but I'd have to make one.

CHAPTER 20

LACIE

"They're all so much the same, and so different at the same time," I said to Nolan as we walked into the lobby of the Houston branch. We'd arrived yesterday after flying in from Florida, but true to his word, Nolan had arranged for us to only do our tour today.

The furniture and style of décor was familiar by now, as was the font on the signage and the navy uniform worn by the staff. What struck me, however, was that Florida was somehow more relaxed than D.C. even though the opulence and style were the same. It seemed like the hotels still managed to maintain the individuality of the city they were in, even if they were part of a chain.

Nolan's eyebrows lifted, a grin spreading on his lips. *Lips that I've kissed. Lips that left my own swollen and tingling. Lips that have been in other intimate—focus, Lacie.*

"I'm impressed that you noticed it, actually. A lot of our guests have been to multiple locations, as have our staff, and very few of them have mentioned it."

"So it's done intentionally?"

He nodded. "No one likes staying in hotels that don't give away where they are. You could be in London, Tokyo, or Paris and everything would feel exactly the same. While the chain does have uniformity, we still wanted the hotel to give an authentic feel of the place it was located."

"I've never been to London, Paris, or Tokyo, but I think I know what you mean. It's a good idea."

"Thanks." He grinned and, spotting Tristan walking up to us, held out his hand to greet the GM. "How are you, Tristan? I'm sorry I missed the meeting last week. Family emergency."

"No problem." Tristan released Nolan's hand to shake mine. "Your protégé here handled the meeting like a pro."

Pride glinted in Nolan's eyes when he gave me a sidelong look. "I knew she could do it. She's the best."

"Right." Tristan grinned and tipped his head. "I received your email about wanting to do the first formal tour of the progress today. That's why I wasn't here to meet you yesterday. I was needed elsewhere."

"We wanted to take some time to look around by ourselves," Nolan lied easily. *To cover for me.*

All because I'd told him I was a little sore. I still couldn't believe he'd done that. It wasn't like I was temporarily disabled. I just hadn't been looking forward to walking around in heels all day long.

I'd tried to tell him not to worry about it on the plane before he'd sent the email, but he wouldn't hear it. All things considered, he wasn't treating me at all as dismissively or as nonchalantly as some of the men had in the stories I'd heard or read about losing one's virginity.

He was attentive, caring, considerate, and had faced everything head on the next morning. Because of how honest and open he was about talking about it, there was no awkwardness between us. Which was great, given how we had to work together in close quarters every day.

Tristan's booming voice and lyrical accent drew me back to the present. "I'd love to hear what you thought. Can I take you through, and then we'll discuss all your notes in one go after?"

"Sure." Nolan smiled agreeably, swiping his hand out in front of him to motion for me to go ahead. "Lead the way, Tristan."

Nolan waited for Tristan to walk out ahead of us, then for me to start moving before he fell into step beside me. "Tell me about the new booking system while we walk."

"We're in the process of implementing it, but we're not having much success finding someone on our usual job portals to man the twenty-four-hour lines. There are also still price discrepancies between the different online booking sites, which remains a cause of complaint."

Before Nolan could answer, an idea struck me, and I interrupted him. I'd apologize later. For now, I was too excited to keep it in. "There are a lot of graduate students seeking jobs in tech support at the moment. They won't stay with the company until they retire, but they'd be good at manning the system. As for the discrepancies in the pricing on different sites, have you added a disclaimer to each site?"

Tristan didn't ignore me, nor was he rude to me, but he did look at Nolan and waited for him to nod before he spoke to me. "We haven't looked at students who have graduated in tech support, nor have we added disclaimers, but those are great ideas. We'll look into them. Thanks."

Nolan flashed me a smile and a thumbs-up once Tristan started walking again, and I couldn't hold back an answering smile that felt like it split my face in two.

"Staff complaints are down, but we're still receiving some about the extended working hours."

Nolan sighed. "That's an industry problem. Everyone works longer hours in our industry than in most others."

"Do the staff here have the same kind of break rooms we do at the head office?" I asked.

Nolan shook his head. "We were told when we wanted to install them at first that it wasn't necessary."

From the tone of his voice, I could tell it had been a fight. I could also tell it had been with Tristan and that Nolan had backed off for some reason.

Tristan huffed out a breath. "My people don't need to play video games on their breaks to keep them energized or from burning out. They can go for a walk outside."

"Walking outside will energize some," I said. "But there are several studies out about how different people need different things in order to avoid burnout. Some will benefit by a walk outside, but not everyone. Napping pods work for those who just need a quiet space to unwind, as well as providing a place to rest or to read."

"You're saying my employees should be allowed to literally sleep on the job?" Tristan asked, unimpressed written all over his face.

"During their breaks, yes." I smiled and reached deep to dig around for the conflict management and resolution skills I'd been taught at college. "If you give everyone the opportunities, within your means and ability of course, to do what they need during their breaks, their work time will be more productive."

Tristan and I went back and forth for the whole tour. I'd learned more than I'd ever imagined from being around Nolan at the office and then in Florida. It was already becoming natural for me to see what needed to be done and then trying to think of a solution for how to get it done.

Honestly, it was exhilarating. I loved every minute of this part of my job. It finally felt like I was getting into a groove, and it was more rewarding than anything I'd ever felt. Even better than straight As, because this was real life. Acing it in academics had taken hard work, but I'd never felt quite like I was flying high in same way as I did today.

Man, this was the life.

I was sure that the orgasms I'd had two nights ago were contributing to how good I was feeling. But all in all, life was pretty darn amazing for me.

Nolan and I sat down for lunch together a couple of hours later. He wore a grin that made him look like the cat that had gotten the canary and the cream, and I was happy to be off my feet for a while.

"What?" I asked as I laid my napkin over my lap. I was becoming so good at this fancy-dining thing that I was doing it automatically now. Mom would be so proud.

"You have a knack for management, and I'm getting to see it come out. I love it. It was such a damn rush watching you stand up to

Tristan like that." He leaned forward and lowered his voice, his eyes sparkling with playful mischief while somehow packing heat at the same time. "It does things to me."

"Don't say stuff like that." I giggled, like full-on, girlish giggled. My cheeks flamed because I wasn't a giggler, but then I relaxed. This was Nolan. He'd heard much worse from me. *Like me screaming his name to the high heavens and making sounds only cats have a right to.*

"Why?" he teased. "I've held them back for long enough. Unless it makes you uncomfortable, in which case, I'll stop and I apologize."

"It's not that. It's just that I'm not... used to it." A smile with a will of its own spread on my lips. "But I think I might like it once I am."

"I'll keep working on it then." He smirked. "But I hope you don't get so used to it that you stop blushing. I think you're adorable when you blush."

"I'm not adorable," I objected. "Besides, you also think it's hot when I stand up to Tristan, so obviously your thoughts are abstract and weird and maybe a little bit creepy."

He threw his head back and laughed, nodding when he lifted it back up. "I'm not going to argue with that, but seeing you go toe to toe with good old Tristan is hot because I know how stubborn and difficult he can be. No one's ever stood on my side against him before."

"Is this about the breakroom thing?"

He lifted his hand and tipped it from side to side. "Sort of. When I was first starting out, Tristan had been managing this very hotel for decades. It was a rundown dump just like the rest of 'em, but Tristan was proud for keeping its doors open. As he should have been. Problem was, he had very set ideas about what had kept their doors open, and he brought it into the new partnership with us."

"Why didn't you just replace him if he was causing trouble?"

"Because he's a damn good manager," he said earnestly. "Also, I'm not the type to fire or replace people just because they disagree with me or have different ideas than I do. I enjoy the challenge."

"Why? You don't have to be challenged when you're at the top."

He shrugged. "But I like to be. It reminds me of where I came from and how I got started."

"Which was?" I was genuinely curious, not having heard much about his story before.

In response, Nolan hit me with the biggest surprise yet. He reached into the inside pocket of his jacket and pulled out a deck of cards. They were smaller than your average playing cards, but there was no mistaking what they were.

"Pick a card, any card."

My eyeballs nearly fell out of my head. "You're a magic nerd? No way."

"Yes way," he said. "Now pick a card."

"Wait a second. How does this remind you of how you got started and where you came from? Are you trying to avoid the topic?"

Shaking his head, he placed the cards right in front of my face. "I always enjoyed magic when I was younger, but it didn't pay enough. This was as close as I could get to the same feeling as a trick really working. Are you going to pick a card?"

I did, and once that trick was done, I picked another. I gave him a hard time and shook my head when he finally put the cards back in his pocket when our food came, but I liked knowing he had a nerdy side too.

Out of all the things I'd summed him up as since we'd met, a closet magic nerd was not one of them. I really, really liked that I'd been wrong.

"We're going to Vegas tomorrow," he said before picking up his cutlery. "For obvious reasons, it's also one of my favorite cities. But you know why else it is?"

I knew it had to be something I could actually guess and not another personal revelation or else he wouldn't have asked. "Because what happens in Vegas stays in Vegas?"

One hazel eye twinkling with excitement winked at me, and his lips pulled into a magnificent smile. "Exactly."

I'd never been to Vegas before, but I had a feeling I was about to find out why people said that about it. And I was abnormally excited to find out what it was that happened there that people weren't supposed to talk about.

CHAPTER 21

NOLAN

Hungover businessmen in sharp suits climbed off the elevator and headed for the breakfast room. A family emptied out of the one beside it, but there was still no sign of Lacie.

Standing in the lobby waiting for her, I looked down at my watch for at least the fifth time in so many minutes. We were running short on time, and worry gnawed at my gut.

In all the time I'd known her, I couldn't remember her being late once. I was considering going up to make sure she was okay when another elevator reached the lobby and opened to reveal her standing right at the front.

She spotted me right away, rushing out and dragging her wheelie bag behind her as fast as the wheels could spin. "I'm so sorry I'm late. I had to do something, and it took longer than I thought it would."

"What did you have to do at this time of the morning?" I reached for the handle of her bag and stood it next to mine.

Mischievousness and excitement mingled in her eyes, shining brightly as she shrugged. "You'll have to wait and see tomorrow. It's a surprise."

"For me?"

She nodded, a radiant smile forming on her lips. "I'm really bad at keeping secrets and waiting to reveal surprises, so don't ask me again, okay?"

I chuckled as I took both bags and turned toward the exit. "You know you probably shouldn't tell people that when they're the one you're trying to surprise. It's going to be really tempting to try getting you to tell me now."

"It's only fair that you be tempted by something, too. Since I'm super tempted to just tell you."

I didn't bother to point out that I was plenty tempted by *her* just about every second of every day.

"I'll do my best not to ask again then." I jerked my head at the doors. "You ready to go?"

"I think so. Have you said goodbye to Tristan?" She fell into step beside me when I started walking, rolling both of our bags behind me. She'd given up on trying to insist on carrying her own bag.

"Yeah, he came by while I was waiting for you. There's a big conference going on that he had to go make sure everything was ready for."

"Ah, that's why I saw so many hungover people this morning."

I grinned, nodding as we stepped outside and into the wide, circular drive. "They're starting with the conference this morning, but most of the attendees arrived yesterday."

"It's seems like there are a lot of them. It's good for the hotel to be hosting such big conferences."

I lifted my hand to hail our waiting driver, who immediately climbed into the black SUV that would be taking us to the airport. "It's one of our big money spinners here, so yes. It's really good. Tristan and his team are aiming to become a premier conference facility as well as one of the top hotels in the city."

She pursed her lips and put a finger to them, narrowing her eyes in thought as the SUV pulled up in front of us. "A lot of the snippets of things he said that I didn't understand make sense now. Is there anything we can do from head office to support them?"

I greeted the driver and handed over our bags before turning to motion her into the SUV ahead of me. "We're already doing all we can. I've approved an additional marketing budget for them, and we've sent out a call for proposals from a couple of big catering companies who are used to providing good quality food at that scale."

"Isn't it cheaper to do it in-house?" she asked, climbing into the SUV and shuffling across the black leather seat to make space for me.

I nodded as I followed her in. "Probably, but the chefs that we have at the moment can't handle the restaurant, the rooftop café, and catering to all the different conference venues. That's part of what we're looking at for their expansion."

The driver pulled away from the hotel and eased us into the traffic while Lacie looked out of the window but kept talking to me. "I'll do some research on the plane. We can add whatever I find into the feedback report I'm preparing for them of our visit."

"You know you can take a couple of hours off to enjoy the flight, right?"

She spun her head around to look at me, amusement dancing in her eyes. "Honestly? I'd rather work than watch those silly movies they have on the plane."

"They're blockbusters," I protested, but then my lips pulled into a smirk. "But you won't have to worry about those today."

"What do you mean?" She frowned, finally giving me her full attention as the city started to fall behind us.

"You're not the only one who has a surprise this morning. I do, too." A shiver of excitement ran down my spine. I couldn't wait to see her reaction when she realized what my surprise was. "The only difference is that I'm not going to make you wait until tomorrow for it."

She bounced a little in her seat, pressing her palms together with her fingers pointed toward the sky. "Please tell me. I'm terrible with surprises. If you don't tell me what it is, I'm going to spend the rest of our trip coming up with all these random possibilities in my head."

"You only have to wait another," I leaned over to peer out my window, getting my bearings, "about ten minutes."

She perked up, smoothing out the navy skirt she had on today and turning in her seat to face me fully. "Will you give me a clue?"

For the next ten minutes, I played along and gave her a bunch of clues. When we pulled up in front of the private jet on the tarmac of the airfield, her lips parted and she sucked in a sharp breath. "Is this..."

"For us, yes." I unbuckled my seatbelt, grinning as I opened the door and slipped out. I popped my head back in. "But you have to get out in order for us to go anywhere in it."

"But what—why?" Lacie stammered, seemingly frozen in place. "How?"

Reaching into the interior of the SUV, I unbuckled her seatbelt for her and gently closed my fingers over her wrist. "Early this morning, I got the notification that our flight had been canceled. I really didn't want to miss out on the extra night in Vegas I promised, so I called Peter."

"Who's Peter?" She finally slid across the seat and climbed out of the SUV. She could have used the door on her side, but I had been tugging at her wrist to spur her into motion, and clearly, she was still too stunned to think about much.

I liked it because when her feet hit the tarmac, I didn't move back. Our bodies were so close together that I could feel the heat coming off hers and smell the sweet scent of her perfume. Resisting the urge to pull her into my arms, I flashed her a smile.

"Peter is my pilot."

"You have a pilot?" Disbelief filled her eyes when she looked up at me. "And you called him just so that I wouldn't miss out on one extra night in Vegas?"

I nodded and lifted one of my shoulders. "It's no big deal. I just didn't want you to be disappointed."

Her mouth opened, but she didn't say anything. When it became clear that she couldn't form words, she threw her arms around my shoulders and pressed her body close to mine, hugging me so tightly it felt like my neck might snap. But if it did, I'd die a happy man.

"You're welcome," I whispered, my lips moving against her shiny black hair. "Come on. Let me show you the inside."

We separated, reluctantly for me, and walked side by side to the steps leading into the cabin. Peter was talking to our driver, who had already loaded our bags on the plane. I thanked him while Lacie climbed into the jet, then I followed her up.

Peter came in last, closing the door behind him and performing a couple of routine safety checks. Before I went to join Lacie where she stood gaping at the interior of the cabin, I stopped next to him. "Everything looking good?"

He nodded. "We're just about ready for takeoff. I apologize again for Emile not being on board today. He couldn't make it to the airport on time. If I waited any longer for him to arrive, I would have been late getting to you."

"That's okay. We don't need an attendant. We're perfectly capable of getting our own drinks." I chatted to Peter for another minute before he went into the cockpit and I went to join my beautiful assistant. "What do you think?"

"I've never been in a private jet before. It's everything I always imagined it would be and more." Her voice was quiet, but I understood why.

The jet was a top-of-the-line marvel of modern mechanics. The walnut paneling gleamed and the carpet beneath our feet was more lush than any we had in the hotels. Four rows of beige leather seats could be spun around to suit our needs on each flight, either taking on the configuration of an ordinary plane or turned to face one another.

There were even coffee tables that folded into the floor that could come up if we needed them. The seats could recline fully, and when they were down, they were about the size of a single bed. A bar took up half of the back wall with a bathroom off to the side of it.

"Its quite something, isn't it?"

"I'd say." A frown flickered across her features as she looked up at me. "Does it belong to you?"

I nodded. "I acquired it about a year ago."

"Why haven't we been taking it all along?" She gave my shoulder a playful push. "Or do you only haul it out to impress the woman you want to sleep with?"

140

"The jet isn't what I haul out to impress the woman I want to sleep with." My lips curved into a smirk. "You should know what I *do* haul out then."

A flush turned her cheeks a rosy shade of pink, but there was a smile on her lips. "True. If it's not that, why haven't we been taking it then?"

I shrugged as I walked to my favorite seat and sat down, patting the chair next to me. "It's an expense I didn't need to have. Rich people don't stay rich by spending all their money on unnecessary stuff like this, and I'd like to keep the money I've made if possible."

"Why buy it then?" She sat down and buckled up but kept her eyes on mine. "It seems like another unnecessary expense to buy it if you never use it."

"We're using it now," I said. "But it's worth it when I have to fly the board or the executives around. Buying first-class tickets for that many people is more expensive than this. Plus, I can always haul it out when I want to impress people, remember?"

Her shoulders shook as she laughed. "True."

The wheels started moving and Peter lifted us off the ground minutes later. Once we were airborne and the fasten seat belt sign had been turned off, Lacie's tongue darted out to lick her lips.

My eyes caught the movement, then the calculating look in hers. "How private is this plane of yours?"

"It's only us and the pilot onboard. Obviously, he's not coming back here." I titled my head, seeing that calculation turn into a deliciously naughty gleam. "Why? What did you have in mind?"

Lacie lifted her shoulders in a nonchalant shrug, but I saw the tremble of anticipation in her hands when she unbuckled her belt. "Nothing much. Just this little thing I've been wanting to try."

"Which is?" My cock was already starting to come to life, sensing that whatever she had in mind might involve it.

When she slid off her seat and looked up at me with an expression that was a perfect mix of soft vulnerability and a sexy-as-fuck woman who knew exactly what she wanted, my blood fled further south and my dick throbbed.

The vulnerability fled when she blinked and pulled her shoulders back, crawling closer to me on her knees. "I want to give you a blowjob. Do you mind being my guinea pig?"

CHAPTER 22

LACIE

Nolan's pupils blew up, sending a rush of satisfaction and empowerment bolting through me. He looked at me through half-lidded eyes, disbelief clear in what little color was left in them.

"You have no idea how much I would love to be your guinea pig." He sounded different again, his voice gravelly and rough. "Please let me be your guinea pig."

My lips curled into a coy smile as I twirled a lock of hair around my finger. "Are you sure? I wouldn't want you to feel too put out."

"Trust me, it's no trouble at all." He sat back in his chair, hands gripping the armrests so hard, his knuckles turned white. "Do your worst."

"Okay." I put my finger to my lips and pretended to think. "If you're sure."

I shuffled forward again, close enough that his thighs touched my shoulders and I'd easily be able to reach his belt. His breathing sped up as he looked down at me. "You're enjoying teasing me, aren't you?"

I nodded. "It's good to see that I can get you as worked up as you can get me."

"I'm worked up, all right." Letting go of one of the armrests, he reached for my hand. I gave it to him, and he placed it right over his crotch. "Feel that? That's how worked up I am."

I sucked in a sharp breath when I squeezed what felt like steel. "Oh, I'm going to like this."

"Careful," he warned. "If you keep teasing me, I might be tempted to repay the favor later."

"Looking forward to it." A rare smirk touched my lips. "I'll just have to make sure that I enjoy this enough now to have something to remember later."

Nolan groaned, his head falling back as I walked my fingers up both his thighs slowly. "Fuck, Lacie."

My pussy tightened at the raw need in his voice. I'd been planning on dragging this out, but even I suddenly couldn't wait any longer.

When the idea to do this had come to me shortly after we'd stepped onto the plane, I figured that if I went slowly enough, he would be too turned on to notice my severe lack of experience. But now I hoped that what I lacked in experience, I'd be able to make up for with enthusiasm.

Fingers trembling as I undid his belt and unzipped his fly, I released his gorgeous cock after he lifted his hips an inch to allow me to pull his pants and boxers off. Since he'd reassured me the pilot wouldn't come out, I took the time to take off his shoes and socks too, getting him totally naked from the waist down.

His cock was hot and heavy in my hands when I reached up and wrapped my fingers around him, licking my lips as I tried to figure out where to start. Nolan was breathing heavily, his fingers twitching on the armrests as if he was dying to touch me, to guide me.

"I don't really know how to do this," I admitted, moving my hands to stroke up and down his length.

The sound he made let me know that he liked it, so I did it again.

"Just like that."

He let his head fall back again as I experimented with speed and pressure. By the time I felt confident that I had this part down, his hips were bucking, and there was the sexiest, contorted expression on his face.

My clit throbbed, and my pussy was drenching my panties, but I ignored my own need and focused on his. Leaning forward and pushing up on my knees, I was immensely grateful for the thick carpet beneath them. It allowed me to do this right, without being distracted by pain or discomfort in my legs.

My lips parted, and my tongue darted out between them to lick the glistening head of his dick. Both of us moaned loudly, but only Nolan trembled.

Giving up their hold on the armrests, his hands landed on my head, and his fingers wound into my hair. I sank my mouth farther down his shaft, loving the feel and taste of him in my mouth almost as much as the knowledge that I was the one making him come apart like this.

I remembered thinking once that nothing and no one could make him lose control, and knowing that I was about to made me feel like a veritable goddess. Opening my mouth as wide as it would go, I took in as much of him as I could and used my hands to work the rest of him.

Nolan's fingers tightened in my hair, and he muttered a string of curses under his breath. Smiling around his length, I took my cues from his reactions and adjusted my game plan as I went along in order to work in more of what I was learning he liked.

My tongue brushed over what felt like a bundle at the underside of his head, and his entire body tensed up. I opened my eyes to look at him, seeing his eyes screwed tightly shut and his features scrunched up in what looked like intense concentration.

Fire blossomed in my belly, making me feel like I was the one about to come apart. I moaned around him, surprised when his lips parted as soon as I did.

"I'm too close," he said through gritted teeth, his dark eyes landing on mine. "You have to stop, Lacie."

I shook my head and pumped him with my hands, tracing my tongue over his slit before going back to that apparently sensitive part under it. A few seconds later, I felt him tap my shoulder, but I didn't pull back.

I knew enough to know that he was warning me, but I didn't want to move back. He'd told me the other night that he wanted to taste me, and now it was my turn.

One more pass of my tongue and the first rope of thick come hit the back of my throat. I would have gagged if he hadn't warned me, but I didn't. I kept going, just like he had with me, and swallowed every last bit of his release before slowing down.

He was panting when I looked up at him again, a mischievous gleam in his eyes when the lust and relief receded. "My turn."

Unlike the last time, he didn't take it slowly now. One second, I was on my knees in front of him, and the next, my back hit the carpet and my skirt was around my hips, my soaked panties off and flying through the air with my heels still on my feet.

Nolan tucked into me like I was that first snack you were allowed after a diet, with such gusto that all I could do was clamp a hand over my mouth to keep from screaming.

It didn't work.

As soon as he closed his lips around my clit and circled his talented tongue around it, I couldn't hold back a shout. They didn't stop as he kept going, making me come in what had to be record time.

I would have been embarrassed if not for the proud smile on his lips when I rejoined the land of the living. He leaned over to kiss me, again giving me a taste of myself I never thought I would like. Since it was on his lips though, there was no way I couldn't like it.

"I forgot I was supposed to tease you for a minute there," he said. "Guess I'll have to keep it in mind for the rest of the flight."

"For the rest of the flight?" I almost squeaked. "There has to be at least two and half hours left."

"Then you'd better hang on to something because I'm not about to go back to work right now." He pushed a finger into me and found a spot at the top that made my whole body shudder. Then he proceeded to make good on his word about keeping me busy for the rest of the flight.

I learned that he didn't need nearly as much time to recover as I might have thought, and was back to full strength soon after my second orgasm. When he eventually sank into me, I cried out before I could stop myself.

I'm so not going to be able to look the pilot in the eyes after this. My cheeks were beet red after we landed when Peter finally came out of the cockpit to say goodbye. Nolan, perfectly put together again with not a hair out of place, thanked him before ushering me down the steps.

"Relax, there's nothing to be embarrassed about," he said into my ear, his hand on the small of my back as we reached the tarmac. "He didn't hear anything."

I turned my head to look at him, probably much closer to me than he should have been. "Are you sure?"

Nolan laughed, his eyes bright and happy when they caught mine. "Absolutely. Don't worry about it. I heard you though, and I'm planning to hang on to those memories for a long, long time. I'm also planning to make a lot more."

CHAPTER 23

NOLAN

"This is what I would call a buffet." Lacie stared at tables upon tables laden with different options for lunch. "Where do we even start?"

"Over there." I pointed with my thumb. "That's where the plates are, so I'm assuming that's the starting point."

"You haven't had a buffet lunch in your own hotel before?" she teased as we wound around the other diners, making our way to the plates.

"Of course, I have, but they keep changing it up. It looks different almost every day." I took the plate she handed over to me when we reached the table. She took one for herself and we joined the line of people trying to decide what to take and what to leave.

She looked at me over her shoulder. "That sounds like a lot of work."

"It is, but so is turning a profit as a hotel in a town like this one." At the front of the room was a window looking out over the street outside. I swept my hand out in its direction. "There's a lot of competition out there, and everyone has something that brings the feet to their hotel instead of another. At the moment, we only have a restricted gaming license. We've applied for the unrestricted one, but there are a lot of requirements and hoops we have to jump through."

"So this branch relies on their restaurant to bring people in?"

"Yes, for now. We also have a live-entertainment license, so we try to get as much live entertainment in as possible. If we want to get to the top here, though, we're going to need that unrestricted license."

Lacie's eyes tracked around the dining room. "It's pretty packed in here. It looks like they're doing well."

"They are, but like the others we've visited, they're just not breaking into that top one percent. Although here, we know the unrestricted license is the big thing holding us back at the moment. There are some other things too, but no matter what we do, we won't reach the top until we get it."

"What else do we need to do?" she asked as we reached the first table.

The ideal we were aiming for was to have no lines at the buffet, but while we'd cut the time down to no longer than two minutes, we just weren't getting to there being no lines at all.

A server dished up some salad onto each of our plates, and we moved along to the next station. "There are a couple of things. The quality of our live entertainment and the full casino once we're allowed to have more than slot machines being the most important. We also need to improve on all our service areas and modernize a little."

"All our service areas?" Her eyes widened. "None are up to par?"

I shrugged. "This isn't like any other holiday destination. Vegas is very difficult and very particular. Our reviews are mostly acceptable, even if they're not the best yet, but there's room for improvement everywhere."

"It sounds like we've got our work cut out for us. Wouldn't it be a good idea for us to extend this part of our trip for more than just one extra night?"

"We can't. We just don't have the time right now. Besides, it's not all going to happen overnight. They've been in the process of upgrading and expanding as long as the others have."

"Well," she said as we finally made our way to our seats, "at least they're doing well in the meantime."

"That, they are." I pulled Lacie's chair out for her before going to my own. Scarlett used to be offended when I tried to be a gentleman, claiming that she could do stuff for herself. Which, of course, I knew she could. But I liked doing it for her, so sue me. *Oh wait, she did.*

Lacie, however, never made a fuss about it. At first, I'd expected her to, considering how assertive and independent she was, but she took it in stride and didn't question me. It was almost like she could tell how much it meant to me and had decided to just roll with it.

Which reminded me. "What was the surprise you were going to show me today?"

Her fork paused halfway to her enticing mouth, chicken momentarily forgotten. "All you need to know for now is that you should be dressed and in the lobby at six. We'll take it from there."

A disappointed sigh left my lips. I hated surprises. When I was the one planning them, as I usually was, I loved them. Being the *surprisee*, however, was not my strong point.

It didn't help matters much that I couldn't remember the last time someone had planned a surprise for me. I really wasn't used to it.

As excited as I was to see what Lacie had up her sleeve, I was also impatient. "Okay, I'll meet you at six, but then I want to know where we're going."

A sexy smirk lifted her lips. "We'll see."

Lacie changed the topic back to work, clearly not wanting to give me any hints about what her surprise was. Throughout lunch, I tried to figure it out. Knowing she'd never been to Vegas before made it difficult because it meant I had no frame of reference for what she might have done here before that she could want to go back to.

Eventually giving up—for now—I enjoyed telling her more about the plans for the Vegas branch and the hopes I had for it. When we finished our meal, we headed up to our separate rooms to get some work done before whatever it was we were doing at six.

Opening the doors to my balcony when I got back to the suite, I fixed a cup of coffee and went to sit outside. Vegas looked like a fairground from up here, so much more innocent during daytime than the debauchery I knew took place at night.

Since I had some time on my hands, I made a quick call to Alec and Karina. He told me they were at my parents' place, having fun and that he was heading out soon.

Karina's little face broke out in a grin when she saw me on the screen. "Daddy! I miss you."

I felt a fissure opening up in my heart. "I miss you too, baby. How are you doing? Are you having fun at Granny and Grandpa's?"

She nodded enthusiastically, her eyes bright. "Granny and I made cookies this morning. They have chocolate chips in them. Grandpa and Uncle Alec watched a game. Then we played catch outside. Granny said we could go to the park later. I wish you could come to the park with us."

Her rambling explanation made me feel a little better. It meant she truly was having fun and despite what she said, wasn't missing me too much. I knew it was only when she spoke to me that she really even thought about me that much.

Alec and my parents were excellent at keeping her busy and distracted. "That's great, Kare-bear. I wish I could come to the park, too. Go down the slide for me an extra time, will you?"

Dutifully nodding, her eyes slid to someone off screen. "Grandpa is waving."

"Tell him I say hi." In my mind's eye, I could see my father standing in their den, wearing his usual plaid shorts and T-shirt combo. No matter the time of year, he insisted that he'd worn enough suits and slacks to last him a lifetime before his retirement and now only wore them when he was going out in the dead of winter. "Have you given him any new gray hairs yet?"

My heart ached to be with them all. Contrary to so many stories of people nowadays not having good relationships with their parents, I adored mine. Despite their move out of the city, we hadn't drifted apart and I really enjoyed spending time with them. *Lacie might have a point about Thanksgiving.*

Karina rolled her eyes at me, pursing her lips. "Grandpa only has gray hairs. I didn't give him any."

I heard my father scoff, then chuckle. "It's almost time to go to the park. Do you need a few more minutes?"

She glanced at him before her eyes came back to mine. I saw the plea in them. "Can we go to the park now?"

"Sure, sweetheart. I'll speak to you all later." I blew a kiss at the screen, told my father who I knew could hear me that I would call them later, and disconnected the call.

Happy to hear that my little girl was doing well and satisfied that this trip didn't seem to be bothering her as much as I'd been afraid it might, I headed inside to get some work done. My thoughts drifted to Karina and my family occasionally, but I actually ended up having a reasonably productive afternoon.

When I closed my laptop, there was time for a quick shower, and then I would have to go down to the lobby to meet Lacie. A strange, new kind of excitement spread through me as I stood in the shower and wondered again where she was taking me.

This flirtation or whatever it was Lacie and I had going on was making me feel things I never thought I'd feel again, such as the electrifying thrill of knowing I was going to see *that* girl again in less than an hour.

Admitting it didn't even scare me. I was into this thing between us and I wasn't ashamed of it. Hurrying through my shower, I got dressed in dark blue jeans and a black button-up shirt before making my way downstairs.

Even though I was five minutes early, Lacie was already waiting for me, looking ravishing even in jeans and a black blouse. Our outfits kind of matched, except that I wasn't wearing heels and I didn't have cleavage to give a tantalizing glimpse of.

I grinned when I walked up to her. "Great minds, huh?"

Her eyes roamed down the length of my body, heating before she burst out laughing. "Oh my God. This is too good. I'm so glad you saw the memo I posted on your mirror."

"Well, at least it looks like I guessed right on what to wear for the occasion. My other option was a tux."

Lacie froze mid-laugh. "You brought a tux with you?"

"Of course, I did." I smirked. "You never know when you might need one."

She rolled her green eyes and nodded at the exit. "Most normal people know you never need eveningwear for a spontaneous occasion. Now come on, Captain Dapper and Well-Dressed. We're going to be late."

"Where are we going?" I asked as we made our way outside and joined the throngs of tourists on the sidewalk.

"You'll see." She tossed me a look over her shoulder, her eyes alive with nerves and excitement. "It's only about a five-minute walk from here."

"You're really going to make me wait until the last second?" God, now I knew where Karina got it from.

Lacie nodded, practically skipping down the street and calling for me to keep up. She kept glancing down at her phone in her hand, obviously following directions to somewhere.

"If you tell me where we're going, I could probably help get us there."

She looked down at the screen again, then up at the building next to us, and shook her head as she stopped. "That's won't be necessary. We're here."

I spun to face the building, my eyes immediately catching on the neon letters advertising tonight's show. My heart did a series of flip flops in my chest.

"Are you kidding me? You got us tickets to this?" My mouth dried up as I tried to process what she had done for me. The performer was a world-famous magician that I'd always wanted to see, but I'd never gotten around to attending one of his shows.

I felt my eyes light up when she nodded, smiling at me. "I had to pull a few strings since it was so last minute, but I got us in."

The flip flops intensified, accompanied now by a fluttering feeling in my stomach. *Butterflies. She's managed to give me butterflies for the first time in my life.*

Fuck, I didn't know it was possible for men to get butterflies. But I sure as hell had them in that moment.

Lacie led me into the theater and displayed printed tickets to an usher, who showed us to our *front-row* seats. My heart was going so crazy, I thought it might pop. *How much better could this night get?*

She answered my silent question a few minutes later when the lights went low and she slipped her hand into mine. I nearly groaned out loud from the rush of pleasurable sensations in my body elicited by all this.

Christ. This surprise had totally been worth waiting for.

CHAPTER 24

LACIE

Who'd have thought Nolan Yates has an inner nerd? I never would have. That was for sure.

But he totally did and he sure was letting it out tonight. As the show started, he jumped to his feet and cheered louder than anyone else in the crowd.

Eyes nailed to the stage, he gasped and laughed and clapped at every trick the magician performed. He was in his element, and I had to admit, I really liked seeing him like this. He was totally entranced, looking younger and more relaxed than I'd ever seen him.

Out of all my own nerdy tendencies, magic had never really been one of them. Until now, at least.

With Nolan enjoying the show as much as he was, I couldn't help falling under the magician's proverbial spell either. It was like Nolan's excitement was palpable and being pushed into me.

For the rest of the show, I was on my feet whenever Nolan was. I clapped and cheered and nearly lost my mind as I watched volunteer after volunteer go up on stage and saw the magician perform his tricks on them.

It was more invigorating than I ever thought it would be, and when the show was done, I knew it wouldn't be the last time I went to a magic show. Nolan was radiant when we left, a seemingly permanent grin on his lips and his flushed cheeks.

"Thank you, Lacie. That was incredible. I owe you one. Several, actually." His hand slipped into mine as we left the theater, and although I knew it was probably a bad idea to hold hands in public, I curled my fingers around his and held them. "No one has ever done anything like that for me."

"Really?" I frowned up at him as we walked, exiting along with hundreds of other gushing fans. "That seems unlikely."

"It's true. I can't thank you enough." He squeezed my hand. "This is the best night out I've had in a long, long time."

"You're welcome. You've done so much for me that you don't even have to thank me. I could afford to take you to something that you'd like." I smiled, winking when I caught his eye. "Besides, you basically bought those tickets for yourself anyway."

He rolled his eyes, but not before I saw the humor shining in them. "Bullshit. You earned the money you spent. I just don't really understand why you spent it on me."

"Like I said, you've done a lot for me. I wanted to do something nice for you too."

"You have done plenty of nice things for me." The naughty way his lips curled told me he was thinking about the plane.

I nudged him playfully with my elbow, laughing as I ducked my face to hide my flushed cheeks. "I meant nice outside-of-the-bedroom things."

Nolan pulled me to a stop, cupping my cheek and making me look up at him. "Well, thank you. It was a very nice outside-of-the-bedroom thing to do."

"Again, you're welcome." I tore my eyes away from his when I realized where we had stopped. "The fountains?"

The words left me as a hushed whisper as I stared at what undeniably had to be one of the most famous things in Vegas to see. I couldn't believe that I hadn't even thought about coming to see them.

The pictures I'd seen hadn't done the fountains justice, with the way the water shot and sparkled and the lights lit up the sky. My feet moved me toward the railing, my hands closing around the cold metal as I stared at the sight before me.

"Beautiful, right?" I heard Nolan say and turned my head to find him standing next to me.

I nodded. "Breathtaking, I'd say."

"Yeah, you're right," he said, but even though I'd turned back toward the fountains, I could see from the corner of my eye that he was looking at me.

Surprise that he could have been implying that *I* was breathtaking rendered me speechless. Considering everything that had happened between us at this point, I knew that he thought I was sexy. He'd even called me beautiful a few times, but that was usually when I was naked.

Breathtaking, however, wasn't a word I'd have used to describe myself or ever expected anyone else to. I was pretty by most people's standards. I'd take beautiful under the circumstances in which he'd used it, but breathtaking?

The moment stretched out between us, the clear night air suddenly feeling laden with sparks and tension that hadn't been there before. It was that chemistry I was slowly getting used to feeling with him, except there was something different about it this time.

There was nothing sexual about it. My body still felt drawn to his like there was that magnet planted in my chest and the opposing pole in his, but there was no ache, no dampening or tightening of anything.

Nolan's lips parted as his eyes remained locked on mine, an unfamiliar softness in them as he seemed to drink me in. I couldn't explain it, but it felt like we were leveling up somehow in our relationship.

"Why haven't you dated since your divorce?" The question came bursting out of me from absolutely nowhere. Sure, of course, I'd wondered.

I'd even nearly started arguing with him that first night we'd been together when he'd told me how long it had been for him. It didn't seem possible that a man like him had not only been single for that long, but that he also hadn't been sexually active at all.

The look in his eyes then had stopped me from asking or arguing.

I'd seen lust and raw hunger there. Nothing else had seemed important when he looked at me like that.

It was important now, though. I wouldn't have been able to tell anyone why, but the information suddenly felt like it was absolutely vital to have, as important as my next breath.

Nolan blinked in surprise, his jaw hardening before he visibly forced himself to relax. It was like I could see his brain give the order and his muscles loosening in response.

"Karina is my life," he said earnestly. "Everything I do, I do for her. She's my beginning and my end. She's been through so much and she's only five. I don't want to add to the trauma by bringing women into and out of her life."

"I can respect that." Even if it did leave a pit in my stomach. "You're a great father, Nolan."

"Thanks." He grinned, but it wasn't quite as warm as before. "We should get back."

"Yeah, I guess we should. We have a flight to catch in the morning." I took his hand when it slid into mine again, realizing just how much I liked having it there.

I was really going to hate when the time came that I had to let go of it for good. And it would come. He'd basically just confirmed it.

"California, here we come." His tone was light again, his grin wider and his eyes brighter. "Are you excited?"

"Yeah, I am." Despite the realization I'd just come to, I really was excited for California. I had a feeling this part of our trip was coming at a good time, since I'd get to see Anna again.

Having a girlfriend lend me an ear and quite possibly a shoulder didn't seem like a bad thing at all. Then again, neither did sunshine, beach, or the opportunity to see yet another place I'd never been to before.

Whatever happened between me and Nolan, my job was still pretty freaking awesome. I would just have to remember that.

CHAPTER 25

NOLAN

"I can see why so many movies and TV shows are set here," Lacie said. "California is beautiful."

She was glued to the window on the passenger side of our rental car. Every so often, I caught a glimpse of her eyes in the reflection of the glass, and they were so bright, it was almost unreal.

They made me want to look only at her. Fuck the scenery around us. None of it compared to her, but since that wasn't what we were talking about, I nodded.

"I've only been to this branch once. I forgot how beautiful it is around here." It was so much more beautiful for having her in it, but I didn't add that.

Something had shifted inside me the last few days. I wasn't sure what it was, but it had been a big shift. I had trouble keeping my eyes, mind, and hands off of Lacie in a way I hadn't before.

Whenever we weren't together, which was a few hours a day tops, I couldn't stop thinking about her. I had to actively work to tear my gaze away from her when we were together, which was very inconvenient considering that I also had to be professional and at least try to appear aloof.

Being alone with her but not touching her was more difficult than ever, which was saying something since I'd itched to touch her from the very first time I met her. My hands wouldn't be told no now and usually had her naked within the same heartbeat that one of our doors closed behind us.

Most nights were spent fucking her to within an inch of my life, and yet, I'd wake up unable to wait to do it again. I'd always had a healthy sexual appetite, except for the couple of years when I'd had none at all, but this was on a different level to where I'd been before.

When Scarlett and I had been newlyweds, we'd gone at it like rabbits. But I still didn't recall it being quite like this. I was totally insatiable for Lacie, desperate again within minutes of recovering no matter how hard I came. And Lacie made me come so hard, I went fucking blind for a minute every time.

If I added to all that the way my lungs wouldn't work around her, my heart worked too hard, and my eyes refused to cooperate, I had a suspicion I was in trouble. My grip tightened on the steering wheel, my mind a mess of incredulity and denial.

"What?" Lacie's voice startled me. "How have you only been here once? I want to come here every chance I get."

Oh, right. We'd been talking about California before my head went wandering. "Wayne has family here, so I came out for the initial inspection of the property, but he used to put his hand up to come after that."

"Any time you need someone to put their hands up to come here in the future, let me know. Mine will always be up." She was still staring out her window like she was searching for treasure out there, intent on not missing a single thing. Even one of her hands was up against it now, as if she was longing to touch the landscape but couldn't. "I can't believe people actually get to live here. I don't think I'd get any work done if I did. I'd just sit and stare out of the window all day."

"I can see that happening." I laughed. "It's happening already."

Lacie's hand finally left the window to flip me off. "Don't blame me. You're the one who brought me to paradise."

There was a retort on the tip of my tongue about how many times she'd taken me to paradise, but I bit it back. I didn't know why, but I didn't want sexual banter right then.

Her wonder at the landscape around us was real and honest, child-like in how captivated she was. I didn't want to ruin it for her. *Yeah, bud. You're in real trouble here.*

"Is that the hotel?" She pointed at the building slowly rising out of the edge of the cliff as we approached, the whitewashed walls blending in perfectly with the stone outcroppings around it.

I nodded. "That's it."

"That's..." She trailed off, finally turning away from the window to give me her wide-eyed stare. "It's incredible, Nolan. I mean, wow."

"I'm glad you approve." A genuine smile climbed on my lips. I didn't know why it meant so much to me that she was so taken by this property, but it did.

We passed through the gates, so overgrown by indigenous greenery and brightly colored flowers that I couldn't see what they had originally been made of. Acres of immaculately tended lawn dotted with old, leafy trees and a multitude of flower beds spread out on either side of the long drive, and then we were pulling up to the wide double doors that welcomed guests into the hotel.

The view from the lobby was spectacular, unobstructed by anything but the darkish tint on the floor-to-ceiling windows that looked out over the turquoise waters of the Pacific and the rocky shoreline below.

The receptionist checked us in, informing us that our suites had been booked from the day before. She also regretfully informed us that Anna was attending a meeting and wasn't available to greet us.

It hit me then that I had lost track of the days since deciding to add an extra day in Vegas, and I hadn't let Anna know. Our schedule had been prepared and forwarded by Lacie, but I'd told her that I'd taken care of everything for our extra night in Vegas.

Lacie smiled at the receptionist as she accepted our access cards for our suites. "That's okay. Please, don't worry about it. We can wait until tomorrow for our tour and to talk to her."

"I can give her a call for you," the receptionist offered, already reaching for the phone lying on her desk. "I'm sure she would come right back."

"No, please don't." Lacie reached out and patted the other woman's forearm. "I'll give her a call myself to let her know that we're here."

It took another few minutes to calm the horrified receptionist, who looked at me like I might pull a giant axe out from behind my back and take her job away with it. I tried to fix a reassuring smile to my lips, but evidently, it didn't work at all.

Lacie eventually sent me out to the bar on the deck to grab a drink while she set the girl at ease. She rolled her eyes at me when we got to the table I had chosen out on the deck, two ice cold beers on the surface in front of me. "Way to organize everything for our extra night. Poor Bernadette feels terrible that Anna isn't here when she's the one who told her to go."

"We had a place to sleep last night, didn't we?" I smirked, pushing the beer I'd ordered for her across the table. "But okay, I also might have fucked up by losing track of the days. I've been preoccupied."

"With what?" she asked, her eyes twinkling almost as much as the ocean below us. They were fucking mesmerizing like this. *And it's official. I have a problem. A big one.*

"You," I said honestly. "You've been keeping me up all night, and my brain doesn't function well on so little sleep."

Lacie laughed, shaking her head as she lifted her beer from the table and let it hang between her fingers. "Really? I'm the one who's been keeping you up? Funny, since I recall a very insistent wake up at three AM this morning when I was fast asleep."

"Yes, but it wouldn't have happened if you hadn't been sleeping naked. Like, right there. Don't blame me."

She swallowed the sip of beer she'd taken, then laughed again. *I love hearing her laugh. It's so lyrical and—Stop it.*

Since when the fuck did I even have thoughts like that? It really wasn't me.

"Okay," she said. "I'll take the blame, but I'm also taking a minute to call Anna before we have to get back to it."

"Go ahead." I sipped my own beer and watched the sun shining off the ripples on the water, its golden light reflected in the rise and fall of the glassy waves. *And since when do I notice stuff like that?*

Meanwhile, Lacie had pulled out her phone and was chatting animatedly to the general manager for this branch.

Suddenly looking right at me, she said, "Hang on. Let me check with him." Then she said to me, "Anna says she can be here in five minutes if you still want to do the tour today."

I shook my head. "No, it's okay. Let's relax. I could use a night of rest anyway."

Lacie pursed her lips as she fought back a smile, conveying my message to the GM. When she hung up the phone, she took another sip of beer and let out a contented sigh. "If we don't have to work tonight, I'm going to go meet up with Anna. Want to come?"

"No, I'm okay." I needed to take some time to either get my head examined or get it straight. "Be careful if you go, though. Okay?"

Fierce protectiveness unfurled in me, making me have to fight the urge to pick her up and toss her over my shoulder. I wanted to carry her to my room, lock her in there with me, and personally ensure that nothing and nobody could ever hurt her.

I didn't know why I suddenly felt so protective of her, but I had an inkling that it linked up with all those other things I'd been trying to explain to myself.

Yeah, that problem? It's bigger than I thought.

There was no more denying that I felt something for Lacie that I shouldn't. I cared about her, and I didn't know what to make of that.

163

CHAPTER 26

LACIE

Walnut Avenue was achingly picturesque. A lane lined with Victorian homes that was transformed into a kaleidoscope of fiery autumn colors.

Anna and I sipped on locally produced, alcohol-free apple cider as we strolled back to her car. "You're so lucky to be able to come here whenever you want."

She smiled, digging her key fob out of the leather satchel that hung across her shoulder. "If only I could come whenever I wanted to. Work keeps me pretty busy, as you probably know by now."

"That's true." I sighed, turning slowly in my spot to take one last mental picture of the street before we headed down to the boardwalk. "Thanks for coming to pick me up, by the way. I really appreciate being able to see some of the town while we're here."

"Of course," she said as she unlocked the car. "You have to take some time to see the places you're visiting. Hasn't Nolan been giving you any free time at all?"

"He has." We spent most of our nights, the only free time we had on most days, in bed in one of our suites, though. "But being shown around by a local is much better than having to figure it out for yourself."

"I guess that's true." She climbed into the car, waiting for me to hop into the passenger seat before she turned the engine on. "It's fun for me to show you around, too. I don't go to any of these places often enough. Showing people around is usually the only time I end up going to any of the touristy spots in town. It's usually work and home for me."

"Isn't it for all of us?" I leaned back in my seat, watching as we left the gorgeous Victorian neighborhood behind and headed back to the ocean. "I read somewhere that we should all take a day sometime to be tourists in our own towns. Peachtree doesn't have all that much to offer, but everywhere we've been on this trip so far sure does."

"Speaking of the trip so far." Anna glanced at me when she slowed at a red light, a knowing smile touching her lips. "How have things been going for you traveling with Nolan?"

"It's been good," I admitted, my teeth sinking into my lower lip as I considered how much to tell her.

Anna and I had spoken on the phone and texted quite a bit since she'd left Washington. I felt more comfortable with her than I had with a friend in a long, long time, but Nolan was her boss too. I didn't quite know how much I could tell her without making things awkward for either or both of them.

Her laughter filled the car as she pulled away from the light after giving me a pointed look. "Oh, come on. You have to give me more than 'it's been good.' You've been so cagey about the details every time we've spoken. Don't make me ply you with alcohol to get the truth out of you."

"You wouldn't." I put my hand to my chest and feigned injury. "There are rules about using a truth serum on your friends."

"No, there are rules against keeping juicy information from your friends," she retorted, a smile etched on her lips. "Besides, this isn't Harry Potter or some other magical universe. I can use truth serum in the form of fruity cocktails or yummy wines as much as I want."

"After the way my head pounded the last time I had fruity cocktails with you, I'm not sure I'm up for a repeat performance."

She shrugged. "You're in California now, my friend. We have

yummy wines by the vat, and we know how to drink them. I'm more than happy to settle for that instead of cocktails."

"You're not going to give up on this, are you?" I groaned, closing my eyes for a second.

Anna waited for me to open them again before reaching over to poke a finger into my ribs. "I'd be a terrible girlfriend if I gave up on this. You're alone with the guy you're crushing on almost all day, every day. It's okay to want to talk about it."

"Yeah, but isn't it weird for you? He's our boss. It feels like it's inappropriate to be talking about him like this."

"Please." She lowered her sunglasses so I'd be able to see her roll her eyes. "I can keep work and play separate as well as anyone. I won't go around spewing innuendo or winking at him when I see you guys tomorrow. I'm here for you as a friend if you want to talk."

"I do want to talk," I admitted quietly, taking a minute to think as I watched the ocean come into view when we crested a hill. "Things are really good between us at the moment."

"And by 'really good,' you mean?" The corners of her lips quirked up. "You're not a virgin anymore, are you?"

"How did you know?" I blurted out the question and forced my jaw not to drop.

Anna laughed. "I could tell the second I picked you up at the hotel."

"What? How?" I shifted in my seat, putting my knee up and turning my back on the window and the gorgeous view beyond it.

"Bosses don't usually wait with their assistants to be picked up," she said as she flipped on her indicator and made a turn. "Also, you had that glassy-eyed, freshly fucked look when I got there. It wouldn't take a genius to put those two things together."

"Oh my god." I brought my hands up to cover my face, separating two fingers to peer at her through the gap. "Are we really that obvious?"

"You are to me." She chuckled, shooting out a hand to lower one of mine away. "Don't be embarrassed. I'm happy for you."

Easing us into a parking lot outside the classic seaside amusement park that was their boardwalk, Anna shut off the engine and turned to face me. "Seriously. You don't ever have to be embarrassed about anything when you're talking to me. Whenever you feel like you should be, just tell me and I'll give you a fact of my own to counteract it."

"Okay." I smiled and watched as she got out of the car. Once I'd joined her on the sidewalk, she linked her arm through mine. I saw amusement dancing in her eyes, but there was concern there too. "Honestly, I've never talked to anyone about sex before so I'm going to be embarrassed all the time. The fact that the sex I'm having is with our boss takes it to a whole other level."

"Fine." She pursed her lips before she giggled, leaning in closer to me conspiratorially. "What about if I told you you're not the only one who had an orgasm before I came to pick you up? Would that make you feel less embarrassed?"

"I thought you were in a meeting all afternoon," I said, remembering what the receptionist had told me. "How did you have an orgasm in the meeting? That has to be against the rules."

"I didn't have it in the meeting, silly. It was after. My meeting ended early, and I went by the house to grab something to eat. My husband was there. He basically tackled me as soon as I walked through the door."

For the first time in my life, I could really relate to this kind of story. "Sounds like there was a lot of that going around this afternoon."

Her eyes sparkled as she nudged me playfully with her elbow. "Okay, now you have to tell me more. Nolan tackled you?"

I took a deep breath, fighting the urge to cringe as I nodded. "We checked in, had a drink at the bar, and went upstairs to get settled. He came to my room when I was getting ready to leave, and it just happened."

Anna released my arm to clap her hands, giving me a cute little bow at the waist. "Bravo, lady. If he's staking a claim on you and practically marking you just before you go out, you know you've got him."

"What are you talking about?" I frowned, feeling like a preschooler talking to a teacher for my lack of understanding. "I haven't *got* him."

With a slight shake of her head, she chuckled. "Whatever you say. Let's just leave it at me being happy the two of you are getting along so well."

"Okay." I was a little relieved that she was letting me off this easily, even if she hadn't really explained what she had meant.

I was perfectly happy letting the subject drop before I had to start going into too much detail, though. Just the thought of having to say some of the things we'd done out loud was enough to make me cringe.

Turning my gaze away from her to the amusement park ahead of us, my stomach flipped when I saw the Giant Dipper. "Can we go on that? I've always wanted to."

Anna nodded. "It's your day, so you can choose whatever you want to do. Just one final thing before we let the Nolan topic go for now, though. Be careful of his baby mama. Rumor has it she's quite the loose cannon."

"Yeah, I've gathered as much." I didn't share any of the information Nolan had given me about her or any of the tidbits he'd let drop from time to time. Those were too personal, and I knew he already felt like his privacy had been violated. "Anyway, do they have arcade games here? I haven't played in ages."

I was desperate not to talk or even think about Nolan's ex. Not only had I heard some of the terrible things she'd done, but I hated to think of how it had torn Nolan apart. It was so clear every time it came up that she really had done a number on him.

A number I wasn't so sure I could undo in order to build anything meaningful with him. It wasn't like I was expecting him to propose or anything drastic like that, but it would have been nice if there had been any possibility of this turning into more than a fling.

As things were, I didn't think there was any chance of that. The thought made my stomach turn even before we got on the roller coaster.

Anna sensed that my thoughts had taken a darker turn, and she spent the rest of the night trying to distract me. It worked pretty well too, until she dropped me back at the hotel after showing me more of the town.

My feet carried me to Nolan's room almost on autopilot. I wanted to see him, wanted to make the most of the time I had with him. But I couldn't bring myself to knock on his door.

The idea of getting in his bed and spending the night with him was enticing, but he'd wanted to rest. Just because I was having these gut-clenching feelings of our impending end didn't mean that I had to disturb him.

No, it's best to leave him be. I refused to be one of those girls who sought solace in a lover's arms whenever they felt mildly panicky.

Besides, even if he provided said solace tonight, it didn't mean he'd do it again tomorrow. I had to be careful, I couldn't go falling for him. We hadn't even discussed what was happening between us. So for now, I would take however many orgasms I could get and forget about a relationship.

Yeah, right. I sighed as I realized I already was losing that particular battle. *And would you like your unicorn to be pink or purple?*

I was so screwed, but I wasn't giving him up. Not just yet. I couldn't.

CHAPTER 27

NOLAN

Lacie's spare keycard was smooth and light where I held it between my fingers. She'd given it to me before she'd headed out with Anna, just in case I needed something from her room for work, but then she'd winked and told me to use it whenever I wanted to.

I wanted to use it now to check on her. All night, I'd tossed and turned, considering whether it would be way too much for me to just go to her room and wait for her to get in.

After a stern talking to with myself, I'd decided to wait until morning to make sure she was okay. There wasn't anything inherently dangerous about a night out on the town with my general manager, so I didn't really have any reason to be freaking out.

All that would accomplish was to make me look like a possessive, protective asshole who was too insecure to let the girl he cared for out of his sight. Channeling Dr. Haversham, I'd also realized that the degree of concern I felt over her girls' night out was probably a throwback to the early days when Scarlett started staying out all night.

Lacie wasn't Scarlett, and I'd do well to remember that. Also, I'd never had these feelings quite so intensely before, but that was because Scarlett had made it hard for me to trust anyone.

Nonetheless, when I woke up and saw that it was morning, I couldn't wait to go see Lacie. The turmoil I'd felt all night had twisted my stomach into knots, the crazy possessive and protective monster that lived inside me roaring when I thought about what I'd do if she wasn't there.

God, Scarlett really has fucked me up six ways to Sunday. It was either that, or something much, much worse. *There's no way I've fallen for my executive assistant.*

Giving my head a firm shake, I swiped her keycard over the reader. The light flashed green, and I stepped into her suite. Relief flooded me when I saw her spread out on her bed, black hair a striking contrast to the crisp white sheets.

Without even really having to think about it, I stripped off my shirt and shoes and lay down in bed beside her. Her lashes suddenly parted and those green eyes flashed with surprise when she saw me. "Nolan? What are you doing here?"

"Just came to check on you." I pushed a strand of hair off her forehead, then bent down to plant a kiss on her mouth. "Is that okay? I didn't mean to wake you."

"You didn't. I've been drifting in and out for a while." A sleepy smile spread on her lips as she nodded and rolled to her side to face me. "It's more than okay. I think I like it."

Scooting over and a little down on the bed, I slid my arm in under her head and crooked the other behind mine, lying on my back with her resting on my chest. It was good, natural. *Too good.*

"How is Anna doing?"

"She's good." Lacie's voice was groggy with sleep, her body relaxed against mine. When she looked up at me, happiness and sincerity shone bright in her eyes. "She showed me around town and we went to the boardwalk."

"Yeah?" I stroked a hand through her hair and felt my own muscles unwinding as I held her. "Did you have dinner there?"

"No." She smiled. "Well, yeah. We had dinner later, but we went on rides and played arcade games first. It was amazing. If we have time, you'll have to come there with me."

I felt my eyes stretch wide open in surprise. "You went on rides and played games on a girls' night out?"

Scarlett's last girls' night out had cost me thousands of dollars that I'd later learned had been spent partially on male strippers and a gaudy limousine. She'd also imported champagne from France for the occasion.

Lacie chuckled and reached up to smooth the frown between my eyebrows. "Why are you so surprised? She was showing me around town, and she said I couldn't miss the boardwalk."

I tightened my grip on her and kissed the top of her head. "I'm just happy you're *you*. That's all."

Confusion clouded her eyes when she looked up at me. "Why are you happy I'm me? I've always been me."

"I know." I grinned. "That's what I like about you."

"There are things you like about me?" A soft smile touched her lips as she poked one of her round breasts that were covered by her adorable "Donut you love me" pajamas. "Other than these, I mean."

"Don't remind me about those." I groaned, ignoring that sudden rush of primal lust I was becoming used to feeling around her. Strangely, talking to her felt more important than giving into that right now. "I'm glad you had fun at the boardwalk. I don't think we'll have time to visit on this trip, but how about I go with you next time?"

"Next time?" Her voice sounded strangled, but then she cleared her throat. "Sure, yeah. That would be fun."

"You and Anna seem to be becoming friends," I said. Throughout the trip, I knew she had been excited to get to California, and I knew it had a lot to do with getting to see Anna.

Lacie nodded, sighing contentedly. "I've never really had a true friend, but Anna seems like a really good candidate."

"Agreed," I said. "I'm really glad you had a good time with her. I'm just hoping that you haven't gotten tired of her company yet because we're due to meet up with her in about an hour and we still have to go have breakfast."

"Crap." Lacie planted a quick kiss on my bare chest, her fingers twisting through the smattering of dark curls on it before she sat up. "I'd better go shower."

Grabbing her wrist before she could climb off the bed, I slid my hand into her hair in one smooth motion and brought her mouth to mine. She tried to mutter something about having morning breath, but I didn't give a fuck about that. Lacie would always taste good to me.

After a kiss that left me hard and aching, I released her. "You better go have that shower. Otherwise, we'll never get to breakfast on time."

Her breathing was labored, and her chest was flushed, but she tossed me a playful wink. "You could always come join me."

"I don't think that's a good idea," I replied, a smirk forming on my lips. "Unless you're planning on having a cold shower, which I really need right now."

"That makes two of us," she muttered under her breath as she finally climbed out of bed and headed for the bathroom.

I heard her turn on the faucet and tried my best not to think about her naked in there, about water streaming down her curvy body, making her skin glisten and—

"Nolan," she called, her voice so muffled that she had to be in the shower already. "Could you please pass me my toiletry bag? It's in my suitcase."

Fuck. That wasn't the request I'd been hoping to get from her, but since she'd invited me and I was hard enough to cut diamonds with my dick, I decided to take the opportunity to join her in the shower.

I grabbed the toiletry bag as she'd asked me to, then quickly shed my pants, underwear, and socks. Opening the shower door, I handed her the bag first. Her wet, warm hand came out to get it. "Thank you. Sorry, I just grabbed my toothbrush out of it last night. I totally forgot I hadn't taken a shower here yet."

"That's okay." I opened the door a little farther, watching as her mouth formed an "o" when she realized I was naked. She gasped, her eyes dragging a trail of fire down my body before she brought them back to mine.

173

"Did you decide to join me after all?" She smiled and held out that same warm hand to me. "What about not making it down to breakfast on time?"

"Fuck breakfast," I growled as I took in how bright her eyes were, how slick her body was, and how her hair hung in a wet curtain to cling to her breasts and waist. "I'll order something up while you get dressed."

I took her hand and let her tug me into the shower with her before closing the door behind me. Lacie put her arms around my neck and lifted up on her toes to press her lips to mine. Her chest mashed against mine as I claimed her mouth with my own, her tightened nipples scraping against my skin.

A low groan rumbled in my chest, one of my hands reaching for the mound of her breast. I dragged my thumb over her peak, loving the way she instantly melted into me. I felt the tremor that shivered down her spine and heard the involuntary moan that escaped between our lips.

"You're so responsive to me," I whispered, pinching her nipple lightly between my thumb and forefinger. Another shiver slid through her.

My own knees threatened to give out even as I felt her sag, and I banded my arm around her to stop her from falling. "You don't know what you do to me, Lacie. I love watching the way you react and feeling whatever you do. I think I'm addicted to you."

She moaned softly but didn't respond. I hadn't expected her to. I'd come to learn that she loved being talked to during the act but found it difficult to reply. Something else I loved about her: she was so pure and honest in her reactions.

There was nothing fake about her or being with her, which was a huge contributing factor to how I lost myself in being with her, in learning what made her tick, and doing it over and over again.

Snaking my free hand in between us, I lowered it to the tuft of hair above her cleft and tugged lightly. Her answering gasp turned into a moan, which told me I was onto yet another thing she enjoyed.

"You like that, do you baby?" I whispered against the shell of her ear before nipping on her lobe with my teeth. Feeling her nod, I smiled against her skin and repeated the action before I let my fingers dip lower. "Oh. Fuck, Lacie. You're so wet for me right now."

"We're in a shower," she finally managed to bite out, a naughty smile I hadn't seen before lifting the corners of her lips. "Of course I'm wet."

I raised an eyebrow, smirking. "Smartass."

Playfulness blended with lust in her eyes. "I think you need to do a site inspection. Just to check whether it's you or the shower that has been making the progress."

"With pleasure." I didn't even have a witty retort for that one. This was the first time she'd actually asked for anything while we were getting busy.

Knowing that I had not only been the one to show her what she liked and wanted, but who was also able to give it to her now that she trusted me enough to ask, made me harder than I'd ever been before.

Kneeling before her, I put my hands on her thighs and gently spread them. "Just so you know, I'd have you for breakfast every morning if I could."

It was totally true. So was my earlier statement. I was becoming addicted to Lacie, and I had no idea how I was going to give her up when she realized how fucked up I truly was.

CHAPTER 28

LACIE

Nolan's tongue darted out between his parted lips and licked a circle around my clit. His fingers massaged my entrance before one slid inside. My knees were numb, and my muscles were shaking, but he had one strong arm around my hips.

Seeing him gracefully dropping to his knees in front of me, watching as he looked up at me with this look of absolute hunger in his eyes before he tucked into me with just as much fervor as he had done before, nearly made me come before he'd even touched me.

Never in my life had I imagined that I'd have a man like him on his knees, looking at me like he really thought I was better than anything else he could've had for breakfast.

Knowing the spread that was undoubtedly waiting on us downstairs, that was saying something.

Yet this powerful CEO, a man who had the world at his feet and could make any woman in it swoon, had chosen me. *For now, anyway.*

Pushing the unpleasant thought aside, I focused only on the sensations he was eliciting in me. His broad shoulders trembled, and I felt his moan vibrating through me, making me cry out.

"Nolan—I—bed."

God, why did he have to reduce me to a stuttering, speechless mess every time we did this?

He looked up at me through hooded eyes and shook his head. "I want to take you right here in this shower."

"I'll fall." I finally found some words through the haze of want in my brain. "My legs. Numb."

Another shake of his head. "I won't let you fall. Trust me."

His eyes burned into mine, and what I saw in them surprised me. There was the lust and the hunger, sure. But there was something else there too.

I was pretty sure it was affection. The kind of affection that promised safety and provided reassurance. Acutely aware that if I was wrong, I was going to end up on my ass on the shower floor, I decided to throw caution to the wind.

"I trust you," I said, my voice so low that it could barely be heard above the pitter-patter of the water against the shower walls.

Although I wasn't sure if he'd heard me at first, the flash of that same something in his eyes assured me that he had. When he gripped my hips tighter and dragged his tongue through my slit again, my neck arched and I surrendered to him. *So what if I fall on my ass? It couldn't hurt that bad.*

Thankfully, it didn't matter how much it could have hurt because Nolan kept his promise. He never let me fall. He worked his magic until I screamed his name when the pleasure building in my lower belly finally broke free, my climax hitting me hard and dragging me to the realm where fairies and stardust existed.

I flew among the stars and reached the heavens above before it finally started to subside. Nolan pushed to his feet when my eyes opened, a turbulent inferno of need raging behind his eyes. "I have a condom, but it's in my wallet."

My heart dropped before it soared when I remembered that I had invested in my own stash. It shouldn't be only his responsibility to keep us safe, after all.

Holding up my finger to show him I needed a minute, I turned my back on him and unzipped the front of the vanity bag he had brought to the shower for me. My fingers closed around the plastic-covered box and pulled it out, presenting it to him on the palm of my hand.

"Don't say I never got you anything," I teased when I saw his eyes light up as he took it.

"Never," he promised as he opened the box and pulled one out. "The gift of the orgasm is the greatest gift of all."

I laughed. "I totally agree with that assessment. Now are you going to put it on and get to it, or do you want me to?"

"Have you ever done it before?"

I rolled my eyes, my lips curving into a smile. "You know I haven't, but there's a first time for everything. Well, first time on a human being anyway. I put one on a banana in sex ed once."

"I'm way too desperate to show you right now, and I'd like to think I'm a little different than a banana." His voice was pitched low and ragged. "Do you mind if I do it?"

I shook my head, watching as he ripped the foil open and quickly unrolled the latex over his shaft. "Wait. You're too desperate? Are you, Nolan Yates, admitting to being desperate for something?"

"Yes." His hands went to my hips, gripping them tightly as he held me captive with his gaze. "I'm always desperate for you. Surely, you've noticed that by now?"

"I have. I just..." I trailed off, not sure what to say.

Despite how desperate he claimed to be, he didn't make another move. He simply kept looking into my eyes. "You just what?"

"I just hadn't imagined that *desperate* was quite the word you would use to describe it," I said. "Horny maybe, but not anything close to desperate."

Nolan's hips trust forward, his hard shaft rubbing against my clit as he tightened his hold on my hips. "Doesn't that feel like desperation to you?"

The turbulence in his eyes grew darker, his voice lower yet. Suddenly using his hold on me to turn me around, he brought his hands to mine and lifted them so I was bracing myself on the wall.

He positioned the blunt head of his cock right at my entrance, making me clench in delicious anticipation. But he stopped.

My hair moved, and then his lips were on my neck, close enough to my ear to allow me to hear the ragged whispers. "You drive me crazy, Lacie. Most of the time when I'm with you, I'm desperate for you. I don't mind admitting it because it's true. I want you so bad it hurts."

He pushed his throbbing length into me but only an inch before he stopped again. "Please don't tell me you doubt me?"

"I don't." I gasped when he slid just a little farther in. Everything was more intense from this angle, making me feel fuller than I ever had before. I tried to push back to take the rest of him, but Nolan moved with me. A frustrated cry tore out of me. "Why are you teasing me like this?"

"I'm not teasing you." His lips planted feathery, affectionate kisses on my neck, like he was apologizing even while he was denying me. "I just want you to know how much I want you. I don't like you doubting me or yourself, Lacie. Trust me. This is more painful for me than it is for you."

I considered his words for a moment. I supposed that he had just made me come, but he hadn't found his own release yet. If he was aching even half as badly as I was, it really did have to be torture to hold back.

"Stop denying us then," I hissed between my teeth, angling my hips so he would slide in just a little farther. A loud moan fell from my lips when it did. "Please, Nolan."

Another soft swipe of his lips against my neck made me shiver. "You don't ever have to beg me, babe. Just tell me you believe me."

"I believe you."

He fed another inch into me. "Say it."

"Say what?" My body was shaking for him, my clit pounding like a bass drum. My brain couldn't really keep up with what he was saying. I needed him too badly.

Without thinking, I let go of the wall with one hand and put it on my clit. Nolan was the one who groaned when I touched myself. "Play with your clit, baby. But tell me that you'll never doubt me again."

"I'll never doubt you again," I said breathlessly as I made a circular motion with my finger like he had so many times. Both of us made sounds of pleasure this time when Nolan buried himself in me in one powerful thrust.

"Don't worry, baby," he practically growled. "I'll make you promise me again when you're not under duress."

I didn't know why he was so adamant about this, but I didn't give it any more thought. I couldn't because my brain stopped working and my body took over.

Nolan's hands found my breasts while his lips kept worshiping every inch of skin they could reach. My head fell back onto his shoulder, my body melting into his. Our hips rocked together and though I couldn't see us, it felt like we were doing some kind of synchronized dance that we'd perfected.

When his thrusts become wilder and less measured, his hand wound around my hips, and his finger landed on my clit, pushing down with just the right amount of pressure. "I can't hold back any longer, baby. Come with me."

As if I had been waiting for him to ask, a tremor traveled through me, and I exploded around him. My orgasm stole my breath and my vision, leaving me gasping as I felt him shudder behind me. He came on a shout, his head falling to rest in the crook of my neck.

We stood there just like that for a few long minutes, neither of us moving a muscle. The water cleaned us up, and when we finally parted, Nolan headed out of the shower to order us breakfast while I washed my hair.

Toweling it dry after getting dressed, I walked up to where he was making us coffee. I couldn't stop smiling, even if I was still curious about those intense moments in the shower before he finally sank into me.

"How am I supposed to be professional with you after all this?" I asked, walking right up to him and pressing a quick kiss to his now-clothed shoulder.

He chuckled and kissed my hair before taking a step back to hand over my coffee. "You have a switch for business mode. I've seen it."

"You sound really confident about that," I remarked, not really expecting an answer.

Nolan's hands suddenly appeared on my cheeks, another stormy look in his eyes even as his lips pulled into a sexy smirk. "I have confidence in you, Lacie. More than you possibly know."

Again, I had no clue what was happening in that brilliant head of his. But I liked knowing he had confidence in me.

It made me square my shoulders and flash him a smile as I took my first sip of liquid heaven. "Maybe you can tell me sometime."

"Maybe." His eyes darted to the door when there was a knock at it. "Breakfast first. Then we have to get to work. Although just know that I'm going to be thinking about my first breakfast all damn day."

Oh, I could live with that. "Only if you promise to let me return the favor tomorrow."

"I can live with that." He smirked, repeating the words as if he'd plucked them out of my own head. "But for now, food and work. We have all the time in the world to return favors again later."

Since I had promised not to doubt him, I decided to trust him. Even if that terrible, ominous feeling was creeping back into my gut. Something was coming for us.

I just didn't know what yet.

CHAPTER 29

NOLAN

"We've reached an agreement with the union," Anna said as she led us through the kitchen of the California branch. "The cleaners seem happy with the increase, and finance has approved it."

"I've read the paperwork." I gave her a nod. "I was impressed with the work you did on the negotiation."

She laughed and pretended to wipe sweat from her brow. "It was a tough one. The representative who came to see us at first was impossible. He refused to make any counteroffers or to see reason. Luckily, he was replaced a couple of weeks later."

"Do you know why?" Lacie asked, a small frown marring her perfect forehead. "I hope he doesn't come back to cause trouble."

Anna shrugged. "The representative who has taken over from him assures me that it won't happen. Our lawyers are drawing up the agreements to be signed as we speak. All the workers are back at work and seem happy, but I want to put this thing to bed as soon as we can."

"That would be great," I said, appreciating that Anna was being as professional as she always was and acting like she knew nothing of our relationship.

Lacie had told me that she'd admitted to Anna the night before that we were sleeping together. As a result, I had thought that things might be awkward when all three of us got together today but they weren't.

Anna hadn't let onto knowing anything at all and was strictly talking business. She hadn't even brought up the boardwalk, let alone my relationship with her friend.

Comforted by the knowledge that we would be able to finish up in California today and not waste time on dissecting personal issues, I grinned when Anna told us she'd arranged for our lunch to be served on the rooftop terrace.

"Thank you. That was very thoughtful of you, but will you join us?"

She nodded, checking the time on the tablet computer she carried. "I'd love to. We're almost done with the walkthrough, so I'm assuming you'd like to discuss your notes and our progress?"

"Yes." I followed her up the wooden set of stairs that led into the spa. "We're going to provide comprehensive reports once we're back at home base, but we're also giving feedback as we go."

"It's to help you know where our heads are at and so we don't leave with you feeling like we've added no value," Lacie said. "Studies show that branches and especially branch managers often see the head office as overly critical paper-pushers who don't know the first thing about the business units."

"I don't think of you that way." A quick wink at Lacie was the first and only crack in Anna's professional veneer. "But I would appreciate if we could brainstorm together on a way forward that we could start implementing immediately. I know those reports are going to take time to compile, but I'd love to have something to do as soon as you leave."

"You will," Lacie said, glancing down at her notes. "We can discuss it more fully over lunch, but I think a good place for you to start would be to start investigating the latest reviews and why people are complaining about the smell in the suites on the second floor."

Anna's nose wrinkled. "I still can't believe we hadn't even known about them."

"Perhaps at the same time, you can investigate why you didn't know about them," I suggested. "Someone on your team must have the responsibility to stay on top of these things."

Her chin lifted a fraction of an inch. "Someone on our team does. I just have to figure out why she hasn't told me."

"Let us know if we can provide backup for you in any way," Lacie said. Since she'd pretty much told me flat out that Anna was her first real friend, I was incredibly proud of her for having flipped the switch to business mode so thoroughly.

Any outsider would have thought these two had worked together before, but they certainly wouldn't have suspected a friendship. When Anna walked ahead of us to place a call, I leaned over and told Lacie what I thought.

"I'm so proud of you. You did an awesome job flipping that switch." My lips itched to kiss hers, my arms aching to pull her into them, but I resisted both urges. The women were being entirely professional, and I had to follow their lead.

Trying hard to concentrate when Anna came back to us to finish up with the tour, I couldn't stop my mind from wandering every once in a while. I hadn't liked the dark self-doubt I'd seen creeping into Lacie's eyes earlier, like after everything we'd done and everything I'd said to her, she still didn't believe how I felt about her.

Sure, I mean, I hadn't told her that I cared for her, but it was just because we hadn't really had time for that conversation yet. I'd have liked to think that I'd shown her despite not having told her before.

I had no idea why she would doubt it or me. It had looked almost like she was waiting for the other shoe to drop, which was something I had hated to see.

I might have nearly killed myself trying to hold back in that moment, but it had been worth it. I had wanted her too badly to leave any space for doubt in her mind when I was so utterly consumed by need and by her.

I'd wanted her to know that I'd put her peace of mind and certainty about us above my own physical needs, but I couldn't find the words in that moment. I also still wanted to speak to her about why she'd looked so surprised when I told her we would go to the boardwalk together next time we came down to California.

Lacie and I were bound to have plenty of trips here together in the future. I didn't understand why she'd been so surprised over the mention of it. It wasn't sitting right with me.

My head snapped back to the present when the smell of spices and cooking seafood hit my nostrils. Anna swept her hand out to indicate the restaurant. "Our rooftop terrace specializes in tapas and anything involving seafood."

She greeted the hostess but walked us to the table she had reserved herself. "I'll be right with you. I just need to check on something downstairs."

"Sure." I smiled. "We'll place the order while you go deal with it. Is there anything you prefer?"

"Here?" She waved her hand dismissively. "I'll have anything or everything on the menu. The choice is yours. Excuse me, please."

Lacie waited until Anna had hurried away before her lips curled into a smile. "You really think I did an awesome job flipping the switch? Because I felt like there was a neon sign flashing above my head, advertising what we did this morning."

"There wasn't," I assured her. "Both of you ladies were totally professional. I appreciate it."

"You were worried?" she asked, incredulity flashing in her eyes.

A sheepish grin touched my lips as I nodded. "She's your friend, and she knows about us. I was partially expecting the Californian inquisition, or maybe just a whole bunch of loaded questions. If you met my friend Alec, you'd understand."

"I'd love to hear more about him sometime." She twisted the silver ring on her middle finger. "If you want to tell me about him."

"I will, but maybe not today." I glanced up through the wooden slats forming the ceiling above our heads, noticing how high the sun was sitting in the sky. "It's getting late already."

Lacie's gaze dropped to her watch. "It's not that late for lunch."

"Yeah, but it's too late for us to fly out today. Getting flights booked and to the airport will take us almost until dusk. Then the wait for the flight and the flight itself? I don't think it's a good idea."

"Does that mean we're staying in California for another night?" A tentative grin started tugging at the corners of her lips.

I nodded. "It looks that way."

"That's great news. Want to go to the boardwalk later?"

Laughing, I shook my head. "I can't tonight. I have a ton of paper-work to get through that Wayne needs tomorrow. I also have to review the agreements Anna and her team have negotiated with the union and get those out before morning. My email inbox looks like a post office for all the little closed envelopes sitting in it."

Lacie inclined her head, a soft chuckle escaping her parted lips. "I know the feeling. Okay, well I suppose we could get some work done instead of going to the boardwalk. Promise me that we'll go next time?"

"I promise." I started reaching for her hand across the table, pulling back when I saw Anna approaching us.

"Sorry to keep you waiting. I just wanted to get some feedback on those reviews you mentioned earlier." She slid into her seat and drew her security pattern on the tablet's screen. "Are you ready for some feedback, or do you want to order first?"

"Let's get started with both." I signaled to a passing waiter and placed our order, then Lacie, Anna, and I spent the rest of the after-noon going over the plan for the way forward for the California branch.

We ended up having an early dinner at the rooftop terrace too, retiring to our rooms after. I wanted to go with Lacie to hers more than anything, but I really did have work to do.

Before I switched on my laptop though, I had to check in with Alec and Karina. When Alec answered the video call, I caught panic in his dilated pupils and flared nostrils. "I was just about to call you. We have a problem, man."

My heart started galloping in my chest, my palms instantly clammy and feeling like I had hornets inside my veins. "What happened?"

"It's Scarlett." He spat her name with as much venom as he could but smoothed his features and trained his tone when his eyes slid offscreen. "Why don't you go play, Kare-bear? I'll bring the phone to you in a minute so you can talk to Daddy."

My breathing came in heavy pants. I shoved to my feet, pacing the length of the room. After waiting for what seemed to be an eternity, Alec's face appeared on the screen again. "She's threatening to call the fucking police on me."

"What? Why?"

He let out a string of curses under his breath, ramming his hand that wasn't holding the phone repeatedly though his hair. "She says that because you're not in possession of Karina, she should be. I refused to turn her over, and now she's threatening me with the police."

Fuck. Fuckfuckfuck.

I had known there was a possibility that this could happen. I simply hadn't wanted to believe it would. My lawyers had assured me that it was okay to leave Karina with anyone listed on the court order, and Alec was one of those people.

Scarlett had been advised on this too, but apparently, it hadn't stuck. "Whatever you do, don't turn her over to Scarlett. I'll be there first thing in the morning."

"I'll do my best," Alec promised. "Just get here, bro. We need you here pronto. I'm scared, bud. The police don't know the story. I'm not related to her, and Scarlett is her mother. We could very well lose her, Nolan."

"I know." By the time we got it all cleared up, it could be too late. "I know. I'll be there, Alec. Give me twelve hours."

CHAPTER 30

LACIE

"You're late," Nolan barked at me when I got to the lobby the next morning. He stood outside of the elevators, his arms crossed and his eyes narrowed.

The charcoal suit he wore stretched over his toned muscles, bulging in all the right places. It would have made my mouth water if his expression wasn't the very definition of pissed off. What was even more confusing was that his suitcase stood beside him, the handle pulled up and ready for him to take it.

I snuck a peek down at my watch. "I'm not late. To be fair, I'm not early either but I'm not late."

"I've been waiting for nearly ten minutes." His arms dropped, and one hand curled around the handle of his suitcase. "I have to go. I don't have time for this."

I frowned, reaching out to put my hand on his forearm. "Don't have time for what? I thought you wanted to have breakfast before we leave."

"We don't have time for breakfast. Are you ready to go?" He shifted, effectively pulling his arm out from under my grip. Annoyance rippled across his handsome features when he realized I didn't have my suitcase with me. "Apparently not."

"Just give me five minutes. I'll go back upstairs and pack my bag. I'll be right back." My tone was calm and soothing, but it didn't seem to be working on him.

"If I wait any longer for you, I'll miss my flight. I can't miss this flight, so I'm leaving." His grip tightened on the handle as he pushed down on it, tilting the suitcase onto its wheels. "I'll book you on the next flight out."

Stepping into his path when he started moving, I brought my hands up and rested them on his chest. "What's going on here, Nolan?"

"I'm going to be late. That's what." Hostility brewed in his hazel eyes as he looked down at me. The green seemed so much brighter, but the blue had faded almost to gray. It made the golden flecks look like jagged holes in his irises.

As mesmerizing as the effect was, it was also downright scary. I refused to back away from him, though. Irritation wafted from him, slamming into my chest with such force that it was like he was trying to push me away.

"Could you just take a minute to breathe and explain to me what is happening right now?" I kept my tone the same as it had been before, but it definitely wasn't causing him to calm down.

If anything, it only seemed to work him up more. Glaring down at me, his eyes narrowed once more. "I really don't have time for this shit. I have to go, Lacie, and I have to do it right now. I'll get you a ticket for the next flight out. See you after Thanksgiving."

Without another word, he stepped around me and stormed out of the hotel. I turned in my spot, my feet rooted there like I'd been planted.

Another of the chain's black SUVs was waiting for him, the sliding door on the side already open. Nolan climbed in, taking a seat in the front row and placing his suitcase down at his feet before slamming the door shut.

I saw the driver start as if he'd been the recipient of another of Nolan uncharacteristic barks. Then he raced around the vehicle and jumped into the driver's seat. Although I couldn't be sure since I was standing inside, I suspected that the tires squealed when he pulled away and promptly impersonated a race-car driver to get them out of here.

For lack of anything better to do while I tried to process my absolute shock over what had just happened, I glanced down at my watch. The entire thing had taken less than five minutes, but it felt like my world had been ripped out from under me during that time.

I had no idea what was going on, but Nolan had left me in the hotel.

In California.

Without a plane ticket or a plan.

Without instructions or the slightest idea of where to go next.

It was Thanksgiving in two days, so I wanted to go home to my mother. But the last time we'd talked about it, Nolan had told me that he was still trying to work it out so that we could go home.

We'd visited all the branches whose GMs had come to the meeting, but there were other branches that needed to be visited for the same purposes. Nolan had wanted to get them all done during these two weeks so that he wouldn't have to go away again soon.

As far as I knew, he'd been in the process of making arrangements for our next visit in order to accommodate going home for Thanksgiving. I'd pointed out that I was his assistant, and as such, I should have been the one handling the planning and logistics.

He wouldn't hear anything of it. Apparently, these visits had been in the pipeline for quite some time, and it was easier for him to keep communicating with the GMs I hadn't met yet than to hand everything over.

Once this round of visits were over, he said I'd handle all future trips. I'd been okay with it, until now. Because now I was stuck.

Stuck in a city where I knew exactly one other person, with nowhere to go that I knew of and no idea why I had been left stranded in the first place.

What made it exponentially worse was the fact that it wasn't a purely professional problem I was facing. Due to my own stupidity, there were feelings involved too. *Lots of feelings.* All *the fucking feelings.*

I rarely cussed, but this seemed like an appropriate occasion. I'd not only been left behind by my boss, but by the man I was involved with. I *cared* about him. I knew he came with more baggage than most commercial airliners carried over the holiday season, but for some reason, it didn't scare me.

I even admired him for it, for the way he kept a company the size of this one going despite the hell he had been through, for how dedicated he was to being a good father and providing stability for his daughter when her own mother didn't give a damn.

He was a man of integrity, or so I'd thought. However, if the events of this morning were any indication, I'd clearly been wrong.

Sighing as I squeezed my eyes shut, I forced my racing mind to slow down. I couldn't stand in the lobby all day staring at the doors he'd disappeared through.

"Is everything okay?" Anna asked as she walked up to me, her brow furrowed in concern. Chocolate-brown eyes flashing with worry and maybe even anger, she glanced at the doors and then back at me. "I just saw Nolan leave without you."

I nodded. "He did, but I have no idea if everything is okay."

"Are you joining him at the airport?" Confusion pulled her eyebrows together. "I can pack you some breakfast to go if you're in a hurry."

"I'm not in a hurry," I said, feeling numbness spreading from my chest to my extremities. "I have nowhere to go."

"I don't understand." She came to stand right in front of me, bending her knees to bring her eye level to mine in the high heels she wore. "Let's go grab a cup of coffee. I could use a good dose of caffeine right about now and I'm sure you feel the same way."

My head bobbed up and down, but no words came to mind. Anna gently touched my hand, worry radiating from her as if it was seeping out of her pores. "Follow me, okay? We'll go to the staff lounge. It should be reasonably empty at this time of day."

My feet carried me to the lounge with her, but my brain hadn't given the conscious command for them to do so. Honestly, I thought I might be in a mild state of shock.

Anna led me through a door marked "Staff Only" and down a long corridor with gray doors spaced evenly apart. I remembered coming through here just yesterday with Nolan, but now it felt strange and unfamiliar.

The staff lounge was situated off to the left at the back of the hotel. It was tastefully decorated with an array of couches, dining areas, and a kitchen. There was a huge balcony with a gorgeous view of the ocean, but I barely noticed it.

I knew the staff lounge was more than just a lounge. It was a large area complete with napping pods in neighboring rooms and even had an entertainment area, but as impressed as I'd been by Anna's dedication to making a comfortable place for her people to take breaks just twenty-four hours ago, I didn't feel anything now.

"Here," she said, handing me a mug filled with steaming liquid. I hadn't even realized she had already made the coffee. "Drink that. Let's go sit outside. Some sunshine and fresh air will do you a world of good."

Following after her again, I stepped out into the breeze. As she'd predicted, the fresh air swept the fog from my mind, and I startled as I sat down in the warm sunshine. "That jerkface just left me here."

Anna's lips pursed as she tried to hold back a smile. "I can come up with a few terms that are a lot more colorful than jerkface, but okay."

"What the hell?" I pulled my phone out of my pocket and checked my emails, noticing a distinct lack of notifications from any airline saying a ticket had been purchased for me. "He said he would book me on the next flight out, but I think he might have forgotten."

She frowned, lifting her arm to look at her delicate silver watch. "It's only been about fifteen minutes since I saw you get off the elevator. Maybe he's still busy booking it."

"No, he's not." I sighed, blowing on the surface of my coffee and watching as the steam danced before it disappeared. *Just like Nolan had.*

"I know him," I said. "He would have booked it on his way to the airport if he remembered to, as soon as he was settled in the car."

She didn't disagree, sympathy softening her eyes. "What happened?"

My shoulders lifted on a shrug, my eyes going round. "I have absolutely no idea. We agreed to have an early breakfast this morning before we headed to the airport. When I got down here, he was packed and ready to leave. He told me he couldn't wait for me to go fetch my stuff and that he had to go. That's all I know."

"That's so weird." She frowned, taking a sip of her coffee as she thought. "Maybe something happened back at the head office or with his daughter."

Despite what he had just done, worry swept through me. "I really hope it's not his daughter."

"Me too," she said. "But it would make sense, I suppose. There are no urgent messages from the office on your phone?"

I checked again, then shook my head. "It doesn't look like it."

Taking a deep breath, she let it puff up her cheeks and kept it there for a second before blowing it out. "Okay, well, we don't know what happened. What we do know is that he left you here. You mentioned earlier that you have nowhere to go. Didn't he tell you anything before he left?"

"Only that he'd see me after Thanksgiving," I said, realization dawning as I uttered the words. "Which must mean that he managed to arrange it so that we could have the holiday off."

"Look at you, finding the silver lining in all this." She smiled softly and motioned up at the hotel. "Why don't you stay here tonight and head home tomorrow?"

"Thanks. I might just do that, depending on when I can get a flight."

"I take it there's no way I can convince you to spend the weekend with my husband and I? We're having a whole bunch of family over, so one more person really wouldn't be a problem."

"I've never spent Thanksgiving without my mother. I'd rather not start now. Thanks, though." I lifted my phone and tapped the icon for the internet. "I guess I better book my flight. The sooner I can get home, the better."

Hopefully by the time I had to head back to D.C. on Sunday, I'd have put all my stupid feelings behind me, and I could get back to work. Since it seemed like our trip had been cut short, at least I wouldn't have to spend another day on the road with Nolan for a while.

Now that? That's the real silver lining here.

CHAPTER 31

NOLAN

All the way back to D.C., my mind was filled with a haze of panic. I'd checked in with Alec just before I boarded the plane, and he'd assured me that if Scarlett showed up again this morning, he would hold her off until I got there.

I only prayed that he kept his promise. *Please, please let my little girl be okay.*

If there was any way I could've paid the pilot everything I had to make the plane go faster, I'd have done it in a heartbeat. Everything I had, I would give just to be with my baby girl right now, to hold her in my arms and know that she was safe and okay.

Unfortunately, there wasn't a thing I could do to get to her right this minute. *Maybe I should invest in teleportation research. I sure could have used the ability right about now.*

I hadn't slept a wink, but there had been no earlier flights. Peter had taken the jet to Japan with a few of our board members who were looking into possible expansion opportunities, so there hadn't been the option to take my own plane.

Even if he hadn't needed to refuel first and his wheels had gone up at the moment I placed the call, he still wouldn't have been getting in until this plane was already in the air. Sighing as my head fell back against the seat, I sent up another silent plea for Karina's safety.

Irrational rage rolled around in my stomach, rattling every cage I had and heating me to the core. *I fucking knew I shouldn't have gone on this trip. I never should have let Lacie convince me.*

I was pissed off at her and even more pissed off at myself. Pretty much the only people who weren't on my shit list right now were Alec and Karina. The general managers who forced this trip on me were all getting fired the second I set foot back in my office, and if Lacie so much as breathed another word about having already made promises that weren't hers to make, she was out of a job too.

Fire licked the insides of my veins, churning in my stomach. Every single one of my muscles was tense, and it felt like I could rip the plane apart with my bare hands. Since that really wouldn't help the situation, I forced myself to sit still.

When we finally touched down, I shoved my way past everyone who stood between me and my daughter and ran flat out to where I hoped David was waiting with my car. He handed the keys over without a word when I got to him, watching as I threw myself into the car and took off.

Just as I was pulling up to Alec's house, I saw Scarlett coming out of it with a screaming Karina in her arms. Tears were streaming down my baby's face, and her arms were flailing, but her mother didn't let her go.

I slammed on the brakes and jumped out, running toward them as fast as my legs could carry me. "Put her down, Scarlett."

Her mouth set in a tight line as she noticed me, eyes wild and out of focus. "No way. She was placed in your custody, and you left her with this irresponsible playboy. Who knows what he's been doing to her?"

Alec came racing out of the house at that moment, a deep scowl on his face as he ran up behind her. "You broke into my fucking house and kidnapped her? That's low, Scarlett. Even for you, and that's saying something."

With Alec behind her and me at the front, Scarlett seemed to realize she had nowhere to run. She tightened her grip on Karina, who was still struggling and cried out in pain. "Daddy!"

Grinding my teeth together, I fought for self-control. "Call the police, Alec. Scarlett, put her down right now or so help me God, I will not be held responsible for my actions."

Alec was already shouting into his phone, but I was barely aware of what he was saying. My focus was solely on Scarlett and Karina.

Putting my hands up with my palms out, I took a step closer to them. "Now, Scarlett. I won't ask again."

"Fuck you, Nolan. You don't control me. Give me my half of the company, and I'll give you back your precious fucking baby." She put Karina down on her feet but kept an arm hooked around her neck and shoulders as she started dragging her toward her car.

Alec's driveway was wide enough that she would be able to get out, even with my car in it too. I saw him come to the same conclusion as I had at the same time.

His eyes met mine, as filled with panic and terror as I felt. Neither of us wanted to tackle Scarlett or to hurt her, but I knew that both of us would if it came down to it. *There has to be another way.*

"Be reasonable, Scarlett." I took another step closer to her, moving only when she did to keep the distance between us even. "Think about what you're doing. This, what you're doing right now, it's a crime. A serious one. Between contempt of court, breaking and entering, and kidnapping, you're looking at prison time. Is that really what you want?"

Her nostrils flared, her eyes hard and defiant. "You wouldn't do that. I know both of you. You're pussies. You wouldn't do anything to hurt me."

I felt a muscle in my jaw tick. "Under ordinary circumstances, you'd be absolutely right. But these aren't ordinary circumstances, Scarlett. You're scaring our daughter, hurting her even."

Silent tears were streaming down Karina's cheeks, her eyes huge pools of dread and horror. I forced my lips into a smile when I looked into those eyes. "You're going to be fine, sweetheart. I promise."

Scarlett snorted, throwing her head back as a wild laugh ripped out of her. "There you go again, making promises you can't keep. Just like our wedding vows."

My brows jumped up on my forehead. "I'm the one who didn't keep those promises, huh?"

It was official. She was out of her damn mind. A shiver of fear traveled down my spine. If she was that far gone, there was no telling what she would do.

Tearing my eyes away from Karina's, I looked up at Alec. He gave me a slight nod, then charged at the same time that I did.

Scarlett didn't have time to react before he was behind her, yanking her arm away from Karina's neck at the same time that I folded my arms around my daughter's waist and lifted her away from her mother.

Screaming tires and sirens alerted me to the police's arrival. There were a few shouts from them, confusion reigning supreme for a moment as Alec twisted Scarlett's arms behind her back and held her wrists together.

"What in God's name is going on here?" one of the officers demanded.

I held my trembling daughter in my arms, burying my face in her hair for a minute as dizzying relief swept through me. *She's okay. She's okay. She's okay.*

Scarlett screamed like a banshee. "These men attacked me and took my daughter from me."

"We didn't attack you," Alec scoffed. He frog-marched her up to the officer. "I'm the one who called you."

The officer looked from Scarlett, to Alec, and then at me. "Who are you?"

I released a shuddering breath and pulled myself together. We had a lot of explaining to do. "I'm her father, Nolan Yates. That's my ex-wife, Scarlett, and my friend, Alec."

After pointing to each of them in turn, I ignored Scarlett's continuing screams and accusations. "I've been awarded full custody of our daughter, Karina. Her mother is only to see her under strict supervision at arranged visits. I've been away on a business trip, and Scarlett here broke into Alec's house, took Karina, and was in the process of leaving with her when I arrived."

The officer's eyes turned hard as steel when he glanced at Scarlett. "Is this true?"

"No," she spat.

Alec rolled his eyes, stepping forward without relinquishing his hold on her wrists. "I have security cameras, you idiot. The guy who owned this house before me was a security contractor. If there's anything left in that crazy brain of yours, you should remember that."

"I'm going to need to see the footage," the officer said after nodding at one of his colleagues. "In the meantime, you keep an eye on her."

The woman he'd nodded at took Scarlett's arm and led her over to the cruiser. Scarlett screamed and thrashed, but the officer seemed unfazed by it all.

"I'm Officer Stuman, by the way," the first man said. "Now, you'd better take me to this footage before we can arrest or detain your ex-wife. Also, do you have a copy of the court order you mentioned?"

"An electronic copy on my phone. I can have my lawyers bring the original." I shifted Karina in my arms, but there was no way I was putting her down.

She was shaking like a leaf with her head buried in my neck, her tears wetting my skin and shirt. Officer Stuman looked at the way she was holding on to me like a koala and shook his head. "No, that won't be necessary for now. The electronic copy will do just fine. We can get the original from you when we start to gather evidence."

"Right this way, officer," Alec said, leading the man into his house. Karina and I followed, but she didn't look up once throughout the entire process.

Alec and I finished answering all the officer's questions and promised him a copy of the footage and whatever else he might need. Then Alec saw him out while I led Karina into the kitchen.

I set her down on a stool, cupping her face in my hands as I looked into her teary eyes. "You're okay now, baby. Daddy's here. I'm not going anywhere."

Another scream from outside made me lift my gaze away from her just in time to see Scarlett getting arrested through the kitchen window. Desperate for Karina not to see that happening, I returned my gaze to hers so she would look at me instead.

"Are you hurt, sweetheart?"

She shook her head as she sniffled. "I'm okay. She held me a little tight, but she didn't hurt me. Why is she so mean, Daddy?"

My heart fractured in my chest, aching for Karina as a fresh wave of tears wracked her little body. I drew it against mine and held her tenderly, careful not to squeeze her after what she'd just been through.

"You don't have to worry about that anymore, okay, sweetheart?"

"But—but I just want a normal family," she managed to get out between sobs. The fracture in my heart turned into a clean break.

I didn't know what to say to that. There was nothing I could say to make it better, so I simply pressed a kiss to her hair and held her. "I know, baby. I'm sorry. I'm so sorry."

Sorry for the way Scarlett had turned out. Sorry that I hadn't been able to help her. Sorry that I had been gone and sorry that I couldn't give Karina the normal family she so badly wanted. Instead of saying any of that, I closed my eyes and breathed deeply.

Karina was safe now. That was all that really mattered. No matter what, I promised myself I would never let Scarlett near her again. And despite what she seemed to think, I kept my fucking promises.

CHAPTER 32

LACIE

Persistent knocking on my door woke me up. Groggy as hell, I didn't immediately realize where I was.

When I opened my eyes and saw the ocean twinkling at me through the window, reality slammed into me with a force that took my breath away. *I'm in California. Nolan's gone. I have an early flight out.*

Another knock came, followed by the sound of Anna's voice. "Lacie, honey? Are you awake? It's me. I thought we could have a quick breakfast together before you leave."

Getting out of bed, I grabbed one of the standard-issue white hotel robes and went to let her in. "Thanks for coming to get me. I set an alarm, but I guess I must have slept through it."

She looked me up and down, a sad smile curving her lips. "You had a big day yesterday. I'm guessing you didn't fall asleep early last night?"

"I think it was four this morning the last time I checked," I admitted, closing the door after she walked into my suite. "Do you mind if I have a quick shower? Everything except what I need this morning is already packed, so we can head right down after."

"Sounds good," she said. "Do you have any preferences for a

comfort breakfast? I'll call ahead with our order. I know you're in a hurry to get to the airport."

"Anything with pancakes and bacon." I managed a small smile. "Thank you."

"You're welcome. I'll take care of it. You go grab that shower." She lifted the receiver on the landline in my suite and pressed a number, shooing me away with her hand as she started talking into the phone.

Leaving the ordering up to her, I rushed through a shower and got dressed in the most comfortable jeans I'd brought with me. After gathering my last few things and giving the suite a quick check to make sure I hadn't left anything behind, I went downstairs with Anna.

"Have you heard from him?" she asked as we sat down in the staff lounge, at a dining area inside this time.

I pulled out my phone and checked it for the umpteenth time before shaking my head. "Not a word."

"So he didn't end up booking you a flight?"

"Not that I know of." I blew out a heavy breath just as a waitress came in, carrying a tray with huge stacks of bacon and pancakes on it. "Wow, is that for us?"

Anna smiled proudly. "Sure is. All the trimmings for the pancakes will be here in a minute. Thanks, Janine."

The waitress nodded at her as she set the plates down. "I'll be right back with the rest."

"Sure thing, thanks again," Anna said to her before turning back toward me. "Dig into the bacon while it's hot."

"Thank you." I plucked a piece of crispy bacon off the plate and took a bite, regretting that I could barely taste what I was sure was delicious.

Anna had a piece too, swallowing it down with a swig of orange juice she'd poured from the pitcher on the table. We ate in silence for a couple of minutes.

Janine came back with balls of real butter, maple syrup, and a bunch of other pancake toppings. No matter how hard I tried though, I struggled to work up an appetite.

"What time was your flight again?" Anna asked when she reached for another pancake.

"I'm provisionally booked for nine. I have to pay for the ticket at the airport. I didn't want to prepay yesterday."

"Because you thought Nolan might still come through?"

"I guess." I shrugged, then popped a bite of fluffy pancake that somehow still tasted like cardboard into my mouth. "I just can't really believe that he left me here and then totally forgot about me."

"I doubt he forgot about you," she said but then rolled back her shoulders. "Either way, fuck him."

"I already have, that's the problem," I replied dryly.

Anna chuckled. "At least you can laugh about it."

"I can try." But it didn't feel like I'd be laughing again anytime soon.

I'd been an absolute idiot for getting involved with my boss. Especially since I knew how much he had going on.

To be fair, I also knew this thing between us would come to an end. I just hadn't expected it to hurt this much. I'd expected a sting, not a searing pain that crawled into my soul.

But that was how I felt.

Somewhere along the line and despite my best intentions, my heart had gotten involved and was now completely broken. How I was going to look Nolan in the eye come next week, I didn't know. I'd have to figure it out, though, because there would be no avoiding him once I went back to work.

This is why people don't get involved in relationships with people they work with, stupid. Anna must have seen the tears that jumped into my eyes because she suddenly reached out and squeezed my hand.

"I'm glad you're going home to see your mother."

"So am I." Home was what I needed right now. I wasn't even a little bit ashamed to admit that I needed my mother. In that way, I was still a little girl at heart. When I got hurt, I wanted my mom, and my heart hadn't hurt this badly in a long, long time. And it had never hurt this badly over a guy.

"Have you told her you're coming home yet?" Anna asked.

I shook my head. "I didn't want to tell her and then have to cancel if Nolan sent me a plane ticket somewhere else."

"You should call her. I'm sure she'll be thrilled to hear you're coming home for Thanksgiving."

"Yeah, you're right. I probably should call her. I think it's safe to say that Nolan isn't going to be sending me a ticket anywhere." Setting my cutlery down, I picked up my phone and hit the first number on my speed dial.

The call had almost rung out before my mother answered. "Lacie, sweetheart. How are you?"

"I'm great," I lied. I knew she heard right through the lie when she made a disbelieving sound, but I didn't want to get into it right now. "I have some good news."

"Oh?"

"I'm coming home today."

There was a brief pause. Then she let out a loud, long squeal. "That's fantastic news, baby. Best I've heard all month."

Mom chatted for another few minutes about how elated she was that I was coming home and then begged off to go shopping for supplies after taking down my flight details.

"All done," I said, feeling a smile tugging at the corners of my lips. "It's amazing how much better she can make me feel."

"That's a mom for you," Anna agreed. "I still go to mine whenever I'm sick or hurt."

"I was just thinking the same thing," I said, even tasting the next piece of bacon better. I tucked into the rest of breakfast with a little more gusto than I had before, washing it down with some orange juice before addressing the next big worry.

"Do you think Nolan is going to fire me?" I asked Anna. She'd been with the company a lot longer than I had. Since she was also management, she knew how these things worked.

"If he does, you'll always have a job here," she said. Her brown eyes went wide, a spark of excitement suddenly entering them. "In fact, if he doesn't fire you, quit. Come work here anyway."

"I knew I found a true friend in you." I smiled. "If he fires me, I might just take you up on that. If he doesn't though, I don't think I'm up for another big move just yet. Can I let you know?"

"Anytime." She packed the cleared plates onto the tray Janine had left behind, standing up when she was done. "Can I give you a ride to the airport?"

"You don't have to take me yourself, but I'd appreciate if you could ask one of the shuttles to take me."

"Done." She opened her arms and pulled me into a hug. "Let me know when you get home safely, and let me know if you hear from the jerkface or if you need anything at all."

"Same goes for you," I whispered into her soft hair, missing my friend already. It sucked that the only real one I had lived so damn far away from me.

Maybe moving to California wasn't such a bad idea after all. I'd get to work with Anna, live in one of the most beautiful places I'd ever seen, and maybe I could even learn how to surf. "I hope you were serious about that job offer because I'm seriously considering taking you up on it."

"I was serious." She laughed as she released me. "Think about it, see how it goes when you get back to D.C., and let me know. We can't offer you the same opportunities in the company that Nolan and the position you're in right now can, but I think you could still be happy here."

"I know I could be." But she was right. My career was important to me, and as much as it would suck to keep working so closely with Nolan, I would be throwing away a lot of opportunities if I quit on him. "If I do it, would I be one of those girls who was throwing every-thing she's worked for away over a guy?"

"There's a reason so many people do it," she said. "I wouldn't blame you."

Maybe not, but I would. "Thank you. I'll speak to you soon?"

"Of course." She gave me another hug, walking me out after letting me go. There was a shuttle driver standing outside, who she asked to get me to the airport safely, and then I was on my way.

My cattle-class seat on the airplane was cramped and uncomfortable after traveling in first or business class with Nolan, but I could take comfort from the fact that I'd bought this ticket for myself. Even if the man sitting next to me reeked of garlic and kept passing me glasses of juice every time the hostesses came by. We weren't even in the air yet, so it really was ridiculous.

Just before we took off, I couldn't resist checking my phone again. I didn't know why there was this flicker of hope in my chest that there would be a message from Nolan, but every time I saw my phone light up, it was there.

Again discovering that the message wasn't from him, I felt it smother and die. Deep inside my heart, I felt another tear opening up, and the pain that came along with it threatened to overwhelm me.

Needing something to drown it out, I grabbed the complimentary headphones and found the hardest rock I had on my phone. Then I turned the volume up all the way and slammed my back into the chair when I leaned into it. *There we go. This is perfect. I'm going to be fine. I'm going to be just fine.*

All the way to Georgia, I listened to my music and repeated my mantra over and over again in my head. When I got off the plane to see my mother waiting for me with her arms already open to give me a hug, I believed my mantra for the first time.

I really was going to be fine. I just needed a little bit of time.

And a new plan.

CHAPTER 33

NOLAN

"How was your trip, Daddy?" Karina asked between bites of her brightly colored cereal. There was a wide smile on her face, and her posture was happy and relaxed.

I was absolutely amazed by how quickly kids could bounce back from something like what had happened yesterday. I, for one, was still rattled. It still felt like there was this fog in my brain, and my heart still raced whenever Karina was out of my eyesight.

Evidently, I was a lot slower on recovery than my daughter. "It went well, baby. Don't worry. I'm not leaving you again soon."

"I wasn't worried." She shoved her spoon into her mouth and munched on the cereal before swallowing. "Uncle Alec and I have fun when I'm with him. Did you have fun?"

"Work isn't really fun, sweetheart. I'd rather have been home with you." *Where I should have been in the first fucking place.*

Yeah, the internal beratement game was strong in this one. A heavy sigh parted my lips. I'd spent the entire night dragging myself over the coals. A second near-sleepless night probably hadn't helped that fog in my brain much.

"But didn't you have fun with your new friend?" Karina asked, scrunching up her nose.

I frowned. "My new friend?"

"Lacie," she said, looking at me like I was stupid.

The mention of Lacie's name shook me. Hard.

I just left her there.

The fog cleared enough for me to think about someone other than Karina, and I was appalled when those memories came rushing back. I'd been so panicked, so afraid and pissed off that I hadn't waited for her when she'd asked for five minutes to go fetch her bag. After I was the one who had told her that we'd have breakfast before we left.

I'd also told her that I'd get her a ticket on the next flight out, which I'd never done. I hadn't checked in with her, hadn't explained anything to her. Hell, I hadn't even sent her a single message to find out if she was okay.

Guilt filled me, thick and hot as it clogged up my veins. A bolt of unexpected pain shot through my chest. *God, she must hate me.*

My throat tightened. *How could I have done that to her?*

"Daddy?" Karina's sweet voice pulled me back to reality, but it didn't make the bitter taste in my mouth or the nauseated feeling in my stomach go away.

I cleared my throat and found my strangled sounding voice. "Yeah, sweetheart?"

"Didn't you have fun with Lacie?" she repeated her question.

"How do you know about Lacie?" I hadn't told her. I knew that much for sure.

"Uncle Alec told me about her," she said, shoving another bite of cereal into her mouth and speaking around it. "He said that you told him all about your new friend."

"He did?" I frowned. I was going to fucking *kill* him. "What else did he tell you? Also, don't speak with food in your mouth, sweetheart."

She rocked her head from side to side, chewing on her bite and swallowing it loudly. "He said that you said she was really nice and that she made you happy."

My heart stuttered to a stop.

Because Alec had been right. Lacie did make me happy, or at least, she had. I doubted she'd ever talk to me outside of work again, but for a while there, I really had been happy.

"She is very nice," I told Karina. "He was right about that."

"I want to meet her," she replied, finishing her cereal and picking up her juice box. "Uncle Alec said she works with you. Can I meet her at the office sometime?"

"I don't know. We'll have to see."

"Why?" she frowned. "Won't she be at the office next week?"

"I don't know." I really didn't.

Lacie wasn't the type to take shit from anyone, even her boss. I wouldn't have been surprised if I opened my emails to find her resignation letter, effective immediately.

But she has that switch, I reminded myself. That switch might be the only thing that saved me from losing her altogether.

She could keep business and personal separate. I'd seen it happening countless times. If she could turn off whatever personal feelings she had toward me, she wouldn't resign. She would stick around because she'd fucking worked for it and deserved to be where she was. Near the top of the hierarchy was where she belonged, if not at the top.

"Why don't you know if she'll be at the office next week if she works there?" Karina questioned, a puzzled expression on her forehead.

Because I fucked up. That's why. "Daddy made a mistake, so she's probably a little angry with me right now."

"You always tell me it's okay to make mistakes," she said. "You said humans make mistakes, but that we have to try to fix them, and we have to learn from them."

"You're absolutely right." Schooled by a five-year-old. Damn it. "I need to go find my phone. Finish your juice. I'll be right back."

Striding out of the kitchen as fast as I could without breaking into a run—I didn't want to frighten Karina—I headed to my room. My phone was still in the pocket of the pants I'd been wearing when I left California. I hadn't even bothered to take it out after we got home last night.

There wasn't much battery power left, so I plugged it in and sat down on my bed to make the call. It didn't go through. Lacie's phone went straight to voicemail.

Fuck. I felt cold tendrils of icy dread spreading out from my stomach to my heart. *Did she block my calls?*

I didn't know if a person could even reach voicemail if someone had blocked your calls, but I had more important things to do than to find out. After checking my emails to make sure my thought about her resignation letter hadn't been an accurate one, I placed a call to Anna.

"Mr. Yates," she said politely when she answered, but I heard the icicles hanging from her tone. "What can I do for you?"

"It's Mr. Yates now, is it?" Laying back on my bed but careful not to yank my phone out of the charger, I rested my forearm over my eyes. "What happened to Nolan?"

"I don't know. Why don't you tell me what happened to Nolan?" Her question came out as sharp as a dagger, making me wonder how bad the fallout from my fuck-up had been. My heart clenched painfully when I thought of what Lacie must have gone through. The confusion and the uncertainty alone would have killed her.

"I had a family emergency to take care of," I admitted to Anna. "I didn't mean to hurt her."

"I had a feeling it was something like that." She sighed. "Unfortunately, what we mean doesn't always matter. Only the end result does."

"Meaning that I hurt her?" I flinched under my arm, feeling a chasm opening up in my chest as my heart throbbed. "How bad was it, Anna?"

I didn't want to hear this, but I needed to. If I was going to take Karina's advice and try to fix it, I needed to know how bad the wreckage was.

"Don't flatter yourself," Anna said. "She was hurt, but she'll be fine."

A tiny part of my aching heart rejoiced. If her friend thought she would be fine, that meant the wreckage wasn't a total write-off. *I still have a chance.*

"Is she still there? I need to talk to her. I need to explain."

"I don't really give a damn what you need right now," she blurted out, followed by the sound of her sucking in a sharp breath. "Crap. I forgot that I was speaking to my boss for a second. Am I fired?"

"No. I deserve it, so feel free to dig into me, but please tell me if she's there first."

"She isn't." Anna paused for a second. "I'm not sure if I'm comfortable telling you where she is."

"Please, Anna," I said quietly. "I'm sorry, okay? I promise you that I didn't mean to hurt her. I wasn't thinking clearly, and I'm trying to make up for it, but I can't do that if I can't talk to her."

"Did you try calling her?"

"Her phone is off."

"Figures." She released a deep breath. "I'm sure if you're thinking clearly again, you can figure out where she is. It's Thanksgiving tomorrow, remember?"

I hadn't actually. But since she'd reminded me, I knew exactly where Lacie must have gone. "She's gone home to Georgia to be with her mother."

"Bingo. When you speak to her, will you remember to mention that I'm not a terrible friend who told the guy who broke her heart where she was?"

"I broke her heart?" I whispered after a beat as I processed what she had just said. Pain lanced through my entire being, my own heart crumbling to pieces.

"Shit," Anna muttered. "I don't think I was supposed to tell you that. She didn't say it or anything, but I know the look. I used to see it in the mirror often enough before I met the one man who doesn't make me cry anything but happy tears."

It dawned on me that I wanted to be that man for Lacie, the one who never made her cry anything but happy tears. *Too bad the ship has already sailed on that one.*

"Fuck," I swore loudly, the word echoing in my borderline-empty, soulless room.

The gray, impersonal decorations and furniture had never gotten to me as much as they did in this minute. They represented the man who had stopped caring about anything except his family and work, but with Lacie, I didn't feel like that man anymore.

She'd brought me back to life in more ways than one. The drab colors in the room reminded me of how dull my life had been without her and how vibrant and colorful it had been with her. I didn't want to go back to being the guy who'd ordered this stuff.

I wanted vibrant and colorful. I wanted that bitter orange, jasmine, and gardenia scent on my pillows, and if I was being entirely honest, eventually I wanted them to be *our* pillows. And I hadn't even realized any of it until after I'd already fucked it up. *God, how stupid could one guy be?*

Flopping over on my bed, I groaned into a pillow and heard my phone beep when it pulled out the charger. *Fuck it.*

Anna chuckled softly at the other end of the line. "You don't sound so great yourself, actually. Lacie values family above all else, Nolan. I'm sure she will forgive you if you explain that yours had an emergency, but promise me that you'll handle it better next time."

"I will." My voice came out muffled, so I flipped onto my back again. "I promise. Got any groveling tips for me?"

"Make sure you mean it when you apologize," she said. "And for God's sake, bring the girl some flowers."

"I can do that." Anna and I said goodbye and hung up, but I didn't put my phone down. I scrolled to the one number I was going to miss the hell out of calling when he left for good one day soon. "Wayne, I need a favor."

"Shoot," he said. "You know I would do anything for you. What's going on?"

CHAPTER 34

LACIE

When I woke up on Thanksgiving morning, the smell of my mother's cooking was already wafting through the house. I inhaled a deep breath and thanked my lucky stars that, whatever else was going on in my life, I had this to come home to.

Climbing out from under the mint green and faded pink comforter I'd had since high school, I stretched my arms out above my head. My body was slightly stiff from the flight, all the crying I'd done over the past couple of days, and sleeping for too long after I got home, but all things considered, I didn't feel too bad.

The dull ache in my chest was still there too, but a good night's sleep in my own bed couldn't exactly cure that. Only time would. Or so I'd heard anyway.

Yawning as I walked over to my dresser, I decided that I wouldn't let Nolan or my silly heart ruin this day for me. I hadn't seen my mother since I left, and I would be heading back to D.C. too soon to waste the time I had with her.

Thanksgiving was her favorite holiday, and I'd be damned if I wasn't going to at least try to enjoy it with her. I pulled out a pair of yoga pants and an oversized shirt. Since I'd be helping Mom cook for most of the day, there was no point putting anything fancier than that on for now. I might even stay in them all day, considering that I didn't think we were having any guests this year.

On the other hand, Mom always insisted that we look good for Thanksgiving dinner, even if it was just the two of us. With that in mind, I set out a neat dress on my bed for later before heading to the bathroom to take a shower.

Once I was done, I went downstairs and found my mother in the kitchen. An apron was tied around her neck, and the entire stove was covered in pots, the light for the oven on. "Jeez, you're cooking up a storm for just the two of us."

She shrugged, handing me an apron of my own. "I'm just used to cooking big for Thanksgiving. Do you mind chopping some potatoes for me?"

"Not at all." I tied the apron on and grabbed the bag of potatoes from the counter, carrying them to the sink to wash them. "What are we going to do with all this food?"

"Eat it for the rest of the weekend?" She grinned and dipped a spoon into one of the pots, filling it with liquid before holding it out toward me. "Taste this. Tell me if it needs anything."

Dutifully tasting the buttery deliciousness, I shook my head. "It's perfect, Mom. It always is."

"Thank you." She set the spoon down and grabbed a spatula, humming under her breath as she got back to work.

I washed the potatoes and got out a cutting board when I was done, carrying it to the island and sitting down beside it. Knife in hand, I realized what my mother was humming and joined in.

The rhythmic chopping and hearing the same song Mom always hummed on Thanksgiving was peaceful, calming my mind and soul for the first time in days.

"How's that boss of yours doing?" Mom asked, shattering the bit of peace I'd managed to obtain since the last time I'd thought about said boss. "Nolan, was it?"

"Yes, that's his name." I carried on chopping without looking at her, hoping that she'd take the hint and change the topic.

"So," she prompted. "How is he?"

"I don't know, Mom. Why?"

A knowing smile lifted her lips, her eyes twinkling with something that looked a lot like amusement. "I still speak to Wayne from time to time, you know?"

"I didn't know, but okay." I stopped chopping and looked at her, my eyes narrowing in suspicion. "What did he tell you?"

"Nothing much." She shrugged, but I could see there was more to it. I didn't have to wait very long before she caved. "He told me you were good for each other. That's all. He was glad you were getting along so well and said that you made a good team."

"We did make a good team." I blinked to ease the sudden stinging in my eyes. I wouldn't cry over him, not again and certainly not today.

Mom frowned, crossing her arms as she cocked her hip against the counter. "Did? Why is that past tense?"

"Because I don't know if we'll make a good team going forward." I sighed, knowing I had just opened the door to having to tell my mother the whole story. Well, the parent-friendly version of it anyway.

Sure enough, she didn't let it go. "Why not?"

"I messed up," I admitted.

When I really thought about it, I wanted to tell my mother this story, and I was glad she hadn't let it go. Talking things through with her had always helped me in the past, and I hoped it would help again now.

Saying a lot of it out loud might hurt, but it was also the only way I knew of to purge some of the pain so the wounds could start healing. Mom flicked on the kettle and took two cups out of the cupboard, starting to fix us hot cocoa as I tried to figure out how best to avoid the parts of the story I couldn't really share with her.

"Tell me about him," Mom said. "And don't worry. I'm not as big of a prude as you think I am."

She winked at me, which I didn't think she'd ever done before. It lightened the mood, and I even had to fight a smile. "I'm going to pretend you didn't just say or do that."

215

The corners of her lips curled. "Whatever you say, honey. Now, stop trying to avoid it and just tell me what happened."

"That's the thing. I'm still not really sure what happened." I explained what had gone down back in California, no closer to having any answers than I had been on the day that it happened.

"Whoa, maybe you should back up a little," Mom said. "Wayne has always told me what a good guy he is, but it doesn't sound like it."

"No, Wayne is right. Despite what happened, I can honestly say that he is a good man." One bad day didn't discount everything I'd seen him do for countless people, everything I'd learned about him in the couple of months that I'd been working for him. "I don't know why he ran off, why he didn't get me the plane ticket, or why I haven't heard from him, but I do know something big must have happened."

My heart gave a pang of worry, just like it did every time I thought too much about what might have driven Nolan to act the way he had. Being hurt by what he had done didn't mean that I couldn't be worried about why he had done it. *Just, please don't let it be his little girl.*

A large lump appeared in my throat. *After everything he's been through, please let his baby girl be okay.*

"Lacie? Are you okay, honey?" Mom walked up to me and put the back of her hand against my forehead. "Are you feeling all right? You just got really pale."

"I'm fine." I lifted my hand to hers and gently pulled it away. "I don't have a fever. I was just running through possibilities in my mind of what might have happened for Nolan to take off like that."

I proceeded to throw caution to the wind and tell Mom all about Nolan, except for the X-rated bits of course. The more I told my mother about him, the more I realized that he really wasn't the type to do what he had done. The more that realization set in, the more worried I got.

Eventually, Mom popped the last of the potatoes in the roasting pan and dusted off her apron as she turned to face me. "It sounds like you really care about this man."

"I do." A part of wished it wasn't true, but it was. "I really do. I just don't know what to do about it now. I'm going to have to face him when the weekend is over, and I don't know how."

A sage smile spread on her lips. "Don't worry about it. It's Thanksgiving. Everything will work itself out."

"You do know Thanksgiving isn't magical, right?" I winked. "The day itself isn't going to work everything out."

She pressed her hand to her chest and released an exaggerated gasp. "Blasphemy. Thanksgiving absolutely is magical. Miracles happen on Thanksgiving."

I smiled. "I think you have Thanksgiving confused with Christmas."

Laughing as she shook her head, she started undoing the ties on her apron. "Let's go get dressed before we set the table."

"Do we have to?" I dragged my hand up and down the length of my torso. "I'm so comfortable."

"Do we have to have this discussion every year?" She propped her hands on her hips and dug out her Mom voice. "Go get dressed, Lacie May. You will not sit down at Thanksgiving in yoga pants."

"Fine," I muttered and followed her up the stairs.

Since I knew how much it meant to her, I even took another shower, did my hair, and put on some makeup. When that was done, I slipped into the dress I'd already chosen this morning and paired it with heels I only wore when I knew I wasn't going to have to walk much.

Walking into the dining room to help Mom set the table, I noticed that she had taken her good cutlery and crockery out already but also that she had taken out six of everything. I frowned as I turned to call up the stairs. "Mom, why do we have four extras of everything out?"

"Because I need you to set up four more places," she replied as she appeared at the top of the stairs. As I'd known she would be, she was dressed to the nines. I was glad I was wearing mascara for the occasion.

"Why?" I asked just as there was a knock at the door.

Mom brightened as she came down the stairs. "Oh, there's our guests. Did I forget to mention I'd invited some friends over?"

She batted her eyelashes innocently, a weird gleam that could only be described as mischievous entering her eyes. But that couldn't be because Mom didn't do mischief.

Curious about what was going on, I followed her to the door. She swung it open to reveal Wayne standing beside a blonde woman about the same age as Mom was.

"Wendy," Mom exclaimed, confirming my suspicion about who she was. The two women hugged before Mom stepped aside to let them in.

When I walked up to greet Wayne and introduce myself to his wife, I realized Mom hadn't closed the door yet. I peered outside, wondering if we were waiting for more people.

There was a man climbing out of a car in front of our house, closely followed by the cutest little girl wearing a red polka dot dress. The man stood with his back to the house, but I would recognize him anywhere. From any angle.

Nolan.

My heart did jumping jacks while my palms grew clammy. I blinked fast, expecting him to disappear, but he didn't.

It was really him. Well, by the looks of it, it was him and his daughter.

Nolan and Karina were in Peachtree? Why?

Mom came to my side, winking as she leaned over and said quietly, "See? I wasn't confused. Magical things *do* happen on Thanksgiving."

CHAPTER 35

NOLAN

Heart thudding like it had been replaced by a jackhammer, my mouth went dry when I looked up at the door and saw Lacie standing in it. The way the light caught her, she looked like a vision in her soft blue dress with her hair lifting slightly in the breeze.

Her jaw seemed like it was about to drop, and her shoulders were rigid, but then she spotted Karina beside me, and her entire posture changed from defensive to warm. Her full lips even curved into a welcoming smile.

Karina tugged on my arm, demanding my attention. "Is that her, Daddy?"

I nodded and reached for her hand, drawing in a steadying breath as I led her across the front yard to the door. Lacie took a step out, her eyes only on my little girl.

"You must be Karina," she said as she held out a hand toward her. "It's so nice to finally meet you."

Karina smiled but hid herself halfway behind my leg. She reached around it to shake Lacie's offered hand. "Nice to meet you, too."

Her voice was quiet, her demeanor taking on that of a shy little girl that I knew she wasn't. She'd been through a lot lately though, and unfortunately, most of it had been caused by her mother. Needless to say, she did better with men nowadays.

I cleared my throat, keeping one hand on Karina's shoulder for reassurance. "Hi, Lacie. Surprise."

"I'd say." She finally lifted her gaze to meet mine, but all the warmth that had entered it for Karina melted away when she looked at me. She opened her mouth to say something when the older woman behind her quietly coughed.

In response, Lacie took a deep breath and stepped aside to allow us entry to their home. "Come on in. Nolan, Karina, this is my mother. Mom, my boss and his daughter."

Lacie's mother came forward to greet us, a picture of elegance with her pearls and her graying hair swept up into a knot at the back of her head. I held out a hand to her, unsure whether to shake or kiss hers if she gave it to me.

My mother and her friends didn't exude this air of old-school grace and femininity at all. They were huggers through and through, but somehow, I didn't think Lacie's mom was the same. "Mrs. Cole."

"Call me Suellen, please." She motioned us inside, taking the choice away from me when she gave my hand a surprisingly firm shake before letting it go. "Welcome to our home. I do hope you're hungry."

Karina had been telling me in the car that she was starving, but she didn't say anything now. She clung to my leg like she'd been surgically attached to it and kept her mouth shut.

Lacie waited for us to come inside and closed the door behind us, immediately bending over to address Karina. "You are a very talented artist, young lady. I've seen some of your pictures in your Daddy's office. They're wonderful. I take it you like drawing?"

She nodded, easing her hold on my leg a little but still not releasing me. "I like painting, too."

"Well, isn't that a coincidence? It just so happens that I love painting as well. So does my mother. We have a small studio in the backyard. Would you like to see it later?"

"Yes," Karina said, enthusiasm in her bright eyes. "When can we go?"

Lacie held out her hand, a soft smile on her lips as she lowered her voice. "We can slip away now if you'd like, just for me to show you. It'll only take a minute."

She looked up at me then. "If it's okay with you."

"Of course." I smiled at Karina and felt the strangest tug in my heart when she took Lacie's hand without hesitation. *Jeez, she warmed up to her fast.*

Watching the two of them walk through the house to the backyard, I couldn't tear my gaze away from the picture they cut. It was like every dream I never knew I had come true.

When I heard laughter trailing after them as they pushed through the door, I actually had to push my hand against my heart to stop it from doing whatever the fuck it was doing. Wayne chuckled, appearing beside me out of seemingly nowhere.

"When they get back, talk to her. Wendy and I will keep an eye on Karina."

I nodded. That was the plan we'd formulated, but I hadn't exactly gotten the chance to ask before my two favorite women had disappeared.

True to her word, Lacie had Karina back within a few minutes. They were laughing again, their heads bent together where Karina sat on Lacie's hip.

Wayne moved with me when I walked up to them. Coming to a stop in front of Lacie, I swallowed down the nerves lumped in my throat and got the fuck over myself. "Can we talk for a few minutes?"

"Karina, do you want to come with me?" Wayne asked. "I have it on good authority that Suellen has a puzzle in the family room that she needs a hand with."

"I'm good at puzzles, Uncle Wayne," Karina replied as Lacie set her down on her feet. Wayne led her away, leaving me alone with Lacie.

I hadn't seen where his wife and Lacie's mother had gone, but it was clear that everyone was giving me space to do what needed to be done. "Is this okay with you?"

Lacie rolled her lips into her mouth, nodding slowly. "Sure, but let's go talk outside."

I followed her through the door she and Karina had just come in through, walking out into a small back garden with a shed that I assumed was the studio and an old swing hanging from the branch of the only large tree.

Neatly kept flower beds surrounded the exterior walls, leaves in every shade of orange and brown covering the lawn. Lacie blew into her hands and rubbed them together, heading for the swing before turning around to face me.

"You wanted to talk, so talk." She wasn't rude, just firm.

Crossing her arms over her chest, she waited me out without another word. It was clear that she wasn't planning on making this easy for me, but I'd expected it. Lacie wasn't the kind of person you could fuck around with and have her forgive you if you batted your eyelashes at her.

"I'm sorry," I started, allowing air to slide into my lungs to calm my racing pulse. "I'm so sorry, Lacie. I left you there without an explanation. I took my anger and my nerves out on you, and I abandoned you without a word."

She sat down on the swing, her eyes on mine. "Why?"

Frustration clawed at my insides. I ran my hands through my hair and shook my head. "There's no excuse for doing what I did. Despite what was happening, I should have handled it better."

She raised an eyebrow but didn't say anything. There was no need to. I knew what she was waiting for.

"Scarlett showed up at Alec's house." I closed my eyes to fight against the shudder wanting to travel through me as I explained the events of that day. "She insisted on taking Karina because I wasn't there with her. The court order allows for my parents and Alec to care for her when I can't be with her, but Scarlett..." I trailed off. It was never easy for me to share the details, even if I had told Lacie some of them before.

"Her mind just isn't right at the moment." There were much worse ways to put it, but ultimately, I guessed she was still the mother of my child. "When I got there, she had broken into Alec's house, taken Karina, and was in the process of leaving with her."

Lacie sucked in a sharp breath, horror clouding the green in her eyes. "No."

"Yes." I sighed. "If I hadn't gotten there when I did, I—well, I don't even want to think about it."

"Is Karina okay?" she asked quietly.

My lips pressed in at the corners as my shoulders rose, falling again under the weight of uncertainty. "She seems to be. Kids bounce back fast, but I just don't know. Even if she is at the moment, I don't know what will happen if she ever has to see Scarlett again."

"Where is Scarlett now?" Her brow was knitted in concern. "Surely, she can't expect visitation to continue as usual after this."

"As far as I know, she's in jail." I watched as Lacie's eyes went wide. "My lawyers are taking care of it for me, but I asked them not to give me any updates over the weekend. Karina and I both need a break after what happened. If there's something urgent, they'll let me know. Otherwise, I'll face this battle next week. Nothing is going to happen over this weekend anyway."

"Karina must have been terrified." The gravity of the worry in her expression surprised me. She had no reason to be invested in Karina's wellbeing. *Except that she has a real good heart, a genuine one.*

"She was." I brought my hands up to hold on to the fraying rope holding the swing in place and dropped to my haunches, my gaze fixed on Lacie's. "To be honest with you, so was I."

"I can't even imagine what it must have been like for you, knowing she was in danger and having to get halfway across the country before you could be with her."

I inclined my head in acknowledgment but didn't look away from her. "It was one of the most terrible experiences I've ever had, hence the way I acted that day. But that wasn't the only thing that terrified me."

Her eyes slid away from mine, focusing on the fall foliage covering the ground at her feet. "I guess knowing that the woman you once loved enough to marry her is in jail must be pretty scary, too."

I tilted my head to one side, then to the other. "I don't imagine that anyone wants someone they care or even cared about to go to jail, but after what she did... It's complicated. I couldn't tell you how I feel about it even if I tried. Scarlett being in jail means Karina's safe, but she's still her mother. She was still my wife, and jail? Well, it's jail. It's not exactly a pleasant place to be."

"Will you try to help her?" she asked, no trace of judgment present in her tone. Many people, my lawyers included, wanted to crucify Scarlett, to nail her to the wall and leave her there to rot.

Lacie wasn't like that. Neither was I. "Probably. A hospital will be better equipped to deal with her. I need to discuss my options with the lawyers, but I think having her committed is the way to go with this."

A slight smile ghosted across her lips. "I was right about you. You are a good man, despite what happened."

"Maybe." I shrugged, releasing the swing to slide my fingers under her chin, and waited for her to look at me. "But that wasn't what I was talking about when I said there was something else that terrified me."

A confused frown slid into place on her beautiful face. "What was it, then?"

"Losing you," I admitted, my voice only barely above a whisper. "When I realized what I had done, I was terrified that I had lost you for good."

She searched my eyes for a long minute. "You very nearly did."

"Does that mean that I haven't?" A spark of hope lit up my chest like the night sky on the Fourth of July.

Lacie pursed her lips, released a breath, and then shook her head. "You came here. On Thanksgiving. Only two days after getting what had to have been one of the biggest shocks of your life. That means something to me."

Finally giving in to the urge to reach for her hands, a relieved breath left my lips when she willingly gave them to me. My thumbs skated across her knuckles. "You mean something to me. A lot, actually. So much that you're the only woman I've ever introduced to Karina. You're the only one I've ever wanted to introduce to her."

I saw the hope I felt reflected in the softness around Lacie's eyes. "Really?"

"Really." A grinned tugged at my lips. "Am I forgiven?"

She wound her fingers around mine and smirked, jerking her head in the direction of the house. "I want to say yes, but you need to be on your best behavior in front of my mother today. You also need to use your manners and show her that you really are a good man."

"You want me to impress your mother?" My eyebrows lifted. "That's it? Because I'm warning you right now. Mothers love me."

The smirk she wore transformed into a challenging smile. "Only because you haven't tried to impress mine yet. She has an excellent sixth sense about people. Bullshit won't baffle her brains."

"I won't try to bullshit her, but I promise I will be on my best behavior."

"Good." She leaned forward suddenly and planted a kiss on the tip of my nose. "In that case, you're forgiven."

CHAPTER 36

LACIE

Nolan took my hand as we walked back into Mom's house. I let him and wrapped my fingers around his until we were about to enter the living room before I released them.

While I thought his explanation more than made up for taking off to get to Karina, I didn't think walking in hand in hand was a good idea. His daughter had only just met me, and my mother had only just met him. This wasn't the time for any big declarations.

Besides, I might have forgiven him, but I still didn't really know what that meant for us. There was no doubting his sincerity when he'd said he was terrified of losing me, but after what his ex-wife kept putting him through, I couldn't blame him for being hesitant about relationships.

I, on the other hand, had learned recently that I wasn't one for casual sex. The way my heart had broken when I'd thought he'd forgotten about me and that it was over had taught me that I hadn't been able to separate sex from feelings.

Lord knew I still had those feelings for him, but we needed to take this slowly for both our sakes, as well as for Karina's. We were all chartering new territory, and I didn't think it was a good idea to storm into it guns blazing.

The understanding in Nolan's eyes and the slight nod he gave me when I released his hand told me he didn't take offense to it. I was pretty sure he even agreed with me on this front, despite us not having said a word to one another.

When we walked into the room, Mom and Wendy flanked Karina, who was building a puzzle on the floor. It was one of my old ones that Mom must have dug out when she learned Karina was coming for dinner. I'd have to get the story about how exactly all this happened before I left, but I was thankful that it had.

Wayne noticed Nolan and I walk in and come to a standstill so close together that we might have still been touching after all. He smiled, his eyes darting from Nolan's to mine and back again. "I take it the talk went well?"

Nolan's head bounced up and down, an appreciative grin spreading on his lips. "Yes, thanks for keeping an eye on Karina."

"It was our pleasure," Mom said, looking up from the puzzle with a surprising amount of fondness and even love in her eyes. "Karina and I have been bonding. We're going to make turkeys out of egg cartons later."

Karina's hazel eyes sparkled with excitement when she nodded. "Grandma Suellen said she'd show me."

"Grandma Suellen?" I said, nearly choking on my own voice.

My mother chuckled as she shrugged. "Her idea, not mine."

When I glanced at Nolan, I expected him to be frowning or to show at least some kind of outward sign of disapproval at the turn of events. What I found instead was a relaxed grin.

"I think it's a great idea, sweetheart," he said as he walked over to join them, sitting down cross-legged on the carpet on the opposite side of the puzzle. "Unless Suellen objects."

"Suellen does not object," my mom announced with a grin wider than any I'd seen from her in a long time. "I do need to go check on our turkey, though. Do you want to come help me, Karina?"

"Yes," the little girl practically cheered as she jumped to her feet. "Cooking is fun."

"Wait until you've been doing it for fifty years," Wendy said with a good-natured wink at my mother. "Then it's not so fun anymore."

Mom chuckled as she stood up from the couch that they'd been sitting on. She smoothed the front of her dress and held her hand out to Karina, who took it and chattered excitedly all the way to the kitchen.

Somewhat awed by everything that was going on around me, I blinked hard as I watched my mother and Karina disappear into the kitchen. She'd always been a loving, wonderful mother. I'd never thought of her as a grandmother, though. I could see now how loving she would be as one. It was an unexpected role for her to have slipped into as naturally as she had.

Karina and Mom eventually came out to call us, telling us the food was ready. Nolan and I had been talking to Wayne and Wendy about their plans for his retirement.

Once we were all seated, Wendy turned toward my mother. "This looks incredible as always, Suellen. Just like the old days."

"They're not that old," Wayne grumbled, shooting his wife a look even though his eyes shone with amusement. "You start talking about retirement, and suddenly, everything is about getting old."

"Wayne told me you guys have been friends for a long time," Nolan said to Mom. "How did you meet?"

Mom and Wendy shared a smile. "We went to high school together."

"We used to go dancing a lot when we were younger," Wendy added. "That's where we met Wayne and Lacie's father, John."

Mom's expression became nostalgic, the lines around her mouth soft and her eyes faraway. "Those were good times."

"I'd love to hear about it," Nolan said, and to his credit, he managed to make it sound like he really did.

Food was passed around the table as we dished up, talking and eating like we'd all been together for years. It was the most festive atmosphere we'd had around the Thanksgiving table since Dad passed and the holiday became that much more subdued.

We ate until no one could fit in another bite, then took a little break before dessert. Nolan and Wayne stoked the fire they'd made earlier, and when all was said and done later, I walked out with them.

"I'll see you on Monday," Nolan said, turning to face me when we got to their rental car. Karina gave me a hug and climbed into her seat, waiting patiently for her father to buckle her in. "Thank you for having us, though."

Mom said goodbye to Wayne and Wendy before coming to stand next to me. She checked her watch with a discreet peek that I noticed. "It's not that late yet. Why don't you go show Nolan and Karina around town? It's not D.C., but Peachtree has got a little something of its own."

I lifted an eyebrow at her and offered Nolan an apologetic smile. "I'm sorry. She must have forgotten that kids have bedtimes."

"It's a holiday weekend," Karina piped up from the back of the car, turning her pleading eyes up toward Nolan's. "I can stay awake a little later, can't I, Daddy?"

Nolan gave her the most indulgent smile after letting out a long sigh. "Sure, sweetheart. Let's go see some of Peachtree. Are you up for it?"

He looked at me as he asked the question. I was surprised, but I tried not to show it. "Sure, I can show you around."

Mom waved me into the car. "I won't wait up for you. Have fun, kids."

Nolan chuckled, and I shook my head at her. He opened the passenger door of the rental for me and buckled Karina in after closing it behind me. Once we were on the road, he gave me a sidelong glance. "Where to first?"

"Make a right up here," I said, pointing at the traffic light ahead. "If we're going to do this, we're going to do it right."

He followed my directions before looking over at me again. "What do you mean?"

"If I'm going to give you a tour of the city, we're taking it on a golf cart." I grinned. "It's the area's most used form of transportation."

"You're kidding." Nolan's eyes widened. "We'll freeze."

At the same time of his disbelieving remark, Karina pumped her fist in the air and let out a loud, "Whoop. I love golf carts."

"When were you on a golf cart?" Nolan asked, twisting around in his seat to look at her when we pulled up at the next traffic light.

Karina batted her dark, long lashes innocently. "Uncle Alec took me while you were away."

"See? It's decided." I smiled. "Karina and I both love golf carts, and it's the only way to explore the city."

"Where will we even get one?" Nolan faced the road again just before the light changed, waiting for the last of the cars to turn before pulling away. "It's Thanksgiving, and it's after business hours."

"The touring companies around here have extended hours for the holiday," I said. "Keep left in front there. We'll pick up a thermos of hot cocoa from the truck outside their offices. We can also rent some blankets. You didn't really think I'd let you freeze, did you?"

Nolan turned his head enough to allow me to see him wink in the dimly lit interior, a smile raising the corners of his lips. "I had my suspicions."

"Let me correct myself, then." I kept my tone light and joking. "I wouldn't let Karina freeze."

His shoulders bounced lightly as he laughed, shaking his head at me. "Fair enough. Okay, where's this touring company then?"

I directed him the rest of the way. Then Karina and I went to get the hot drinks and blankets while Nolan rented the cart. We piled into it with Karina on the seat between us, all of us bundled up beneath more than a few blankets.

The night air was crisp and cold. There wasn't a cloud in the sky, and thankfully, there also wasn't any wind. We'd missed the usual holiday rush out on the paths which happened around sunset.

There would be more tourists and locals alike coming out again later, but we'd had dinner a touch on the early side and had hit a bit of a sweet spot.

Nolan drove, but I acted as the guide. "This is how you discover life at fifteen miles an hour. One of the city's hallmarks is that we have a hundred miles of paths for pedestrians, cyclists, and golf carts.

Depending on how long you guys are up for staying out tonight, we can wind through wooded greenbelts, drive around the scenic lakes that connect the city, or go see the lights displayed by many of the hotels and shopping centers."

Nolan's eyebrows lifted. "Something tells me this isn't the first time you've given a tour like this."

I shrugged. "I used to do it in high school. It's not a bad way to earn extra money. I got to be outside, learn about the city I called home in real life, and I met the most interesting people from all over."

"You never mentioned that on your resume," he said.

I waited for him to look at me before I smiled. "It's like you said before, I'm full of surprises."

The carefree laugh that rumbled from his chest warmed my own. With my arm around Karina's shoulders and Nolan in the driver's seat, I felt like I was part of their family. It was a good feeling, even if I was cautious about getting too attached to it.

Eventually, Karina's eyelids started drooping, and Nolan called it a night. They dropped me back off at my mother's, and after checking that Karina was asleep in the back, Nolan caught my hand when I made to climb out of the car.

"Good night, Lacie. Thanks again for everything." His free hand came to rest on my cheek, but he didn't make any other move.

The ball was in my court. He was leaving the decision of how this goodbye would go up to me, and I knew just how I wanted it to happen.

Although it was uncomfortable to try doing it without climbing out of my seat or ending with my ass on the handbrake, I looped my arms around his neck and gave him the biggest hug I could manage.

We held on for longer than was normal, and when I finally let go, he brushed the lightest of kisses against my cheek. "Good night. I'm already looking forward to seeing you on Monday."

"So am I." I smiled, pressed a kiss to my fingers, and placed them against his lips. "Enjoy the rest of your weekend, Nolan. I'll see you on Monday."

CHAPTER 37

NOLAN

"Would you look at that?" Alec joked as he slid onto a stool at the dining nook in the kitchen, tossing a wink at Karina. "Your old man is cooking us dinner for once."

I rolled my eyes as I flipped the chicken breasts in the pan, checking the temperature on the oven when I was done. "I cook you dinner all the time. Which begs the question, why are you here for dinner again?"

He flashed me a lopsided smile, his eyes alive with humor. "Just making sure you don't burn the house down. Who knows if you remember how to cook after all those weeks getting spoiled by the hotel chefs?"

"All those weeks?" I scoffed. "It wasn't even two weeks."

"Yeah, well." He shrugged and rolled his shoulders back. "In that case, I'm letting you spoil me for a change. A nice, home-cooked Sunday dinner."

"As opposed to the junk food you eat when you're at home?" I shot him a look over my shoulder, my lips lifting into a smirk. "I guess you can stay. A nice, home-cooked Sunday dinner is the least I owe you."

This time, it was his turn to roll his eyes. "Stop it with that sh—"

He cut himself off. "Crap. You still up for our movie marathon tonight, Kare-bear?"

"Movie marathon?" I asked as I lifted the pan off the heat. "What movie marathon?"

"We had it planned before you came home early and crashed the party. We're watching the sequels of the movies we watched last weekend." He took a sip of the beer he'd snagged from the fridge when he walked in. "I guess you're welcome to join us if you want."

A knock at the door interrupted my answer. "I'll get it."

Alec fist-bumped Karina as I walked past them. "It's good to have him home, isn't it?"

She nodded, shooting me a sweet smile. "But not only because he cooks dinner and gets the door."

Alec's laughter followed me out of the kitchen, and I couldn't stop a grin of my own. Man, it was really good to be home.

Another knock followed the first just as I got to the door. I swung it open, my body going still when I saw Lacie standing on my doorstep. She was wearing jeans and a thick black jersey with leather boots that came to her knees.

Her dark hair fell past her shoulders in soft waves, framing her beautiful face. Black liner under her eyes made them seem greener and brighter than ever. She quirked a brow at me, a smile playing at the corners of her lips. "Well, are you going to stand there staring at me all day, or are you going to let me in?"

"Lacie?" I stepped aside, fighting the urge to pull her into my arms. It wasn't easy. "What are you doing here?"

Light danced in her eyes as she followed me into the entrance hall. "My flight got in this afternoon. When I got back to my apartment, it was just so quiet, I couldn't stand it. Figured I'd pop in and see what you guys were up to."

"We're about to have dinner. Would you like to join us?" I allowed the door to swing shut, turning just in time to see Karina barreling out of the kitchen.

"I thought I heard your voice," she said as she came to a stop in

233

front of Lacie. "I'm so happy you're here. Too many men. Come meet Uncle Alec."

"Whoa there, sweetheart." I put out a hand to ruffle her hair. "Let Lacie get her bearings first. Can I get you something to drink?"

Lacie shook her head and opened her arms as she dropped to her haunches, pulling Karina into a hug. "I'm happy I'm here, too. How are you?"

Karina beamed at her, stepping back and putting her little hands on Lacie's face. The boldness of her actions surprised me, but I guessed it shouldn't have. The two of them might only have spent a day together back in Peachtree, but Karina had taken a liking to Lacie and hadn't been able to shut up about her since.

"I'm good. Are you going to have dinner with us?" Karina's eyes were round with hope as they darted from me to Lacie.

"I just asked her the same thing." I grinned, raising my eyebrows expectantly as we waited for her answer.

Karina even held her breath, which made Lacie laugh before she nodded. "Sure, I'd love to join you if it's not too much trouble."

"None at all," I assured her. "There's plenty of food to go around, and if you ask nicely, Alec might even let you have one of the beers."

"Let who have one of the beers?" Alec asked with mock indignance dripping from his tone, his hand pressed to his chest as he walked out of the kitchen. When his eyes landed on Lacie, his mouth formed a surprised "o" and he dropped the act. "Sure. Of course, she can have one of the beers. I take it this is the famous Lacie."

"Famous?" One of her brows swept up as she stood, her green eyes finding mine. "I didn't know I was famous."

"Oh, you're definitely an A-lister around here." Alec winked and stuck out his hand. "I'm Alec, by the way. Chief cook and bottle washer, as well as the glue that holds them together."

Lacie laughed as she shook his hand, her eyes lighting up with humor. "Lacie. It's nice to meet you."

"You too." He released her hand just as an irrational flare of jealousy sped through my gut. *Jesus. It's just a handshake. Calm down.*

Alec snorted when he saw the expression I was undoubtedly wearing, a grin forming on his lips. But he also took a deliberate step away from her and surreptitiously raised both his palms, holding them out for a fraction of a second to let me know discreetly that he was backing off.

With a nod of thanks to him, I swept my arm out toward the kitchen and caught Lacie's attention. "Ladies, if you'll follow me, dinner is about to be served."

"We're having chicken," Karina piped up as she took Lacie's hand and led her to the dining nook. She even patted Alec's coveted spot beside her and shot him an apologetic look as Lacie took it.

He released an exaggerated huff of air, shaking his head as he took the seat opposite her. "Fine, I'll just squeeze in here next to your dad. Word of warning though, we might get stuck. This thing was not designed for two guys our size to sit next to each other."

Lacie frowned as she looked at him. "I'm sorry, am I in your spot?"

"Yeah," he said as he reached out and picked up his beer. "But that's okay. This way, I get to look at you two. It's a much better view than having to look at Nolan."

I rolled my eyes, but I didn't argue. I'd rather look at them too. "Okay, guys. Grub's up. Everybody dig in."

After grabbing an extra plate and cutlery for Lacie, I carried the food to the table and set it down. About halfway through dinner, Alec gave me a grin that let me know he was up to something. I shot him a warning look, but he winked and cleared his throat.

"Hey, Kare-bear, do you want to come stay with me tonight? We can have the movie marathon at my house. My TV is bigger than your dad's anyway."

"Bullsh—" I cut myself off. "Our TVs are the exact same size, but you can go if you want, sweet pea."

Karina bounced in her seat. "Yes! I love Uncle Alec's house."

She turned to face Lacie, lowering her voice but not so much that we couldn't hear her. "He lets me stay awake until the movie is finished. Even if it's after bedtime."

"That was once," Alec burst out, grinning at me. "Okay, maybe twice."

Under normal circumstances, I might have rehashed the old argument about the importance of bedtime. As it was though, I kept my mouth shut.

I knew what Alec was doing, and it was a monstrous favor.

"Thank you," I mouthed at him when the girls started discussing the movies Alec and Karina had decided to watch.

He nodded, then speared a bite of chicken and popped it into his mouth. They left soon after dinner, leaving me and Lacie to do the washing up.

I tried insisting on doing it by myself while she had a drink, but she pushed her sleeves up to her elbows and came to stand next to me to help rinse everything before it went in the dishwasher. She bumped her hip playfully into mine. "So, what did Karina think of Peachtree?"

"She loved it," I said earnestly. "In fact, she loved it so much that she's asked me if we can move there."

"Really?" She bent over to place the plates I had already rinsed in the machine, giving me a front-row seat to the best view in town for a second before she straightened out again. Just that one glimpse was enough to rouse that same insatiable need for her that I'd had on the road.

Forcing my brain to stop conjuring up pictures of what that ass looked like naked, I nodded. "Yeah, she thinks it's way better than D.C."

"Well, she did have a pretty amazing tour guide." Lacie smiled as she loaded more of the dishes I'd rinsed. "And the best food Peachtree has to offer at Thanksgiving."

"Your mother can definitely cook," I agreed. "Speaking of your mother, how did she feel about us? Did Karina and I pass the Suellen Cole manners test?"

"Karina did," she said, then jumped back when I reached out to tickle her into telling the truth. Laughing as she backed away, she shrugged. "Fine, you did too. She loved both of you. Even told me to invite you over again for Christmas."

"Is that so?" I cocked my head and shut off the faucet before stalking up to her. She let out another shout of laughter but only backed up another step before stopping to let me plant my arms on either side of her, gripping the counter behind.

"That is so," she said, the atmosphere between us changing suddenly from light and joking to heavy and serious. "Would you be interested?"

"Absolutely." Looking into her eyes, I couldn't help the way my heart burned. I wanted to kiss her, to touch her, and to know for sure that everything was okay between us. But I couldn't.

I'd lost that right the day I'd left her standing in that lobby staring after me. "I'm so sorry, Lacie. I know I've apologized before, but I—"

There was no warning for it.

Lacie's hands came up to my chest, her fingers curling into the fabric of my T-shirt at the same time that she pushed up on her toes and silenced me with a firm kiss. I was surprised, but I sure as shit didn't object.

My arms wound around her and yanked her against my frame, holding on to her tightly as I deepened the kiss. Her lips softened as our mouths moved against each other. My fingers tangled into her loose hair, and I felt a shiver running down her spine.

Drowning in the taste of her mouth, I lost myself to her touch, to the way she fit against me, and the feel of her body pressed to mine.

Lacie sighed into the kiss, breaking away from me to look me in the eyes. "You can stop apologizing now, Nolan. I forgive you, really. I've met Karina, and she might not be mine, but I would lose my head if I knew someone was trying to hurt her. I understand."

She emphasized the last two words, then repeated them firmly. "I understand."

The knot that had formed in my heart the day that I realized what I had done suddenly slipped free, releasing with it a flood of emotions it'd been preventing me from feeling.

They hit me all at once, causing me to kiss her harder, hold her tighter, and lift her against my stomach as I groaned beneath the force of them all. Lacie didn't break the kiss to question the sound or the intensity of my actions.

She relaxed against me and wound her legs around my hips to

hook her ankles behind my butt. My hands slid to her thighs, and I gripped them, carrying her to my bedroom as fast as I could without dropping her or crashing us into something.

I couldn't be responsible for hurting her, not now and never again. Whether I'd told her yet or not, she was mine to protect now. Mine to hold and mine to kiss. Just mine, really.

Yeah, buddy. I wouldn't tell her that just yet. It's way too soon. I shut my brain down and felt my heart swell as it cheered. *She's mine, and this time, it really will be forever.*

My eyes popped open at that thought, but then I shut my heart's whispers down too. Everything flying through my mind was true, and the fact that it didn't scare me one bit was all the confirmation I needed.

CHAPTER 38

LACIE

"What are we doing in here?" I whispered when Nolan laid me down on his bed. Giving him a playful nudge as I waggled my brows at him, I planted another kiss on his kips. "You didn't think you were getting lucky, did you?"

"I already am getting lucky," he replied, his eyes closing as a smile much sweeter than I'd have thought him capable of spread on his lips. "You've forgiven me and now you're kissing me. That makes me feel pretty lucky."

I arched a brow up at him, bringing both of my hands up to cup the nape of his neck. "Is that why you brought me to your bedroom? To tell me how lucky you feel?"

He shrugged, grinning when he tried to back off and I wouldn't let him go. "Yes. I've never used this bedroom for anything but sleeping and talking so get your mind out of the gutter, woman."

About to argue, I remembered that he hadn't been with anyone but me since he separated from his ex-wife. Which meant he was probably telling me the truth about this bedroom, since I knew he and Lacie had moved in here after the divorce.

I didn't know why I felt special to be the first woman he brought in here, but I did. It felt like the start of something real instead of the temporary moments we'd had in hotel rooms that didn't belong to us.

Well, technically, they all belonged to Nolan, but I digress. Being here with him, in the bed where he slept at home, with him lying half on top of me and looking at me like I'd stolen him a star, I finally got the feeling that what we had was real.

It didn't feel like it was all about to be snapped away from me at any moment. I wasn't afraid he was going to run, and I didn't worry about what was going to happen in the future.

Winding my fingers into his soft hair and looking up at him in the relative darkness of his room, only ambient light streaming in from the outside allowing me to see him, I felt like I belonged to him. What was more was that I was one hundred percent okay with it.

Nolan lowered his mouth to mine again, stopping when he was a hair's breadth away. "Except, you know, if it's comfortable in the gutter. If so, you won't find me complaining."

I smiled against his lips, arching my hips against his growing hardness. "You definitely won't find me complaining either. Now, are you going to talk about it all night, or are you going to do something about it?"

"I told you. All I do in this room is talk and—"

I didn't let him finish.

Lifting my shoulders off the bed, I wound my arms around his and pressed my lips to his mouth. Nolan responded with a low growl, parting his lips for me and stroking my tongue with his when I did the same.

Sparks of pleasure traveled through me with every swipe of his tongue, every slight touch of his body over mine. My hands roamed over the hard planes of his back, feeling his tightly coiled muscles beneath his shirt.

I found the edge of the fabric and broke our kiss to pull it off. His lips crashed back to mine the instant the shirt passed over his head. A moan broke free from my chest when I ran my hands along his smooth bare skin.

Nolan made a low sound of pleasure at the back of his throat and slowed the kiss before lifting his mouth from mine, his eyes burning with heat as they raked down the length of my body. He undressed me slowly, dragging his knuckles and his fingers over my ribcage and inner thighs.

My back arched, my entire being desperate for his touch. But I didn't hurry him up.

As much as I wanted him, I wanted this, too. The anticipation, the togetherness, this feeling of coming together like we never had before.

Because we hadn't done this before. What was happening between us now felt like more than just sex. It felt like discovery. It felt like an exploration of the feelings inside as much as each other's bodies.

It feels like making love.

The thought stopped me short. It was too soon to be thinking that word, but that was definitely what it felt like.

Nolan knelt on the bed between my legs after removing his pants and boxers, his chest rising and falling on fast breaths, but his eyes had come back to mine. Our gazes locked, and what I saw in his warmed me all over.

When I finally tore my eyes away from his, I took a moment to take him in, to soak in the feelings coursing through me.

He was so gorgeous, so indescribably perfect. My legs spread wider for him, my arms going around him to bring his bare skin to mine. Our mouths met in another searing kiss that ramped up my need to a level I'd never experienced before.

Nolan let out a moan that nearly made me combust spontaneously, then slowly broke our kiss. "I need to be inside you."

"I need you to be there," I whispered.

With heavy breaths that ghosted across my skin, he leaned over and opened the drawer of his nightstand.

He came back with a condom, his white teeth flashing in the darkness on a naughty smile.

I cocked an eyebrow at him. "I thought all you did in here was sleep."

"Had to go somewhere with them after we got back." He rolled his shoulders, but the movement was tight. "I figured it was as good a

241

place as any. Besides, I might have been hoping I'd get l again someday soon."

"Am I that predictable?" I asked, taking the foil package out of his hand and bringing it to my mouth.

Nolan moved it aside to press a kiss to my lips. "It's called wishful thinking. That's a far cry from predictability."

"You don't say?" I waggled my eyebrows at him as I brought the foil back to my mouth, tearing into it with my teeth.

He groaned. "Okay. I promised you I'd show you, but go easy on me, okay? It's been a while."

"It's been less than a week," I pointed out, but I couldn't stop a smile from forming on my lips. "Although for you, it must seem like an eternity."

"Without you, it has been." He looked into my eyes as he said it. "I mean it, Lacie, I've missed you so damn much."

"You?" I questioned, giving a pointed look at his beautiful cock. "Or him?"

"Both." He grinned as he leaned down, his lips brushing against mine. "Mostly me."

"I missed you too." I felt him taking the condom out of my hands and the motion of him putting it on.

One day, I'd do it. But my hands were trembling too much, my body shaky and needy.

Nolan positioned himself over me, his hands gliding into my hair and his mouth claiming mine as he slid into me.

It was one of those moments that I knew I would remember forever, just like the night I'd lost my virginity to him. Only this time, I'd remember it as the first time I made love to him.

I didn't care if it was too soon to be thinking about that word because that was what it was. In movies, it was almost like the cameras slowed down when the characters were making love instead of fucking.

That was exactly how I felt in this moment. Like everything had slowed down.

All that existed was our bodies moving together, our sighs and our moans as my shoulders lifted with his. My hips moved to a pace he set, and my mouth followed suit.

An hour or a lifetime later, I couldn't hold back anymore. My clit was on fire, and when I let go, the flames exploded from my core and disintegrated every part of my being.

Nolan put me back together again, better than before. Then his own climax hit, and he shuddered against me. His brow clenched tight as he called my name and finally stilled above me.

"Why did you come to me for Thanksgiving?" I asked him quietly once I'd caught my breath.

The only light that was on in the room was the lamp on his nightstand, casting a warm orange glow over us on the bed. Our limbs were tangled together, our heads resting on pillows smashed up against one another.

It was the serenity, the domesticity even, of the moment that had given me the courage to ask him the question that had been on the tip of my tongue from the second I'd seen him climb out of that car.

Hazel eyes soft and alight with joy, he placed his hand on my face and stroked my cheekbone with his thumb. "I came to you because I couldn't stay away. I needed to see you to explain in person, but I also just needed to see you. To be near you."

"Why?" With all the emotions tugging at my chest, I needed to hear him say the words.

A smile curved on his lips as he leaned forward to plant a chaste kiss on mine. "I care about you, Lacie. A lot. More than I thought I would care about a woman again, more than I was prepared to care for a woman again. You came out of nowhere and knocked me clear off my feet."

"I care about you, too." I ran my fingers through the coarse smattering of hair on his chest, unable to look away from his eyes. "But where does that leave us?"

"It leaves us here, if this is where you want to be." His expression was open, honest. "I want to give this, us, a real chance. If you want to continue being casual—"

"No, I want to give us a real chance, too."

His smile turned into a radiant grin, his arms sliding around me as he rolled to his back and took me with him. Resting my head on his chest, I listened to the steady thrum of his heartbeat and I looked up at him. "The whole casual thing wasn't working for me anyway. Not with you. I don't think I ever stood a chance with it when it came to you."

CHAPTER 39

NOLAN

Flames licked the underside of our steaks, filling the yard with the mouthwatering smell of grilling meat. Alec and I stood beside the fire with tongs in our hands, each searing a piece of prime ribeye before taking it off the grill.

"Can you believe he's really retiring?" Alec asked with a tilt of his head in Wayne's direction.

The man of the hour was standing with his wife and Lacie's mom, who I'd flown up as a surprise guest for his retirement party. This one time, I'd allowed myself the unnecessary expense of sending the jet for her. With Lacie on it.

What can I say? I wanted to impress my girl's mother. What was the use of having a jet if you couldn't flaunt it every once in a while?

In the month and a half that had passed since Lacie and I had agreed to giving a relationship a go, I'd pulled out all the stops for her, and I didn't plan on stopping now. Or ever.

When I'd started making money, I'd realized that I loved spoiling the people I loved. The only time I spent real money was when I could spend it on them.

The effort had been wasted on Scarlett, who had taken everything for granted and never viewed anything as good enough. She'd always wanted more.

Spoiling Lacie, however, was a whole different kettle of fish. Her eyes lit up with surprise and elation over every little thing. I loved seeing her get all excited. I loved the build up to the surprise and how she couldn't stop asking for clues.

She'd told me that flying her mother over for the party had been the best surprise yet, though. I'd accepted her comment as a challenge to top it soon.

After more than a month of being an official couple, I still couldn't keep my eyes off her. Even now, I watched her out of the corner of my eye. She was playing with Karina on the other side of the yard, laughing as Karina talked a mile a minute while hanging on her monkey bars.

Lacie caught me watching them and smiled, then jerked her thumb in Wayne's direction. His cheeks were red from the cold where he climbed up the steps to my patio. Seeing him reminded me that Alec had just asked me a question.

"No, man, I can't really believe it. It seems impossible." A full beer dangled from the fingers of my free hand. I raised it to my lips and took a sip of the liquid, deciding immediately that it was too cold out for beer today. "I tried everything I could to get him to stay, but he says it's time."

"That's because it is." Alec drained his beer and took another steak off the grill. "He's done his time. Let the man relax. Besides, he found you a pretty incredible replacement, didn't he?"

My eyes automatically went back to Lacie. "Yeah, I'd say. Before she started, I didn't know what we were going to do without him. We'll still miss him, but now I know we'll be okay once he leaves."

"How's it going between the two of you?" he asked, following my gaze across the yard.

Lacie's black hair was loose, a bright purple beanie on top of her head. Her head fell back as she laughed, a hand shooting up to keep the beanie from falling off.

In her faded blue jeans, purple coat, and a turquoise scarf around

246

her neck, she was the most beautiful woman I'd ever seen. "I can't even tell you how well it's going. It's just..."

"What?" he questioned when I trailed off, so mesmerized by her that for the second time, I'd forgotten I'd been in the middle of saying something.

"I love her."

Alec's eyes went wide, but it didn't look like it was because of surprise. "Are you only realizing that now? Because I've known for a while, dude."

I tore my gaze away from her to look at my best friend. "How could you have known when I only figured it out last night?"

He shrugged. "I'm smarter than you."

I punched his arm but not hard enough to hurt. "No shit."

"No shit." Alec grinned before his gaze drifted away from mine and back to where Lacie was now helping Karina off the jungle gym. "In all seriousness, though, I have known that you were in love with her for a while."

"How?" I was genuinely curious. I'd known that I cared deeply about her for months now, but love? I hadn't wanted to admit that one to myself until I couldn't deny it any longer.

That had only happened approximately twenty hours ago. We'd been standing side by side, brushing our teeth before turning in for the night. She caught my eye in the mirror and smiled, and something just clicked inside me.

Love hadn't been in my plans again, but it had snuck up on me and left me no choice in the matter. I didn't fear it though, not with Lacie.

"If you had seen the way you look at that girl, you'd have known too," Alec said. "Have you told her yet?"

I shook my head. "I should probably do something about that."

"Probably." He grinned and picked up his empty beer bottle, shaking it at me. "Can I bring you another one?"

"Nah, man. I'm freezing my balls off. Who organizes a barbeque in January?"

"You," he quipped and ducked, dancing out of my way when I tried to punch his shoulder again. "You sure I can't get you anything?"

"I'm all good for now," I said as I removed the last of the steaks from the grill. Placing them on a tray Lacie had brought out before the guests started arriving, I carried them to the kitchen and checked on the sides in the oven.

Satisfied that all the food was ready, I went outside to tell everyone. They followed me in out of the cold, taking their seats around the dining-room table.

Lacie sat on my one side and Karina on the other, but Karina quickly poked me in the ribs and glanced longingly at Lacie. "Can I swap with Granny Suellen? I want to sit next to Lacie."

Suellen heard her request and paused behind her seat. "Sure, honey. I'll sit next to your daddy. I have a bone to pick with him, anyway."

My heart slammed to a skidding stop until I saw the smile ghosting across her lips. When we had spent a few days in Peachtree over Christmas, I'd learned that she might look uptight, but she had a wicked sense of humor.

We got along quite well, much to my relief. She was Lacie's only family, and she was starting to feel like ours too. She took her seat beside me when Karina vacated it, leaning over to whisper to me.

"The jet was a nice touch, but you know what would impress me more?"

I turned my head toward her, seeing a curious gleam darkening her eyes. "What?"

"Telling me what your intentions are with my daughter." She held my gaze. "I know it hasn't been official for very long, but she's crazy about you. I also know you've had a rough past where women are concerned. I need to know if I have to worry about my baby girl."

"I'm crazy about her, too," I replied, keeping my voice low so Lacie wouldn't be able to overhear us. "You don't need to worry about her. I'll take care of her. I promise."

"You better." She glanced down at the butter knife resting in the dish in front of her place setting. "Else I'll use that to cut off an appendage I'm sure you're rather fond of."

I winced, sitting back as far as I could. "If I ever hurt her again, I'll hold still for you, but I'm pretty sure Lacie will beat you to it."

She nodded serenely. "That's a good attitude to have."

Wayne interrupted us by standing up and clinking the side of his glass with a steak knife. Not exactly elegant, but certainly effective. "I want to thank you all for coming tonight. It means a lot that I can get together with you one last time before Wendy and I head out in the RV."

Lacie's voice was suddenly murmuring in my ear when Wayne paused to look at Wendy. "They're really doing that?"

"They are." I gave her a sidelong grin. "Why? You want to follow in their footsteps once we retire?"

She shrugged, then pulled a lock of her hair forward over her shoulder and twisted it around her finger. "We could, if you think I'm going to be able to put up with you for that long."

Wayne ended his pause with a meaningful look at me. "Nolan, you've become a real friend to me. Thank you for throwing this little soiree, but I need to thank you for so much more. You've been the best protege and the best boss I ever could have asked for. The company has flourished under you and I can honestly say that it's been a privilege standing by your side and seeing it happen."

I inclined my head in acknowledgment, but he wasn't done yet. "You have someone else standing by your side now. Make sure you keep her close because she's a keeper, son. I hope you know how lucky you are, and I hope you tell her every day."

When he was done, he lifted his glass, and the rest of us followed suit. While everyone else was dishing up, I slid my hand into Lacie's and squeezed her fingers to get her attention. "Can I steal you away for a minute?"

Wayne was right. I should tell Lacie how lucky I was every day, but there was also something else I couldn't hold back anymore.

She nodded and got to her feet, following me to my bedroom. "What's up?"

I closed the door and walked up to her, slid my arms around her waist, and looked right into those captivating green eyes. "I was

249

talking to Alec earlier, and I realized that there was something I haven't told you yet."

"Oh, yeah?" She dropped her head to one side. "What's that?"

"I love you." I slid one hand up her side and underneath the silky curtain of her hair to cup the nape of her neck. "I love you, Lacie Cole."

Bringing my lips to hers, I kissed her more deeply and with more feeling than ever before. Lacie sighed into the kiss, moving her mouth with mine as her hand came to rest lightly on my cheek.

"I love you too," she whispered when we finally broke apart. "I love you with all my heart and all my soul."

She smiled and took a step back, taking hold of both of my hands and tugging me in the direction of the door. "But if we don't get out of this bedroom right now, I'm going to tackle you to that bed and make you prove it to me."

"With pleasure." I planted my feet and refused to move another step, but then she released my hands and sashayed backward to the door.

"The pleasure will be all mine but later." She turned the doorknob and winked as she opened the door. "I knew you loved me, by the way. I'm glad you finally got all caught up."

With that, her lips titled into a full-blown grin, and she stepped out of the room, calling back over her shoulder, "Now come on, lover boy. We have a party to host."

EPILOGUE

LACIE

"This is nothing like the tour Anna and I took," I said as I followed Nolan and Karina to the upper deck of one of Alec's company's buses. "Where are the rest of the people?"

"We are the people," he replied, a wide grin spreading on lips that I'd been kissing whenever I wanted for a full year now. *I can't believe it's our anniversary already.*

Knowing that my boyfriend—butterflies still exploded through my stomach every time I thought about Nolan and that term in the same sentence—was up to something, I reached out to grab his forearm. "What do you mean by that?"

The grin turned impish. "I mean that I rented it out for the three of us for today."

"Just us?" Karina called from the landing, her eyes lighting up when we heard the doors closing up front. "That's awesome, Daddy."

She ran the rest of the way up, squealing in the excitement when she got there. I raised an eyebrow at Nolan, suspicious about what was going on. "What are you up to?"

He climbed down the step below the one I was on and dropped his forehead to mine as he wound his arms around my neck. "Did you really think I forgot?"

My heartrate sped up as I looked into his eyes. "Maybe. You didn't say anything this morning."

We had woken up together, but he'd simply rolled out of bed and went to fix Karina's breakfast. I'd gotten a quick good-morning kiss, but nothing else.

As was our routine most mornings, even though I wasn't officially living with them yet, we'd showered together in his massive shower. We'd had coffee and breakfast together and then left the house. All without a word about what today was.

He grinned at me now. "That's how a surprise works. Remember Vegas? You made me wait thirty-six hours. I only made you wait four."

"So this is payback?"

"In a sense." He lowered his head to mine and kissed the living daylights out of me. When he lifted his lips from mine, I was practically panting. "Maybe not payback so much as thank you, and that I owed you something incredible."

"You already gave me something incredible," I said, my voice low but masked by the sound of the bus's engine turning over anyway.

"What's that?"

"That orgasm last night," I joked.

Nolan laughed, shaking his head as he pressed a kiss to the tip of my nose. "You're incorrigible. You know that?"

I shrugged. "You're the one who did this to me."

"True." Pride shone in his eyes and puffed up his chest. "Even after a year, you're still insatiable."

"So are you," I pointed out. He shrugged and nodded, but I went on. "That wasn't the incredible thing you've given me, though."

I reached up and placed my hand on his chest. "This is. You are."

The love that I saw reflected back at me in his eyes was pretty incredible, too. "So are you. I love you, baby. Happy anniversary."

"Happy anniversary." I offered him my mouth, and he took it in another passionate kiss before he released me, leading me up the stairs.

I had an anniversary surprise of my own for him, but I was planning on giving it to him at sunset. It was his favorite time of day with

Karina and me, and I was about to agree to be there every day to spend it with them.

Nolan had asked me to move in, but I wanted to check with Karina before I gave him my answer. He'd assured me that he had spoken to her about it and that she was excited about the possibility, but I figured a little girl-talk was in order.

When I'd picked Karina up from school a week or so ago, I'd taken her to an ice-cream parlor and finally got the chance to have the conversation with her. After getting her blessing, I'd decided to save my answer as a surprise for him on our anniversary.

As far as he knew, I was still thinking it over. Little did he know that I'd swiped his house keys while he'd been in a meeting earlier this week and had my own made. It was in my purse now, on a keyring that had a picture of the three of us taken over Christmas on it. I'd had a matching one of those made for him, too.

Alec's voice called from above. "Are you two lovebirds coming up or what? I want to get this show on the road."

Nolan rolled his eyes but held out his hand to me. "Relax, bud. We're not on a schedule or anything."

Alec scoffed, his head popping out over the top of the railing to look down at us with a smirk on his lips. "You might not be, but I am. If we don't get going, we're going to run into too many other tourists when the tours get started for the day."

"We're coming, we're coming," Nolan said as we ascended the stairs.

Alec gave him a saucy wink. "I'd hope you're not. You're in public, man."

Nolan flipped him off, but I saw the grin he was trying to hide. "Maybe being out in public does things to me."

Alec threw up his hands and grimaced, laughter shining in his eyes. "That's not something I ever want to think about."

Joining in the banter as we reached the top, I made sure Karina was out of earshot before I added, "It's true. Nolan has a thing for public places."

Laughter rumbled out of Alec as he shook his head. "It's not fair how you guys gang up on me."

"If you'd settle down," Nolan said, "you'd have someone who constantly had your back too."

Alec shrugged his wide shoulders. "Nah, that's okay. I got my own back. There's less drama that way."

"Hey, I haven't caused any drama," I protested.

Alec shot me a mischievous look as he affixed his headpiece and adjusted the microphone in front of his mouth. "Yeah, but you're already taken. Unless you're considering your options."

I held up my hand, which was still adjoined with Nolan's. "Thanks, but no thanks. You're right. I'm very much taken."

"But you did walk right into that one," Nolan said to me. "Did you really think you could object to that and not have him make a pass at you?"

"I suppose not." I smiled and walked to the nearest row of seats, seeing that blankets and a thermos had already been set down on it. "But I felt like I had to stand up for myself anyway. Not all women cause drama, you know?"

"You're the only one I know of who doesn't thrive on drama," Alec said, faking a solemn expression as he looked at Nolan. "You caught the unicorn, man. Now the rest of us are doomed to be single forever."

"Your sense of humor is what doomed you to be single forever," Nolan quipped, grinning at his best friend.

"I have no problem with that." Alec shrugged again, then motioned to Karina to come take her seat. "Come on, Kare-bear. Let's get going."

Karina skipped over to us from the back of the bus, where she'd been leaning on the railing and admiring the view. Her eyes were bright and excited. "I've never been on one of these tours before."

"I've certainly never been on a private one," I replied. "This is going to be my first time too."

She settled in beside me, taking one side of the blanket when I handed it to her and tucking it in beneath her. Nolan did the same with the other side, stretching his arm out on the backrest behind us.

Alec called to the driver that we were ready to go, then flashed us a charismatic smile when the wheels started rolling. "Welcome to the best tour of this city you're ever going to have. Lacie, if you look to your right, you'll see a man who is so whipped that he turned down a beer with his best friend this morning."

I turned my head to plant a kiss on said man's cheek before pursing my lips at Alec. "That's because it was morning. It had nothing to do with me."

"That might be true." He laughed, then launched into the actual tour. Even though the air was crisp and cold, the view from the top of the bus made it worth having to bundle up.

Leaves the color of burnt orange and fiery red blanketed the parks and stood out against the clear blue sky where they clung to branches. There wasn't a cloud in sight, making it one of those beautiful days that highlighted the foliage and natural beauty of the city since you could see for miles in every direction.

I settled in for the tour, laughing at Alec's jokes and absorbing the wealth of knowledge he had about the landmarks and the city. My tour with Anna had been nothing like this. Alec knew things the other guide hadn't and seemed to really enjoy sharing them.

We were coming up on our next stop, but the bus started slowing at least a mile early. My head rested against Nolan's shoulder while my arm was around Karina. She suddenly sat up straight and flashed me the biggest smile I'd ever seen from her, her arm shooting out to point at something I couldn't see from my vantage point.

"Lacie, look!" She pushed the blankets off her lap and jumped to her feet, standing against the railing and waving me over excitedly. "You have to see this."

"What is it?" I pressed a quick kiss to Nolan's shoulder and shivered at the rush of cold air when I climbed out from under the blankets. The bus stopped unexpectedly, Alec exchanging a look with Nolan that made me frown.

When I joined Karina at the railing, the way they were all acting suddenly made sense to me. But at the same time, I struggled to process what I was seeing.

Right there under the cherry blossom trees that would be the stars of springtime in Washington D.C., a magician performed with an array of elaborate movements. The next thing I knew, the words "Will you marry me, Lacie?" on a banner appeared out of seemingly nowhere.

I whirled around to see Nolan down on one knee, an intricate ring in a velvet-lined box resting on the palm of his hand. "So, will you?"

So stunned that I could barely form a thought, never mind words, the most unexpected question burst out of my mouth. "Did you ask my mother?"

"Of course, I did." A beautiful smile lifted the corners of his lips, his hazel eyes shining with so much love that it made me tear up. "Anything else you want to know before you give me an answer?"

I shook my head, my hands flying up to cover my gaping mouth as tears rolled silently down my cheeks. "Yes. Of course, I'll marry you."

The words were muffled by my shaking hands and the tremor in my voice, but Nolan heard them loud and clear. With the most stunning grin I'd ever seen from him, he rose to his feet and took my hand, sliding the ring onto my finger.

"Thank God. You had me sweating for a minute there." He leaned over to press a kiss to my lips with his hand still in mine. "I love you, Lacie."

"I love you, too." Pushing myself up on my toes, I couldn't resist kissing him again. My brain was still struggling to catch up to the fact that I was now engaged to the man of my dreams, but there was one thing I knew for sure.

This time, he would get his happily ever after. And so would Karina and me, as a family. Which was exactly the way that we belonged.

The End

ABOUT THE AUTHOR

Hey there. I'm Weston.

I'm a former firefighter/EMS guy who's picked up the proverbial pen and started writing bad boy romance stories. I co-write with my sister, Ali Parker as we travel the United States for the next two years.

You're going to find Billionaires, Bad Boys, Mafia and loads of sexiness. Something for everyone, hopefully. I'd love to connect with you. Check out the links below and come find me.